Operation Oboe

Miller Caldwell

Best wishes

Miller Caldwell

authors OnLine

Visit us online at www.authorsonline.co.uk

An AuthorsOnLine Book

Published by Authors OnLine Ltd 2003

ISBN 0-7552-0090-X

Authors OnLine Ltd
Hertford
England

This book is also available in e-Book format from
www.authorsonline.co.uk

MILLER CALDWELL

Miller H. Caldwell graduated from London University's School of Oriental and African Studies in 1980 after he had spent five years in Ghana as a fraternal worker to the Tema Council of Churches. He is the former Regional and Authority Reporter to the Dumfries and Galloway Children's Panels, branch Chair of the Scottish Association for the Study of Delinquency and past President of the Dumfries Burns Club. He is a direct descendant of the poet Robert Burns and a Founding Fellow of the Institute of Contemporary Scotland.

He has had articles published in New Society, the Scottish Review, the Christian Herald, and Good Health. Operation Oboe is his first novel.

He lives in Dumfries with his wife and his collie, Tache.

ACKNOWLEDGEMENTS

I had always thought I had this story to tell but structuring the tale required a concentrated period of time. The third ingredient was a group of reliable confidants who could keep me productive. Accordingly, I am grateful to my neighbour, Roy Shearn, who took a copy of the script to the Isle of Islay, where in leisure, he produced constructive criticism. My friend Tony Barbour gave his German expertise and our shared love of Ghana to my aid. Thanks also go to both Linda Ramsay and Margaret Heron of the Local Heritage Centre of Elgin Library for unearthing Vera's escape from Germany and confirming Fleur's family details. My thanks go to Baroness Symons, the parliamentary under-secretary of State at the Foreign and Commonwealth Office, for her report on 'Women in Diplomacy - the FCO 1782-1999' and her researchers. Joyce Bell, my badminton partner and friend, graciously undertook to create the cover design. Thereafter the book's defects whether in length, style or content are mine alone.

The novel drew precision from the following historical and philosophical books and I am grateful for copyright permission granted from passages of these publications:

August 1914 copyright © Barbara Tuchman by kind permission of AM Heath & Co Ltd
The SS: Hitler's Instrument of Terror by Gordon Williamson published by BCA by arrangement with Sidgwick & Jackson
The Ethical Mysticism of Albert Schweitzer by Henry Clark published by the Beacon Press, Boston, USA
The Presbyterian Church of Ghana 1835 - 1960 copyright © Noel Smith published by Oxford University Press
A Social Survey of Takoradi by KA Busia published by the Crown Agents for the Colonies
African Myths & Legends by Margaret Carey by kind permission of Hamlyn Books

Most of all, I benefited from the close attention to detail which characterises my wife, Jocelyn. Her support for this project during my ill health has given me more love than I could ever deserve.

For

Jocelyn, Fiona, Laura and Tache

REVIEW OF OPERATION OBOE

A family game of trivial pursuit was the conception of this absolutely brilliant historical novel.

One of the geography questions opens a flood gate of memories for Vera. The family sit round with silent enchantment as she recalls her own experiences and those of her aunt, Fleur.

Fleur is a music lover and an accomplished oboe player. She meets her German husband at one of the musical concerts and moves to live in Germany. The first part of the story tells of how Vera goes to stay with Fleur and the First World War breaks out. They all know that Vera is in severe danger and try to get her out of Germany and to safety. A series of traumatic journeys are explained with vivid attention to detail and suspense mounts.

The second part of the story dwells on Fleur's experiences of war, her music and the birth of her son. Just prior to the Second World War, she is invited to take up a post in Africa. The boat trip alone is hair raising, a murder on board leads to much suspense.

She is invited to play her oboe along with members of the ship's company and some of the most wonderful strains of music are mentioned.

The research into this work has been painstaking and extensive, but well worth the obvious detailed effort. We learn of the Ashanti and the Twi language and many proverbs, we would do well to practice today.

World War Two sees Fleur on a mission, where she learns of many mysteries surrounding her family.

Her assignment acknowledges her flair for the oboe.

The whole book is steeped in historical events and I found it difficult to put down. My hope is that Miller Caldwell digs his heels in and treats us to another helping of such splendour.

Wendy Lake
Submissions Editor
Authorsonline.co.uk

FOREWORD

If this historical novel had a date of conception, it was 27th December 1991. Yet it is a novel which spans that whole century.

This is a work of fiction. It is however tentatively based around the remarkable life of my great Aunt Campbell (Fleur). Her niece Vera, my godmother, set in motion the events of 27th December 1991 which took place at our home in Troon, a year before we moved to Dumfries. With the exception of these two women, my family in the first and final brief chapters and identified historical personalities, the characters and incidents in this novel are entirely the products of my imagination or adapted from my own experiences in Ghana in the 1970s. They have no relation to any living persons.

One significant encounter helped me to consolidate this story. I met Hiroshi Murikami, a trained Kamikaze pilot, on 15th December 1977 at my home in Tema, Ghana.

Most importantly, I have valued the support and love of my wife Jocelyn and our daughters Fiona and Laura. They knew I was harbouring this novel for many years. They never gave me cause to abandon the project and, once it was begun, they gave me constant support. Our ageing collie Tache accompanied me on many necessary breaks to clear a fuddled mind. Gratitude to him will be ensured hopefully through many more walks in the years ahead.

Finally, I have earned time to write this book while combating mild cognitive impairment. I have found relaxation in bringing this story together and have no hesitation in recommending creative writing as a constructive pursuit to challenge and defeat a troubled mind.

The mind is its own place and in itself
Can make a heaven of hell, a hell of heaven.

Milton: 1608-1674

'Netherholm'
Dumfries

PART 1
Operation Oboe

CHAPTER ONE

Just occasionally, you find yourself in touch with history. Such opportunities often lurk in innocuous beginnings. Yet if the interest is nurtured and explored at a steady pace, an intricate tale often emerges. For some, it is mere history. A lesson learned. For others, it is a reawakening. A lesson to extol.

For more than two decades, my godmother Vera and her Wiltshire husband Tim, had joined my parents to celebrate a Christmas meal each year in the manse. These were Glasgow days, in the fifties and the sixties. Troon had been our home since 1984 and seven years later, whilst hosting this four generational gathering, this story emerged.

Lunch was over. All had retired to the lounge. Then the soporific warmth of the fire, generated by logs recently gathered from Fullarton woods, ensured twenty winks was enjoyed by the older members. Fiona and Laura had respected their need for a nap but impatiently awaited their stirrings. In time, eyes opened, limbs stretched, wristwatches were consulted and Fiona took centre stage.

'Let's play a game,' she challenged.

'We'd rather hear you play your violin, Fiona,' proposed Tim.

The tattered violin case was opened with little enthusiasm. Her younger sister released the bow from its lid, then tightened the horsehair bow. Fiona played twenty eight bars of Dvorak's Largo from the New World Symphony only making two errors, which showed more on her face than in the listening ears. Mild applause rewarded her efforts, but that was all that the audience was to hear.

'OK. Now, let's play Trivial Pursuit. I'll be on Uncle Tim's team. Laura you can go on Aunt Vera's.'

'All right,' replied Laura, keen to be involved in her big sister's planning.

Mutterings of …not being sure how to play…. were overcome by Laura. She had played the game twice since her mother had opened this Christmas present, though never winning. Her enthusiasm cautioned any other detractors. Soon chairs were positioned around a glass-topped, Ghanaian bubinga wood coffee table and the board lay open. Laura placed a cushion on the sapele wood Queen Mother Ashanti stool, and sat on it.

Fiona clarified how the game was played. Coloured wheels were lined up. No effort was made to give a choice of colour to the players. She distributed the yellow to Nana and Papa; the brown to Vera and Laura; the pink to Jocelyn; the orange to Miller and the green to herself and Tim. The game was underway.

Vera landed on History. 'What blew up at Lakehurst, New Jersey on 6th May 1937?' I asked.

Vera had no hesitation in replying. 'The Hindenburg. It was an airship, Laura.'

Four on the dice took them to Geography. 'Which British islands are the farthest north?'

'That will be the Shetlands.'

'Well done.' A single spot on the dice took her to Entertainment.

'What's tattooed on Popeye's arm?'

'Oh.... I know...' shouted Laura. 'It's ...um...er....spinach.'

'Sorry,' I answered compassionately, 'it's an anchor. Good try though Laura.'

The game proceeded with coloured pies appearing within wheels and a welcome cup of tea was served by rotating non-playing members. The game was proving to be a success, though it was clear to see that categories of Entertainment and recent Sport questions were left to the minds of the younger generation.

Tim rolled the dice and glided his wheel anticlockwise.

'No,' shouted Laura 'go the other way. Land on Geography. It's a pie.'

'I see.' Tim realised his mistake. 'Let's hope it's an easy one.'

'Which two countries span the Brenner Pass?'

Tim looked towards the ceiling for a moment. 'I've been there you know. I was there in 1920. It's Italy and Austria.'

'Correct. That proves that travel broadens the mind, Tim.'

Laura reached for the blue pie and placed it alongside the previously won brown Art & Literature pie. Their duo was doing well.

Then taking a deeper interest in his reply, Fiona asked why Uncle Tim was at the Pass. Tim recalled he had crossed the border from Austria into Italy, by going through the Brenner Pass whilst cycling with a friend on holiday but told Fiona, 'If you want to hear a real adventure, ask Vera where she was when the First World War was declared!'

All eyes turned to Vera. She was very aware that she was the focus of the family's sudden attention. 'Well,....as a matter of fact.... I was in Germany. I was in Hamburg, staying with Aunty Fleur and her husband, when war was declared. I remember on 4th August 1914, feeling sorry for Fleur, because she was married to a German doctor. She had a remarkable life. Her story would make a good book some day. But at that time, they were more worried about me, especially as I was suddenly an enemy, facing capture.'

That evening in Berlin, the British Ambassador, Sir Edward Goschen, presented the ultimatum in a historic interview with the Chancellor. Hardly noticing the phrase that was to resound round the world, Goschen included it in his report of the interview. He concluded that, if for strategical reasons it was a matter of life or death for Germany to advance through Belgium, it was, so to speak, a matter of life or death for Britain to keep her solemn pact.

Britain's declaration of war, coming immediately after Italy's declaration, was seen as the last act of treason and infuriated the Germans. A large number surrounded the British Embassy. Some began stoning the windows. Britain became overnight, the most hated enemy. '*Rassen Verrat'* – Race Treason was the favourite hate slogan heard that evening in the streets of Berlin.

'So how did you escape?' Fiona asked excitedly.

Laura sought the security of her mother's lap. Vera began to recall the events of 77 years ago.

'I suppose I featured early in Fleur's story. ....Let me tell you both stories......where should I begin? .... It was such a long time ago.'

She sat up, repositioned the cushion at her back, smiled at the girls and gave them the age-old preamble, 'Are you sitting comfortably?' Both girls nodded silently. 'Then I'll begin.'

Vera was once again, a girl of eighteen.

CHAPTER TWO

The spirit of adventure was not equally divided between the two daughters of Colonel James Bruce. Ada, the elder daughter, was a keen tennis player and classics enthusiast. She married the town's banker, William Caldwell and they had three daughters, Vera, Edith and Hilda.

Vera's grandfather had served a distinguished military career, in the Scots Guards as an Infantry officer. He had ensured his place in history, during the Ashanti invasions in the Gold Coast, between 1886 and 1901. He retired from the Army in 1908 to Forres in the highlands of Scotland where, with his wife, he ran the town's Moray Hills Hotel.

Fleur was fifteen years younger than Ada. Despite a hefty appearance, she had an exuberance of life and two dimples that gave her a warm soft face. She had been an avid reader as a child and, inspired by her father's military adventures and stories of Africa, her interest in political and international affairs flourished. She was musical too, playing the oboe at every opportunity she could, with friends, at parties and in local concerts. Although fluent in French, German was her first love and in 1911, after graduating in modern languages at Aberdeen University, Fleur sailed from Aberdeen to Hamburg to visit Germany, whilst considering her future.

She spent her first night abroad in Hamburg and was taken by its cosmopolitan character. It was June and the continental summer was warm. The tree-lined avenues and brightly coloured flowerbeds added an air of sophistication to the cobbled grey streets of the city centre. She thought she would like to take more time to get to know the city, but perhaps later, during her return home. She wanted to get to the rural heart of Germany, the parts where she would meet people who might respond to her willingness to speak with them and learn from them. Fleur travelled south of Lüneburg, seeing similarities in the purple heaths and moors with her native Knock of Braemoray in August. She marvelled at Celle's ducal palace which combined Gothic, Renaissance, Baroque and Rococo styles, before spending several weeks at Göttingen University, where she engaged in part-time English teaching. She enjoyed her time there so much that, with winter approaching, she decided not to proceed on the Baltic-

Alpine road to Munich. On this occasion, her first visit to Germany, she felt she had made a good start. She could return to see more another year, so it was time to return to Hamburg and sail home.

The Hamburg air was autumnal and it took a little longer for the morning sun to deliver its warmth on her return. She went to the shipping office at the Alster Pavilion, on the Jungfernstieg and discovered a ship was sailing to Harwich in three days time. On the other hand, if she could wait a further two weeks, there was a sailing to Aberdeen and that information pleased Fleur immensely. She could spend two more weeks in Germany's Gateway to the World. It had been a thriving town, even before the Holy Roman Emperor Friedrich Barbarossa granted it trading privileges in the year 1189. Hamburg was also the home of Johannes Brahms (1833-1897) and Felix Mendelssohn (1809-1847). Fleur loved their music and had played pieces of both composers' works at home in Forres. Taking an instant liking to the city and its culture, Fleur's holiday would go out with a flourish. She bought her ticket for Aberdeen and secured it in the tartan purse in her handbag. She had just sufficient funds, from her casual teaching opportunity at Göttingen, to prolong her holiday.

She found accommodation in a second floor flat overlooking the Grosse Wallanlagen Park on the Holstenwall. It gave her a sweeping view of the park and the residential area beyond. She noticed that the sun would enter her bedroom in the morning and, by evening, it would circle round to her sitting room. She was very pleased with her accommodation find. After unpacking, she washed her face, combed her long auburn hair, then set out mid afternoon across the Holstenwall, into the park.

Prams, children and nannies traversed the gritted pathways. It was a time for nannies to meet and compare their charges and their social news. Fleur wondered if or when she would have a pram and whether she would find such a well laid out park, on a pleasant afternoon such as this, in the place she would finally settle. Where might that be she wondered?

She followed a path to the Hamburg Museum, which was situated in the corner of the green expanse. There would be much to see here, but it surely merited a full day's attention. Preferably a full wet day she thought. So she approached the Museum with little intention of entering. Instead her eyes followed the public notices outside the building. Intimations of when the Sunday park concerts had been held had not yet been removed, but the city's late autumn flower show was still to take place. There was also a dog training class being started and the notice sought to attract suitable owners and young dogs to attend.

Towards the end of the notices was mention of a Brahms concert taking place that evening at 7.30pm. Brahms Symphony No. 4 in E minor, opus 98 was to begin the concert and in the second half was to be the Tragic Overture, Opus 81. It seemed so pertinent. His Fourth Symphony was like a great autumn landscape, its autumnal colouring sometimes subdued and sometimes tinged with harshness. Meanwhile, the tragic mood was more like the resignation of a philosopher withdrawing into himself as he grows older. These sentiments seemed to mirror Fleur's feelings. Brahms was a lonely and solitary figure in his later years. He never married. Fleur felt a further kinship with this work. Hamburg had also been his birthplace. What fortune to have noticed this concert. She lost no time in returning to the flat and prepared for the evening performance.

The concert took place in the Künsthalle, on the far side of town across the Binnenalster pond. After making enquiries, she boarded the tramcar and arrived almost one hour before the performance. This ensured her obtaining a modestly priced seat and gave her time to read the concert notes in the evening's programme.

It was a large domed building ornately plastered and with long crimson velvet curtains framing the orchestral stage. Fleur hoped that the music would not be smothered by such heavy drapery but correctly assumed that the conductor had taken this into consideration.

The hall was filling with young and old couples. Complete families quickly filled some rows. Many chaperoned females were ostentatiously directed to their seats, by an assortment of young male suitors and relatives. She detected even a few reluctant or merely dutiful partners. There were a few young men, on their own. Fleur's eyes followed each one as they entered the hall and made their way to their seats, guessing where they would sit, what they did, and how well they might know the works of Brahms. She had played many mind games in her travels, over the last few weeks.

Her preoccupation with this playful diversion had blinded her to the approach of a well-dressed man, whose seat ticket brought him next to her. He excused himself as he took his seat, but Fleur had not heard him and gave no indication that she had noticed him approach.

All rose to sing the National Anthem. When she resumed her seat, she became aware of the charm of the young man as he ensured she was seated before him. She focussed momentarily on his hands. They were quite beautiful, gentle, sensitive hands. Long thin fingers she noticed. Hands of a musician. A pianist perhaps, or a violin player maybe. Fleur wondered who he might be.

The second movement, the Andante moderato, was in the style of a romance. It opened with a call on the horns, then the clarinets entered with pizzicato strings accompaniment and sang a beautifully tender and wistful melody. The emotions of the music were distilled into Fleur's mind, her veins, and her hopes. The interval approached.

As the applause died down at the end of the first part of the performance and the orchestra was leaving the stage, the young man turned to Fleur and smiled. Their eyes met fleetingly.

'Did you enjoy the first half?' he enquired.

'It was beautiful,' Fleur replied. 'I see how much Brahms means to the people of Hamburg.'

'You are not from the city then? Well, let me guess. Perhaps you are from Lüneburg. No? Well, perhaps much further south. Perhaps I detect a Munster-Osnabrück accent? Am I getting closer?'

Fleur was enjoying this game. 'Further north, well, north-west in fact.'

'I think you are teasing me. North-west takes me to the North Sea!'

'Indeed I am not teasing you, Sir. You are assuming I am German.'

'But your German is so good. Your accent is remarkable. *Fabelhaft! Dies ist herrlich.* I can't believe you are English.'

'I'm not. I am Scottish, from the north of Scotland.'

'Permit me to offer you a refreshing glass of Riesling with which we can toast each other's nation.'

They arose and made their way towards the café in the hall. Fleur became aware that her companion was responding to the greeting "Good evening, doctor."

'I was wrong then. I thought you might be a musician,' she ventured.

'Just because I attend a concert, I am a musician?'

'No.' Fleur felt hurt. 'Because I noticed your hands. They are artist's hands. They would please a pianist or a violinist. I am sure you do not work in industry.'

'My apologies. You are right. I am a general practitioner, of three years experience and yes, I do play the piano, when I find time.'

Two glasses of white wine were served. 'To the people of Scotland!' Willy raised his glass.

Fleur raised hers 'To the good people of Hamburg.' she replied. They sat down. This time they were face to face.

'May I introduce myself to you. I am Dr Willy Richter. It is a pleasure to meet you.'

'I am Fleur, I mean, Fräulein Fleur Bruce. I am a graduate of Aberdeen University, where I studied French and German and, during the last three months, I have been travelling in Germany, improving my language. I will be sailing home in two weeks time.'

'Ah, so soon?' Fleur could think of no answer. She tightened her lips and nodded.

'Well, anyway let us enjoy this evening and forget about tomorrow. Then we can enjoy the rest of the concert.'

'What, may I ask, made you decide to attend the concert this evening?' he enquired.

'I strolled by the Grosse Wallanlanger park this afternoon and saw the notice. I do not get the chance to attend many concerts at home and, of course, I liked the programme I saw. *Ein Konzertstück von Brahms.* I also knew Brahms was born in the city and that added a certain thrill, which I did not want to miss.'

'You know Brahms' father, Jakob, played double bass in this same Hamburg City orchestra.'

'Really?'

'Indeed. He had quite humble beginnings. I have one criticism of Brahms though.'

Fleur thought she was getting out of her depth musically. She need not have worried.

'Brahms should have married Clara Schumann. Instead he

suffered a breakdown. He died, only sixteen years ago you know. What makes us proud here is that he founded a women's choir. It is very difficult to get into. They demand such a high standard. That too is always a very well attended concert.' He turned to face her. 'Do you play an instrument?'

'I used to play the clarinet, but four years ago I changed to play the oboe.'

'Ah, the instrument which sounds the solo 'A' note to tune the orchestra. I can imagine you playing the oboe. The discipline of controlling the double reed is demanding, I understand, but if I may say, I can see you have an advantage.'

'An advantage?'

'Yes. Your dimples!' Fleur blushed. Willy was taking an interest in her. 'Such taut cheek muscles are an advantage, I would have thought.'

Willy wondered if he was being too personal for a moment. Her response was slow in coming and thwarted by the sound of the stage bell. Willy resorted to an escorting role. 'It's time to resume our seats..... After you......'

They made their way back to their seats through the gathering audience. Fleur was aware of people noticing that she was with the doctor. She was also aware of a warm, frightening, unsure feeling deep within her. What did this night mean to her? How would it end?

The second part of the concert was ominous. The Tragic Overture. Was its turbulence associated with Goethe's Faust or that of Hamlet? Or was it a threat to a brief relationship? The two pieces this evening had been juxtaposed, mirth and sadness. Willy and Fleur's emotions for the music diffused and transposed to those for each other.

When the concert ended, Willy insisted that she shared a carriage home with him. He hoped that his intent was not too obvious, but he wanted to know where she was staying. He also knew that, if he wanted this budding relationship to linger or even grow, he had only two weeks in which to make his mark, or his intentions known.

The covered horse-drawn carriage sped its way past the Raathaus, past the Michaeliskirche, towards the gates of the Grosse Wallanlagen. How he wished the horse would pick up a limp. Any delay would do. Perhaps a wheel might dislodge. It was not to be.

'This is where I am staying, on the second floor. It's really quite comfortable and there is a marvellous view across the park.' She looked into his eyes. 'I thank you for a most pleasant evening. I will not forget it.'

Willy took her hand as she descended from the carriage. As Fleur stepped down, he raised her hand to his lips and kissed her. Fleur smiled.

'Neither will I,' he replied.

'Permit me to give you my card. The Clinic, Brachvogelstrasse, Hamburg, is where I work. As you can see, my surgery is not more than three kilometres from your residence. I live above the clinic. May I invite you to dine with me tomorrow evening?'

'That would be most kind.'

'Shall I say 7.30pm?'

'Perhaps 7pm..... if... that is as convenient?' She was shocked to find herself encouraging him by saying this.

'Then 7 it is. I will be here prompt at 7pm.' Willy stepped back and for a last fleeting moment that evening, their eyes coupled once more.

'Good night, sleep well,' they said simultaneously. Then he returned to the carriage and was gone as suddenly as he had appeared, almost four hours earlier that evening. Fleur entered the stairwell, her emotions in turmoil.

CHAPTER THREE

The next week found Willy and Fleur in each other's company daily. They spoke of families, of religion and politics and found their backgrounds were similar. They visited parks and took walks in the countryside. They spoke of music and poetry, of culture and literature. They shared their knowledge of science and nature and created a future, in their minds, that they wished to share. Willy was very aware that this relationship was becoming public knowledge, but he did not care. There was something special about their alliance. Fleur was not tainted by the local social milieu. Indeed she was seen as something almost exotic. She spoke German well and with style. She was of sound health and mind. Deep down Willy knew that Fleur was his partner for life.

Accordingly he made overtures to his brother Karl and his wife Renate. He proposed to Karl that Fleur could stay with them for a while and be the English tutor to their two children. After a family lunch with Karl, Renate, their children and an unsuspecting Fleur, Karl communicated to Willy that his family would be delighted to provide free accommodation, while regular lessons in English would be taught to the children to compliment their school studies. If only Fleur would agree, pondered Willy. He had yet to present his well-laid scheme, to retain Fleur in Hamburg.

Willy took Fleur to lunch on the Saturday, three days before she was due to return to Aberdeen. He chose to dine at *Der Radfahrweg.* The Cyclist's Track was a popular eating place for couples. It was a forty-minute cycle ride from Hamburg on the Bremen road, near to the village of Apensen. It had been known to him since his student days, when he cycled to the Cyclist's Track to consolidate his medical studies in his mind, only to muddle his learning in the light beer which was served in chilled, wide-rimmed glasses. The interior consisted of a series of alcoves, which almost looked like confessional boxes, but gave the couple the privacy they sought. The food was traditional, plain and wholesome. Willy joked that he would order *die Forelle* as the trout sounded like Fleur's name.

'Then I shall have trout too!'

'Trout, potato and cabbage it is then! A good choice.' The waiter took that as a double order.

They were speechless, but comfortable in the moment's

silence. They looked into each other's eyes. Willy moved beside Fleur, his left leg resting against her long skirt. His warmth was transferred to her and hers to him. They held hands. They wished this moment to last forever. He turned to her and kissed her cheek.

'Darling, it was fate that brought us to that concert. Had I met you on the street, the moment would have passed with no opportunity to catch your eye. How upsetting that would have been for me. Like focussing on a beautiful bird only for the attention to cause flight.'

'Oh, I am sure we would have passed that spot over and over again, until we met! You know, my mother has a saying "What's for you, will not go past you." I suppose I always used this to get over disappointments in the past, but for the first time I see what she meant.'

She smiled at Willy. 'We have not known each other very long. It has all been so quick. I need not have....'

The waiter arrived with two oval plates on which two trout lay alongside cabbage and potato. They placed serviettes on their laps and raised their cutlery.

'You were about to say something Fleur?'

'Oh, it's so hard to explain. It's just,.....oh,...I don't know...' She began to sob. Her emotions poured out.

Willy put his knife and fork down. He placed his arm round her. Then he said 'The symptoms are clear. Neither of us can possibly eat in this state....when parting is drawing so close ...and.....we are both ....so very much in love.'

Fleur looked into Willy's eyes.

'Yes, Willy, I love you so very much.'

Willy was right. Fleur knew it was love, but could see no way for it to flourish any further, with her impending departure. She probed in vain.

'Willy, you could be a doctor in Aberdeen. Would you think about that?'

'I had.....but no. Fleur, you remember we went to Karl's home on Wednesday. Did you like them?'

'Yes, of course I did. Why?'

'Well, until we sort ourselves out, give ourselves a little more time to think about our future, you know....some breathing space, Karl and Renate would wish you to live with them and you can give English lessons to their children Jurg and Liesel. Would you consider that?'

'Does that mean we still see each other regularly?'

'Of course it does. Very often, I assure you. It gives us time to be sure – even though I am already!'

Thoughts raced through Fleur's mind, her family, her travel plans, her future …her future!

'Then you know what I must do?'

'What?'

'I must go to the Alster Pavilion tomorrow and cancel my sailing.'

Willy held Fleur close to him, hugged her while resting his cheek next to hers, then kissed her not once, but four times. 'Oh Fleur, I love you so much.'

Fleur cried quietly. 'Willy I have made the most important decision in my life. I love you too.'

The waiter approached.

'Is the fish not to your liking. Shall I take the plates away?'

'Not yet,' replied Fleur, regaining her composure, 'My appetite is returning.'

The winter of 1912 gave way to the spring, in which Willy and Fleur announced their engagement. In the autumn of 1913, Willy married Fleur at the Michaeliskirche, in Hamburg city centre. Although Fleur had no family present at their wedding, telegrams from home were read out in both languages. To make amends, their honeymoon took them across the North Sea to Forres, where Willy was introduced to her family and friends. Vera met the couple and practised her basic German with them. Vera was thrilled when Willy suggested that she come to visit them one day, to improve her German.

So it was, a year later, as an eighteen year old young lady, in June 1914, that Vera stepped ashore at Bremerhaven and took the coastal train via Cuxhaven and Buxtehude to Hamburg where she was met by Aunty Fleur.

They embraced at the platform and when Vera bent down to collect her baggage, Fleur noticed the unmistakable shape of her black oboe case. 'Vera, you've brought my oboe?'

'Yes. Your father thought you would be missing it by now.'

'How right he was. That's wonderful. Oh, what a pleasant

surprise. It was silly of me to forget it on our honeymoon last year. I'm lost without it.'

Vera stayed with Fleur and Willy at Brachvogelstrasse throughout the summer. Willy and Fleur soon gave presentable performances on oboe and piano while Vera sang. These were very happy soirées that the trio enjoyed that summer.

Vera soon began to go shopping for the family. She read the papers and pictorial news sheets over and over until she could read them fluently. Fleur was always at hand to translate the awkward or unknown phrases.

Like Fleur before her, Vera enjoyed the warmth of a continental summer. At weekends they would frequently visit the city parks and on Sundays, after church, they visited friends and she widened her acquaintances. Vera was attracted to the oldest part of the city, lying to the east of the River Alster. Paradoxically the most recent buildings were there now, after the great fire of 1842. She felt at home in Hamburg. It was a vibrant city, with an open door to the world. Ships came and went regularly and the artefacts of the Orient and Africa were to be seen in gift and antique shops. Sailors sometimes had monkeys on their shoulders. They were always an attraction for the children to see.

She enjoyed her visit to Hagenbeck's Tierpark at Stellingen. There she saw antelope, bok, gnu, zebra, giraffe, pelican, adjutant stork, black swan and flamingo. All these creatures and many more could be seen, not in the perimeters of the zoo she had seen in Glasgow, but in such a disguised captivity, which gave the animals the advantages of freedom, with the additional advantage of safety. Her impression was that this was how zoos should be. There could be no more congenial home than this for them, at Stellingen.

On one Saturday in the height of summer, they travelled by rail down the banks of the River Elbe, to Glückstadt where they enjoyed a sumptuous picnic of cheeses, sausages, chicken and cakes. They came back before nightfall, glowing. Each day her confidence in speaking German grew and her fluency and accent got better all the time. Fleur complimented her on her efforts and told her she would soon be talking like a native German girl.

Vera purchased a local summer dress. It made her seem so grown up. She had never experienced such a hot summer. At times, it was difficult to keep cool. Nevertheless, she knew it would not last. The summer wore on, turning June into July. She felt that the three-month excursion would be enough for her, on her first long journey away from home. Maybe she would have some days next summer to wear her new clothes in Forres. She opened her purse. In the leather stamp slit, she had no stamps. Instead it contained her return ticket. 16:00hrs Sailing Bremerhaven – Harwich. Saturday - August 29th 1914. Nothing in her mind gave any indication that she would miss the boat.

CHAPTER FOUR

Vera arrived in Germany, exactly one week before Sunday 28th June 1914. On that fateful day in Serajevo, Gavrilo Princip, a Serbian student and member of a secret movement Mlada Bosna (Young Bosnia), using weapons supplied by the Serbian 'Black Hand' movement, assassinated Archduke Franz Ferdinand, heir to the Austrian throne, and his wife the Czech Countess Sophie.

Had Vera planned to arrive three weeks later, her trip would most surely have been put off. The stacked pack of cards, which represented European alliances, tumbled dramatically over this period and the implications were ominous for both Vera and Fleur. On 23rd July, counting on Germany's support, Austria gave a ten-point ultimatum to Serbia, the perceived instigator of the trouble. Although most points were accepted, Serbia refused to agree to the demand that Austrian officials should be involved in the investigation of the assassination plot. On 28th July, Austria-Hungary declared war on Serbia. A mere two days later Czar Nicholas II ordered general mobilisation in support of the Serbs.

The whole network of alliances was consequently called into play, plunging Europe into catastrophe. When Russia failed to respond to a German ultimatum, calling her to stop her mobilisation, Germany herself ordered mobilisation and declared war on Russia on 1st August 1914.

Willy was a troubled man. Vera could not stay any longer and certainly not wait for her sailing on 29th August. He would arrange for her to sail to England as soon as possible. He was confident that this would not be too difficult as Britain was thought likely to stay neutral, but if not neutral, then quite likely to come to aid Germany.

Sunday 2nd August 1914.

Germany presented Belgium with a note to demand right of passage through her territory.

As they sat down to eat that evening Willy reported the day's events.

'I went to the shipping company office this afternoon, to arrange for your return home, Vera. They say that due to our mobilisation and declaration of war on Russia, England has suspended all sailings. The government ordered steamship lines to cancel all merchant sailings on 31st July, but this is a temporary measure I am told. However, as soon as the situation improves, sailings will continue. After all our countries are not at war. I have asked to be kept informed of any boats going to England. They know how to reach me.'

Monday 3rd August 1914.

Germany declared war on France.

Vera's situation was becoming more difficult. She was trapped and yet she was with her family. A feeling of helplessness clouded her mind, mixed with her concern for Fleur. Was Fleur now German by marriage and therefore safe, or was she as alien as Vera herself was becoming? How could she be an enemy, while her aunt was not? If Fleur was not, then she surely was not, she thought. Her youthful reasoning was faulty, but she needed to grasp a token comforting emotion.

Vera watched mesmerised as she saw the 47th Infantry Regiment, part of the 10th Division in Crown Prince Wilhelm's Fifth Army, march to the military band down Glacischussee, on their way towards north eastern France. An Infantry division, all so familiar to Fleur's father, but for their tunics and the spikes on their helmets, which glinted in the sun as did the brass instruments and their highly polished brass buttons. At the rear, was a strong large horse, a Clydesdale in all but name, bearing a drummer with two drums astride his saddle. Vera enjoyed the martial music, while fearing the menace it represented.

Tuesday 4th August 1914.

Germany's troops invade France. 11am Germany is now at war with Britain.

The crystal set in the doctor's living room, reported Britain's betrayal to Germany and, over the airwaves, Ambassador Edward Goschen's embassy step declaration suddenly altered the military equation.

'Patients are mentioning our situation. I tell them my wife is German now, but Vera I must arrange for you to leave. Karl and Renate will keep you in hiding, until we get you out of Germany. Tell no one where you are staying and you must keep out of sight. Remember Karl and Renate are doing this to protect all of us, while placing themselves at risk.' How strange and ironic this was.

Karl and Renate had provided a safe haven only two years ago, that enabled Fleur to elongate her stay and in due course marry Willy. Now their hospitality was to conceal Vera and aid her speedy departure.

Tears welled up in Vera's eyes. She knew she was helpless and so dependent, but there really was nothing she could do other than co-operate fully, protect her helpers and avoid contact with all others.

'We are trying to get you home as soon as possible. I assure you we're all working hard,' reassured Fleur.

'It would be better if I gave you one of my German suitcases. Your case looks as if it might give you away, Vera. Come, let me help you pack your things into this one. I got it in Hanover in March. It's a strong case. You could even sit on it if you had to!'

That night as dusk fell, Willy took Vera to Karl's home, making sure no one was around to see her enter the house. Vera was taken up to the loft, where a mattress had been prepared for her comfort.

'I'm afraid we have to take precautions. That's why you are in the loft, Vera.' said Renate. 'When it is safe, you will hear this knock…rat a tat taat. Then you can come down, but if you hear anyone sneeze, or pretend to sneeze, then make your way quickly and quietly, up to the loft. That means there may be danger around. Do you understand?'

Vera nodded. Had this been a game it would have excited her, but it was not. The full impact of being an alien in an enemy country was now upon her, and her adrenaline flowed to camouflage her fear. She must do nothing to offend or disappoint her benefactors.

On Saturday 8th August 1914 at four in the afternoon, Willy called. Vera heard the knock and came down. Arrangements had been made for her to sail to Sweden. It would not be a comfortable crossing and it might be long, but it was possibly the safest in the circumstances. Willy explained that Vera would be smuggled on to a fishing trawler, at the port of Wismar on the Baltic Sea. This would mean a day travelling through Lübeck and Dassow by rail. She would then be met at the port of Wismar by a trawler skipper named Franz. On arrival at the Swedish port of Halmstad, the skipper would give Vera enough money to get the train to Göteborg, where the British Consul would be able to assist her back to Scotland. It was best that these details were not written down and indeed, Willy suggested it was best to forget the details, but be assured and aware that a plan had been prepared. It was her duty to see it through, not to question it.

Clearly some considerable money must have passed hands to arrange this crossing. She even wondered how trust could be ensured? How many people knew about the arrangements? These questions Vera put to Willy.

'Don't you worry about the cost or the planning. It is a life we are saving. It is the best we can do in these troubled times. Believe me, I have confidence in what we have arranged. I have a friend in Stockholm, a doctor too. I will try to contact him as well. We must succeed and I am sure we will. We can not wait much longer. Please trust us, Vera.'

On Sunday 9th August, Vera was woken early with a cup of coffee, a slice of buttered black bread, an apple and a few grapes. 'Eat well, your meals will not be regular for a few days,' said Renate.

True to Willy's word, at 8.15am an elderly man arrived. Renate opened the door. He introduced himself as a retired chemist and patient of Dr Willy Richter. They had been expecting him. He was prepared to help to get Vera, an innocent young lady, back home no matter what was happening all around in Europe at this time. He was Herr Hugo Kleist.

Hugo was a widower of seven years, whose only son had been killed in a train derailment four years earlier, at his work in the Hamburg rail yards. His circle of friends was diminishing, but he saw in the young doctor, a compassionate and caring individual, who had time for his occasional medical complaints. Last week, he had sought an appointment, because of a cold he could not clear. The doctor suggested, in addition to a bedtime ointment, which he prescribed, that he took the sea air, to assist his breathing. Little did he know where this prescription was leading him.

'Oh, what a good suggestion. Thank you, Doctor. I can now have a reason to visit my nephew at Wismar. I have not seen him for some time. He has a fishing trawler business. He's a fine young man. I suppose he'll be called up by the Navy soon.'

As Willy pondered his patient's response, Hugo ventured to enquire of Vera. 'That young girl you have staying with you,

Doctor. Is she not British?'

'She is a young Scottish girl, who was visiting us this summer.'

'I see your predicament. If she could only get away to a neutral country.'

'Well then, Hugo, what would you do in my position?'

'I suppose.... I'd ask my nephew at Wismar. He lands fish in Sweden sometimes. That would be my best option.'

'Could it be mine too?' Willy felt an opportunity emerging, which he could not let slip.

Hugo paused. Had he heard the doctor correctly? Was this a dangerous commitment he was being asked to undertake, for himself and his nephew?

'Let me make some enquiries. I'll get back to you in a few days.'

The next few days had been anxious ones. In the evening, to break the tension, Fleur played her oboe and Willy accompanied her on his piano, but there were no opportunities for Vera to sing in English. Fleur warmed-up by playing exercises by Wilhelm Popp, but together they played the Soldier's March by Robert Schumann, the Waltz by Johannes Brahms and the oboe accompanied Willy playing Schubert's piano quintet, The Trout. This was certainly not the time for any non-German music to seep beyond Vera's sanctuary. Yet the music calmed their anxieties and carved memories that they would recall in happier years to come.

There was a hint of an easterly breeze on Sunday 9th August as the armies of Europe were gathering and Hugo, Vera and her new brown suitcase, set out for the station at Hamburg.

Hugo bought two adult tickets to Wismar. The journey involved two trains. The first would take them only as far as Lübeck. Hamburg station was busy, with soldiers standing in groups of six or so. Their packs were on the ground and six rifles rested on each pile, pointing upwards. Hugo overheard that this was part of the German First Army, commanded by Colonel-General Alexander von Kluck, but he was not present. This was a north Schleswig-Holstein brigade heading for Dortmund and a rendezvous with the rest of the First Army. Fortunately, the train they would board was heading north-east to Lübeck, in the other direction. That was a relief for them both.

Keeping close together at all times and with Vera forbidden to speak, they boarded the train on platform 3 and sat in a second class compartment. At precisely 10.10am the train pulled away from the station.

As the train passed through the outskirts of Hamburg, Vera relaxed and saw the labours of gardeners ripen in rows. Would they benefit from their work this year, or would the war require troops to be fed from these gardens? Apples, pears and plums ripened in some garden orchards, while in other gardens, regimented rows of sweet peas, potatoes, cabbages and beans awaited their call for service. The rich green wands of hidden carrots grew well in this sandy soil not far from the North Sea.

By 11.00am the train had crossed the rivers which served the health spa of Bad Oldesloe. Twenty minutes later they crossed the Elbe-Lübeck Kanal and pulled into Lübeck. This was a smaller station, with no sign of troop movement on their arrival. They disembarked and made their way towards the ticket box. A policeman stood beside the ticket collector. Vera was told sharply to say nothing and look sad. '*Verstehen Sie?*' '*Ja, Herr Kleist.*' She understood fully.

The ticket collector clipped both tickets. Then as they left the platform, the policeman enquired where they were going. Vera's heart missed a beat. She remembered to look sad and say nothing. Herr Kleist took the policeman to one side and spoke quietly to him. Was he handing her over? Vera felt her heart pound. Was this the moment of betrayal? Oh, how she wished for Willy and Fleur to be with her now. Then the policeman came forward, placed his hand on her shoulder, and patted it twice. '*Ich spreche Ihnen mein Mitgefühl aus.*'

Vera nodded without a word, recognising that his condolences were being offered. As they crossed the station forecourt, Hugo told her he had informed the policeman that she had just learned of her mother's sudden death and he was taking her to her home.

'I may have to use this excuse again. It went down well, Vera.'

'I may shed a tear next time,' she retorted.

There was a wait of two hours before the train to Wismar left Lübeck. There was much movement of luggage and people both civilian and military. Possibly more were in naval uniform than in army uniform. They required horse drawn carriages to move items to and from the station. The stench of horse droppings, yet to be cleared, mingled with the steam from the trains fuelling their boilers. Newspapers were in considerable demand and all declared the same word *KRIEG*. Vera tried to nap, letting sleep overcome all thoughts of war.

Hugo noticed her tiredness. He drew his arm around her shoulder and gave support to her head as she catnapped. He had not been as physically close to anyone for years. It reminded him of his son when he was small, snuggling up to his father at bedtime. It was an infrequent and tender moment for him to treasure in his old age. He had no wish to consider that she was the enemy. How strange to find such purpose in life in these circumstances. Why, when war tore people apart, was it capable of bringing the enemy close to him? His thoughts were overcome by his responsibility resting beside him. Had he had a daughter, he would have hoped for one like Vera. She would have made the perfect sister for his late son, he thought.

He saw the station clock approach 14:40. It was time to waken Vera. 'Platform 2 for Wismar,' he whispered softly in her ear. She woke from her comforting dreams and eased herself from his side.

They boarded an empty carriage, but by the time the train gathered pace departing the station, two other passengers had arrived. One was a priest and the other was a woman of around fifty-five years of age. The woman was clearly a parishioner of the priest. She spoke incessantly about her fears for the war. How suddenly it had seemed to come upon them.

'Was war an act of God?' she asked, but gave no time for the priest to reply. 'Why were Italy and Britain not supporting Germany? How long would the war last? How many Germans would be killed? What if we lost the war? No, that was unthinkable.'

'Many will die on our side as well as their side. God has given us this right to chose, but we must continually pray that He enters the minds of those who make the decisions as well as those who suffer.' Then the priest turned towards Vera.

'And you, my child, I pray that there will be good men folk after this war, to renew faith in our land and give you the families that our country needs.'

Vera was unable to follow the priest's every word and felt that repetition of the death of her mother by Hugo would lead to further pastoral intrusiveness. She chose to break her agreement not to talk.

'*Entschuldigen Sie. Mir ist sehr übel.*' On announcing her

feeling sick she rose to her feet and made for the corridor. To ensure she was not followed, she remarked with growing confidence '*Ich glaube, ich habe eine Vergiftung.*' This was really most unlikely. Vera had not eaten since breakfast and was actually feeling rather hungry!

Hugo was relieved that the priest and his parishioner left the train at Dassow. Vera returned from the corridor feeling very much alive. She apologised for breaking her silence but felt it was necessary. Hugo admitted he was worried she would be found out, but pleased to report her accent caused no interest and the message got through.

'We are unlikely to meet such a combination again. I think the old routine will stand the test next time.' Vera agreed.

The train slowed down as it approached Wismar. Vera could smell the sea in the air. They were very close to the shore. The screech of the brakes and a sudden halt meant they had arrived. They disembarked and proceeded along the platform. Then Hugo exclaimed. 'There he is, my nephew, Franz. Remember, Vera, he knows all about you. He is a good man.'

Franz gave Hugo an embrace, then shook Vera's hand. 'Come, let's go. I do not want people asking too many questions.'

Taking her case, he crossed the line behind the departing train and made for a cutting through the town, towards his home. Uncle and nephew spoke incessantly about his health, Hugo's fishing business and, of course, the war developments. At no point did they seek Vera's thoughts. She dutifully followed them in silence.

CHAPTER FIVE

Franz had been a fisherman since he left school in 1885. He knew the Baltic coastline intimately. He knew the boats and the nationalities of those who sailed these waters and he knew how kind and how treacherous the Baltic's moods could be. But what troubled him most were the consequences of failure in this undertaking. He knew he would be shot if he was caught exporting an enemy. What defence could he have? She was a young woman, not a combatant. Her uncle by marriage, was a respected German. Yes, but was her grandfather not a British military man? Was it blind loyalty to an ageing uncle which had set him off on this foolish mission? He had many reservations.

He put these thoughts to reality. Was there not a greater cause? Was he not doing the right thing by God? He turned towards Vera. This was his cargo. This was his mission. War had brought the situation upon them both. He knew what he had to do. With a sudden clarity of purpose, he explained what must be done.

It was arranged that they would visit the trawler around 8pm that evening. Vera would be taken on board and hidden but the boat would not sail. The following day, Franz would approach the harbourmaster and notify him of his intention to sail to a non-German shore. This was standard practice, but in view of the war which was now upon them, harbourmasters had been given the authority to search every boat leaving harbour and ensure no smuggling of any sort, human or otherwise, was being entertained. At night, there were patrols of old mariners assisting the police in finding illegal practices at the harbour. They did not begin their patrol until around 9.30pm. That is why Vera had to be secured safely on board before then.

One further problem existed. There would be two other crew members on board. They were not privy to the arrangements. Franz could not afford to mention Vera before she arrived and to make sure, neither fisherman had been told nor would they be told, until they were well under way. It meant that even after setting sail, Vera would have to stay hidden until Franz introduced her to them.

Vera was taken to a shed at the bottom of Franz's garden. She was told to wait there until Franz returned. There was some food and enough room to lie down. Vera was hungry. She ate the onion pie heartily and thought of how Fleur might cope with a war against Britain. Yet she knew Willy would support her throughout the war no matter how long it lasted. Having eaten well, sleep came over her. She stirred only when she heard Franz approach some two hours later.

'It's time to go. Please do not speak to anyone and, remember, when you are on board, you must not attract any attention. Movement means sound and the harbour is a quiet place at night. You may be aware of voices or footsteps on the shingle approaching the boat. Someone may even board the boat. You must stay hidden and silent. Do you understand?'

'Yes, I do. Honestly.' Vera noted the business like tone of Franz. He had never mentioned her by name. She knew he had thought this through thoroughly and respected the fine detail of his planning.

Der Fischhaken lay partly on the shale of the beach, partly in the water at the harbour. Vera was prepared to be trapped by this 'fishhook' but fully intended to be the fish that got away in the end. As she approached this functional craft, she knew it was her only hope, her lifeline and, whatever discomfort it might have in store for her, it was a small price to pay for her freedom. They climbed down eight metal rungs and boarded when no one seemed to be around. Franz took Vera below deck. 'You will not be hiding here, I regret. First, I have a thick sweater for you to wear. It will keep you warm. I will take you up to the bow of the boat when all is clear. It has a high covered area with a life belt fixed on a plank. This plank is attached to a series of seven others, to form a wooden panel. It has been brought forward to give enough space for you to stand or lie down in. You can bolt the panel from the inside. This makes it look flush with its surroundings. I warn you, it will be pitch black when you are enclosed. To prevent any inspection coming too close, I have placed an old oily net with a dozen creels on top. Inspectors might examine the net to see if it hides anything beneath but they should not go beyond that unless they have been tipped off. For your toilet, there is a bucket. It will be emptied at sea, after I release you. On the ledge above your head is fresh water and some bread. It will not be comfortable you understand? Do you have any questions?'

'How long will the journey take?'

'Forgive me for forgetting to tell you. It will take three and a half hours to enter Danish territorial waters and a further four hours to arrive at Halmstad in Sweden. But you will be on deck by then, I hope. So, are you ready for your incarceration now?'

'Yes, I am and thank you for making this possible. Let's hope the war is over soon. You are a very brave man.'

Franz secured Vera behind the wooden panel. Complete darkness hit Vera. It frightened her. Then suddenly Franz opened it again.

'I forgot to give you these Swedish krona. There are enough for you to get to Göteborg. It's best you take them now. Right, don't forget to secure the board.'

Vera heard the oily net being dragged towards her hiding place. She ensured the bolts were firmly in place. She counted the lobster creels being dropped on top. Had she missed one out? The smell of the sea, of nets and fish was strong. She had to get used to it. She listened intently, but no noise could be heard. She could not sleep as the shed nap had driven her tiredness away. She sat on the side of her suitcase, with her hands cradling her face.

With not a speck of light intruding this blackness, she knew sleep would come to her eventually. She turned her thoughts to her worried parents. What must they be thinking? What a surprise they will get when she arrives unannounced. When would that be? In two days time, she wondered? No, perhaps four or five days would be more likely. A smile came to her as she remembered the comfort in which she had arrived in Germany, compared to her incarceration now, on her departure. Thoughts of how a modern war might be fought occupied her mind. Why were so many countries involved? Would the Commonwealth, the great British Commonwealth, come to our aid? Would the German Navy latch on to Der Fischhaken in the Baltic? Then she thought of herself. How uncomfortable the next day would be. What sort of state would she be in by then? Would the crew be civil towards her? She put her hands together and silently prayed to God, that she was not alone during these hours of fear and darkness. Then she prayed for Franz and his crew and all those who had made this attempted escape for her possible. God seemed to answer in a challenging way.

Suddenly, a murmur of voices was heard. Vera froze in her seated position. The noise was from a distance, but was approaching. Perhaps two, or three voices. She must stay calm and stay silent. Feet dragged along the shale, then crunched as full weight was applied to each step. The newcomer spoke quietly with a coastal accent that Vera could not fully understand. It seemed they were there for a long time, but in fact, only for as long as it took to light a cigarette, gaze out to sea and reminisce about happier days.

Vera lost count of the hours until the moment some five hours later, when a deputation came on board. She heard Franz greet the harbourmaster. The voices grew louder and suddenly she felt a tug on the boards. The lifebelt had been lifted and then replaced. She heard the crashing of the creels and the scuffling sound of the net being disturbed. Then it fell silent. The voices went down below and from under her feet she felt a probing. How long would this last? She heard Franz's reassuring voice. It showed no signs of anxiety. Then the two crew members arrived. Greetings abounded.

The trawler blurted into life. Woken like a sleeping giant, the engine warmed up. Fumes pinched her nasal tracts. The boat then moved slowly in reverse. She heard the shale slide away from the bow beneath her, while above, she was perched rigid like a weather-vane. The last contact with German land slid out of earshot as Der Fischhaken pirouetted round to face the open sea. In three hours time or so, they would be outside German territorial waters. That moment could not come soon enough for Vera.

Tuesday August 11th 1914.

Fortunately the German Navy was inactive in the Baltic. The belief was that an early victory on land would not necessitate any risk in the performance of the Navy function, their intention being merely to ensure that sea-lanes were open for the commerce of the country. The Kaiser's reluctance to use his beloved Navy was a godsend for Der Fischhaken and for all on board.

It was far from plain sailing however for Vera. An hour after setting sail, the wind got up creating a swell through which Der Fischhaken pitched and rolled. Vera was thrown round her confined space and banged herself so hard that she was sure she would have been heard. Then the retching and sea sickness followed, filling the bucket at her feet. Fresh air was what she craved. None was forthcoming. She thought she was losing consciousness but it was only her body resisting the heaving and swaying of the bow as it crashed into high waves, dipped then rose. Then no sickness was left, just headache and misery. Her energy had sapped from her weakened body.

Her clothes stank. Her spirits were low. She wondered how long she could endure this hardship. She tried to take long, regular breaths. For a good five minutes she breathed deeply. Her water was finished and the weightless bottle freed itself from the improvised shelf above her. It fell breaking its fall on her back and giving her a momentary shock. She stooped to pick it up to prevent it causing a commotion. A groping hand in pitch darkness tried to locate the rolling bottle. She caught it by the neck eventually but then hesitated before deciding what to do with it. She held it for a further few moments before ramming it into her waistline clothing.

Spray and foam dashed heavily around the deck. Gigantic waves hit every twenty minutes or so. Vera could hear the sharp hissing sound but she could not see these waves approach with unearthly deliberation, heavy as lead. Waves were slowed down by their own monstrous bulk, but they left no room for Der Fischhaken to avoid their path. It was easier for the crew, who braced themselves below deck as best they could. Vera used every muscle in her body to wedge herself between the walls of her prison. Yet still she felt like a cork in the sea. Like the Lord's most worthless being in the universe. A universe at war with itself while Vera was at war with her hostile environment. She felt forgotten, neglected and even despised. She longed for the comfort of her home, even Fleur's home in Germany at this moment. This was blind horror she was experiencing. And no end to her misery was in sight.

It lasted only a further twenty minutes, when catching her off guard, the long awaited knock on the panel came to save her sanity. She was pleased and relieved to hear Franz again.

'Vera, open up. Come out now. It's safe. But take care. Hold on to me. The seas are still very rough.'

Vera unbolted each side and slid the panel away. The light blinded her instantly. Her state was appalling. Her hair was a mess covered in sickness. The stench of the enclosed space thankfully fled to the salt laden winds.

Three faces looked on her with pity. Franz held out his hand. 'I'm sorry it took so long. There was naval craft around for a while. Then the seas got angry. They may diminish slowly. Perhaps, in half an hour. …… Come over here. …There is a large bucket of water to wash your face and your hair….. let me tie this belt round you and fasten this rope to it. You'll be safe if you hold on to the wooden rail at the wheelhouse. Then come down and have some ersatz coffee. It's warm down below.'

Vera was glad to have fresh air to breathe and see the seas, whose menace had been engaging her mind. She washed her face and hair vigorously, with some difficulty, as the boat pitched. The water was not as cold as she had feared but as soon as it had left her face, the wind combined to bite her skin. It was a further misery, but she felt glad to experience the open air and the promise of hot coffee awaited her. She rubbed the towel over her hair and face and then made her way to the galley. She was introduced to Hermann and Helmuth. Helmuth was not willing to speak. He had felt betrayed. Had Franz told him before sailing of the human cargo, he would not have come. He might even have told the authorities. What if they had been caught? He felt he would have been shot and his family probably too. Yet, he respected Franz as a seaman and a friend. It had been a real shock for him to learn of Vera's presence and Franz's deception.

Hermann on the other hand, being the older of the two by almost fifteen years, had a more philosophical approach.

'The war has only just begun. It would be different if it had been going on for a year. Anyway I have a granddaughter about her age. If she had been in England, I would have welcomed the enemy sending her back. And she's a girl not a boy heading straight back to fight us.'

Vera appreciated Hermann's point of view. She finished her coffee and offered to help. Helmuth was quick to seize the opportunity and gave her potatoes to peel. Vera was pleased to make herself useful. It was a welcome distraction.

The work took her mind off the heaving waters, which had not yet fully subsided. Franz brought her fisherman's trousers, a waterproof jacket and a woollen hat.

'Cover your hair with the hat. We are approaching busy sea-lanes and it is wise not to be seen as a woman on board. If word got out we could face trouble. After all it would be very suspicious.'

The coastline of Siaeland, Denmark's eastern island appeared. It gave greater protection from the winds and the seas reduced accordingly. Vera was surprised to see how near Sweden's city of Malmo was to Denmark's Copenhagen. Was this not a model of harmony between nations, which so many other countries were trying to achieve through war? Several inland boats approached Der Fischhaken taking an interest in her progress. Franz flashed his port of destination as Halmstad in Sweden and the Danish boats drew back.

Four hours later Der Fischhaken dropped anchor at Sondrum, the port for Halmstad. The harbourmaster boarded the trawler. Vera was introduced as a refugee making her way back to Scotland. Der Fischhaken promised not to land, save for depositing Vera. It would revert to fishing and return to Germany. Vera took Franz' hand to shake it. He pulled her towards himself and hugged her. 'May God protect you. Auf Wiedersehen.' She turned to Hermann. He hugged her too and wished her well. Helmut stepped forward and shook her hand without strength or warmth. He was glad she was leaving the boat.

Vera made her way to the station at Halmstad. When she attempted to purchase her ticket, she was asked for her name. This took her aback. On hearing it, the stationmaster smiled, reached for the wire basket on his desk and informed her that she had a letter. She wondered how this could be possible. The stationmaster handed her a long ivory-coloured envelope. She retreated from the booking counter and retired to a wooden seat in the waiting room. She sat down and studied the envelope. It had the seal of the British Ambassador to Sweden embossed on the rear. She opened it slowly and carefully, unfolded the letter and read:

Stockholm
Sunday 9th August 1914

Dear Miss Caldwell

It is my sincere hope that you receive this letter. I welcome you to the hospitable shores of Sweden.

I understand you found yourself in enemy territory, in Germany, at the outbreak of war and that by good fortune and brave undertakings on your behalf, you have been brought out of Germany and find yourself in Sweden, en route home to Scotland.

I enclose second class rail tickets, for you to travel from Halmstad to Oslo in Norway and a little money for you.

On your arrival, please report to the British Embassy in Oslo, where arrangements are in hand for your onward journey to Scotland.

I trust that you have not been too distressed by your recent experiences and that you will travel safely to your home in the very near future.

God Save the King.

I remain
Yours sincerely

Sir Peter Brookes-Kimber
His Majesty's Ambassador to Sweden

Vera read the letter twice then folded it and replaced it in its envelope. Somehow, she thought, Willy had managed to convey her movements to the authorities in Sweden. She recalled him talking about his friend. How else could this letter have reached her?

The stationmaster observed from a distance. He had a friendly face, behind a flowing white beard. His stationmaster's hat sat on a stack of equally white hair as it had for many a year. His pocket watch, at rest in his waistcoat pocket, gave his ample stomach a slight bulge. A heavy gold metal chain secured it to his person. Navy spats protruded from his trousers, almost covering highly polished black boots. This was a man who took pride in his appearance and his duties.

He had given Vera time to read the letter and gauged her resultant demeanour. It was obviously important news.

She approached the ticket office once more.

'I won't need to buy tickets after all. See, I have been given tickets to take me to Oslo.' She handed her tickets over for inspection.

The stationmaster put them to one side and began to draw on a sheet of brown paper.

After a moment or two, he handed this piece of brown paper to Vera. He had drawn a snaked line. At the top of the page was marked Oslo. He pencilled the names of stations down the line OSLO – Fredrikstad – Sarpsborg – Halden – Kornsjo <u>xxxx</u> Ed –

Dalskög – Mellerud Trollhatten- GÖTEBORG zzzzz Kungsback - Varberg – Falkenberg – HALMSTAD.

Then he pointed to the xxxx. He placed two pencils together in an attempt to show this was the border between Norway and Sweden. Vera thought as much. Her thoughts raced on to the zzzz. She wondered if staying overnight in Göteborg, was suggested by his letters. But her tickets only showed a change of trains there. Vera pointed to Göteborg then placed her hands together at an angle and placed her face on them as if to sleep.

'Ja, Jaa i Göteborg, Sove err sleep, ja sleep,' he nodded vigorously.

An overnight stop was confirmed. On another piece of paper he wrote the times of each departure and arrival. Vera consulted her watch, it was 16:35.

Wednesday 12th August Halmstad 17:10 – Göteborg 19:45
Thursday 13th August Göteborg 9:00 - Oslo 14:20

Fortunately, Vera had enough krona together with Sir Peter's Swedish notes, to stay in a modest hotel that night in Göteborg. The rhythm of a train was heard faintly but sufficient for Vera to step on to the platform with her case moments before the station-master. Then she saw the steam column belch and the dark green train steam along the platform. A bicycle protruded out of the guard's van followed by its youthful owner. A blond family descended from the first coach beyond the train's tender. The stationmaster held the door open for Vera to board and he followed her on board to find her a seat and secure her case in the overhead rack. He knew the train would not leave without his signal.

The train set off at a sedate speed, gathering pace in the few flat pastoral stretches that lay between more rugged coastal cliffs where it took the curved track more cautiously. It passed by Falkenberg and Varberg as the brown paper map correctly indicated. Göteborg duly appeared and Vera was heartened to see its cosmopolitan heart beat.

She had a craving to see the town before it was too dark. She made her way from the station to the open Vasaplatsen. She sat amid the colourful flower borders of this clean and fresh city. It was a Swedish summer's early evening. She absorbed the scents and the airs of this port and noticed how the sea, the North Sea, had gently penetrated the banks on which the city flourished. This was in such contrast to Hamburg, which lay many miles from the open sea. Yet the same results were there to note. Prosperous cities built on divided banks by the sea. Her thoughts took her mind to the many great rivers dividing land and creating great seaports. The Clyde at Glasgow, the Thames at London, which she had yet to see, and the Avon at Bristol, recalled from her geography lessons, a mere year ago. There would be countless others around the world. But this night she was delighted to be in Göteborg.

There was a much lighter atmosphere here than in Hamburg, but a developing European war left no one immune from the anxiety of the future. What pleased her most, was that there was no sight of military or naval uniforms or troop movements. She felt safe.

Vera strolled down the Vasagatan two blocks and approached the Linne Hotel. She obtained a room for the night and requested to be wakened at 7am in time to catch a train at 9am. The manager arranged for Vera to be driven to the station in good time the following morning.

Vera entered the room, closed the curtain and after a warm bath, slipped into clean fresh white sheets, on a high wooden bed, lay her head on two feather pillows and let her thoughts, her dreams, but most of all her exhaustion, render her to a deep satisfying sleep.

CHAPTER SIX

Friday 14th August 1914.

At precisely 7am there was a quiet knock on her bedroom door. She was not sure if she was dreaming. The sound stirred her without wakening her. She was disorientated. Where was she? The knock was repeated a little louder.

'*Enschuldigen Sie bitte. Warten Sie auf mich.*' Vera wrapped a woven blanket round her as the door opened.

'*Sprechen Sie bitte langsamer,*' the maid replied. Vera smiled with embarrassment. No wonder she wanted her to speak more slowly; she was not a German speaker! How silly of her she thought. Of course, she was in Sweden.

The maid approached bearing a tray on which a glass of cool apple juice sat. 'I'm sorry,' said Vera. 'I am not German. I am Scottish. I have just come from Germany.'

The maid smiled, placed the juice on the bedside table and turned to leave. What a strange guest, she must have thought. As she left the room, she said in perfect English 'Breakfast is served at 7.15.'

Vera dressed and went downstairs to the breakfast room. There were several tables occupied. She chose a square table near a diamond paned window, overlooking the hotel lawn and its bordering beds of early autumn colour. Guests were not served. Instead they gravitated towards a long table by the kitchen door, gathered some food and returned to their seats. Vera followed their example. She approached the table and took a large white plate with her as she had seen others do. It was a cold plate. She turned towards the table where her eyes were met by the gaze of a dozen gleaming fish. Fish she had never seen before. Large open-mouthed fish, much of which looked raw. She recognised the green and black backs of the mackerel, the skate, haddock and cod but a large wedge of red meat with black skin was unfamiliar. The waiter caught her eyeing the whale meat. More recognisable cuts of sliced meats and cheeses lay beyond the whale and by sampling what took her interest, she managed to fill her plate, leaving just enough space for bread and wafer thin water biscuits. Raw fish for breakfast was surely an acquired taste, she concluded.

She paid her bill by 8.20am and waited in the hall for her transportation to the station.

The open car arrived and took her to the station entrance. She followed the driver, who took hold of her case and led her to the platform. Vera opened her purse and gave the driver several coins. She had little idea of what they were worth but his smile reassured her. After all she would not need any more Swedish krona.

The day was bright. The blue sky matched the background of the Swedish national flags, freeing yellow crosses to flutter in the breeze from the sea. It was a marvellous day on which to travel. Her rest had revived a stressed, worried and anxious body, which now eagerly anticipated new and safer horizons, each getting closer to home.

At 9am the train for Oslo steamed its way out of Göteburg city station. Vera settled into a compartment. She viewed the suburbs, wondering what winter would look like in this clean and colourful city. She admired the red roofs on the white painted wooden houses and recalled seeing the coloured roof tiles in Culross in the kingdom of Fife the previous year on a summer visit. Why were there not more beautifully coloured roofs at home to brighten up towns so effectively? She made a note to suggest this to her town council one day.

As the town gave way to country, Vera chose to sit on the seaward side of the carriage. There, she set her eyes on a typically west of Scotland coastal seascape. Inlets, islands of differing shapes and sizes, small craft keeping close to shore, seals, sails, seaweed and, farther afield, fishing trawlers heading north with their catches, seagulls following their progress in anticipation of nourishment.

Vera opened the food parcel, which the Linne Hotel had prepared for her journey. Mackerel, salami, cheese, two slices of buttered bread, a tomato, a pear, a cake of marbled hue and a bottle of water had been packed for her. She would chose her time and landscape for lunch around noon. This would be a picnic to remember, like the ones she had had with Willy and Fleur on the banks of the Elbe.

At Svinesund the train stopped briefly to acknowledge the crossing from Sweden to Norway. How polite and void of commotion was the chore. The ticket collectors of each nationality stopped to chat amiably. Only a cursory glance at her ticket was made.

Norway had gained its independence from Sweden only nine

years before. It had been a most civil agreement, ending an eighty year association, having previously been in unison with Denmark. The Norwegians' adoption of universal suffrage in 1898 launched a final bid for recognition as a nation. This was graciously accepted by Sweden. Vera felt this was the amicable way in which international affairs should be conducted.

The train picked up speed and progressed north to Oslo. Mountains hemmed the rail track close to the sea until several mountain tunnels had to be entered. Vera chose to lunch in Norway as the train left Sarpsborg. Each mile was a celebration of her progress towards home. Passengers joined the train heading for the capital. Soon Vera's compartment was full.

Even fuller trains were arriving at Amiens on this day. Sir John French, along with Major Sir Hereward Wake, oversaw the detraining of the British Expeditionary Forces. They further advanced to an area around Le Cateau and Maubeuge. As they moved forward to these positions, General von Kluck's army, whom Vera had observed in Hamburg, began moving south from Liège.

The further north the British marched, the greater was the French enthusiasm. They were kissed and decked with flowers by villagers. Tables of food and wine were set out and all payment efforts were refused. A red tablecloth, with a blue cross sewn onto it, was decked over a balustrade. Soldiers tossed their regimental badges, caps and belts to smiling girls and admirers, who begged for souvenirs, until the British Army was marching, with peasants' tweed caps on their heads and their trousers held up by string. The advance to Mons was 'roses all the way' and no wonder. This was not the regular British Army with its NCOs, trained for overseas duty. Rather this was a homeland defence. These were the enthusiastic conscripts, reduced from six divisions to four as a result of an invasion scare. They were the face of British indignation for the violation of Belgium and that was how they felt. A gun had not yet been fired in anger. Nor was there any imminent intention to do so in these circumstances.

A whistle blew and the train dived into a short dark tunnel once more. On its emergence this time however, the city of Oslo appeared in the distance. It seemed surrounded by mountains with soft-fringed firs climbing high into the sky. Yet the suburbs of Oslo were not dissimilar to those of Göteburg. Bright wooden homes with mainly red roofs appeared and there was much vegetation in the gardens. Tall spires located Lutheran kirks and, by their number, Vera deduced she was in a God fearing country.

The train came to a halt and a gentleman took her case down from the roof rack. Vera thanked him for his kindness. Leaving the station, she enquired of the British Embassy and was directed to Thomas Heftyes Gate 8, two miles north-west of the station in the Skillebekk district. A horse drawn carriage took her there.

She walked up a flight of steps and rang the doorbell. A butler answered. She introduced herself.

'Miss Vera Caldwell, the Ambassador was expecting you. He has been recalled to London at present. The first secretary, Mr Ian Pierpoint will be pleased to meet you. Come in please. Let me take your suitcase.'

Vera entered a long wooden vestibule, adorned with paintings of figures unknown to her, except for one of King George V dominating the others. Opposite her King was an equally grand painting of King Haakon VII, draped in the Norwegian colours of red and blue. She followed the butler to a door on the right. They entered.

'Please be seated. Mr Pierpoint will be with you shortly. In the meantime I will take your case to your bedroom. I understand you will be staying here for a few days.' This was indeed news for Vera.

These were also reassuring words. She was keen to return home, but she was equally keen to stay for a few more days in this peaceful city and in this fairytale home. She wandered over to the fireplace in which silver birch logs were sparking behind a wire fireguard. She looked at the French clock on the mantelpiece and admired its artistry. As she did so, it responded, striking three o'clock. As the final bell chimed, the butler reappeared with a silver tray on which a silver teapot sat with three cups, three saucers, three plates, a sugar bowl, a milk jug and a slop bowl. The tray was placed on a side table.

'The tea needs to brew a little longer,' the butler announced, probably to ensure Vera did not impatiently serve herself. He left the room, once more leaving the door slightly ajar. He returned this time with a three-tier wooden cake stand. Fresh pancakes were mounted on the top tier. A selection of sweet and plain biscuits covered the second tier and on the paper doily of the lower tier, was a fresh-cream sponge cake. Vera could hardly remember drinking her last cup of tea and, as for the home baking, she wondered if it would be impolite to have a second pancake before descending to the biscuits, while making room for a slice of the cream sponge.

Footsteps were heard coming along the great hall. An elegant man appeared.

'Miss Vera Caldwell, I am extremely pleased to meet you. I am Mr Ian Pierpoint, acting in the absence of the Ambassador. He was sorry not to meet you himself. He was recalled to London four days ago. This is my wife, Mrs Susan Pierpoint.'

'I am pleased to meet you,' Vera said coyly.

'Do sit down Vera. Let me pour the tea. What do you take?'

'Milk and no sugar please. You know, I have not had a cup of tea for several weeks.'

'Ah yes. It's coffee morn, noon and night in Germany isn't it? You were caught up in Germany at the start of the war. You must tell me what it was like,' urged Ian.

'Oh darling, first things first. Let Vera have some pancakes. There's fresh cream and strawberry jam to put on them. Your visit gave me an opportunity to do some home baking. Our Embassy cook usually bakes waffles. Good though they are, I thought this was an occasion for pancakes.'

The assembled three sat down and, relaxing with her afternoon tea, Vera unwound and told of her recent experiences.

She recalled each step of the way. She spoke of her concern for her aunt, the kindness of her uncle and their good friends. She opened her purse. 'And here is the return ticket to Harwich. It's still valid by date but these sailings will have ceased for the duration of the war I suppose.'

'That will make a good souvenir in the years to come,' remarked Susan. Ian reached forward to read the ticket. Susan emptied her cup into the slop bowl and poured a second cup. 'Now Vera, a biscuit perhaps, or shall I serve you a slice of cake.'

Vera decided to go straight for the sponge.

'I think you have chosen wisely, especially if tennis is on the cards later.'

Ian stretched for a biscuit. 'I say, quite an adventure you have had,' he commented. 'You were very fortunate you were able to get out of Germany. Things have probably tightened up since last week. It's a nasty business. Norway is certain to remain neutral and that could mean you are the first of other visitors to come our way in due course. They will all have a story to tell and bit by bit it can provide useful information for our forces.' Vera realised the significance of his statement.

'Vera, if you do not mind, I am going to ask that you retell this story to one of the shorthand secretaries tomorrow. The military attaché will assist you in prompting your memory for detail. You see, as one of the last people to leave Germany, you may have information that may prove to be useful. I assure you the process will be quite painless. But I have arranged that for tomorrow. Tell me, do you play tennis?'

The change of subject took Vera by surprise. 'Yes, I do play, but usually with my two sisters at our local club in Forres. But I certainly do not have my racket or shoes with me.'

'Don't worry, Susan will kit you out. We have a court in the back garden and a daughter, Anne, about your age as well. I think we'll be able to play a game of doubles this evening.'

Vera smiled at the prospect. She was a keen sportswoman but opportunities had not come her way recently. She wondered what standard she would face.

'It's a pity wars were not fought by tennis matches,' Vera remarked.

'Indeed,' agreed Ian. 'Probably best of three would do. But who would umpire?'

The butler came to clear the tea tray.

'Susan, will you show Vera around the public rooms and to her room. Let's say tennis at 5.30pm. Yes, that will give us time to change for dinner. Agreed. Then, if you will excuse me for now?'

Susan took Vera back to the hall and remarked that this was a good place to get her bearings. 'That was the sitting room we have been in. Across here is the library. Of course most of the books are in English, all sorts really. Novels, children's books, encyclopaedias and maps. There's even a section of German, French and Spanish books around. I suppose they arrive with some of the diplomatic staff, who have served in these slightly warmer climes. You are most welcome to read any of them. You may prefer to look through our collection of magazines. I love the photo journalism of David Harvie in the Daily Sketch. He's a Scot. A good friend of King George V. The only thing I must tell you is that the library is open to all our staff and some come to read in peace and quiet. So this really is the quiet room too. You can take books out of the room, as long as you return them in due course.'

'Oh I don't think I'll have time for a novel, but I'll look out for the Sketch. May I ask if you know how long I am to be in Oslo?' asked Vera.

'Well, of course I am not privy to such decisions.....'

'Oh I did not mean to quiz you.'

'No, no. I know you must be anxious. I understand. What I would say is that arrangements are being made for you to return to Scotland but I do not know the details and I do not know when. My advice is for you to relax and enjoy however long you are here, technically in a small part of Britain. Let's go through here. This is the dining room, where we will eat this evening. In fact we eat all meals here, so this is where breakfast is served too. That door leads to the kitchen.'

Just as she said that, the kitchen door flew open and Anne came through with a partly eaten pancake in her mouth.

'Anne, this is Vera. She will be staying with us for a while.'

'I am pleased to meet you, Anne.' Vera was not sure whether to proffer a handshake, but Anne put the rest of the pancake in her mouth and offered a wrist to shake.

'Oh really, Anne!' frowned her mother.

'But we have not had fresh pancakes for so long, Mum,' Anne appealed.

All three smiled at the unfolding scenario. 'Anne, why don't you show Vera her room and I'll look out some tennis attire for her.'

'Oh great. It's a super sunny afternoon for tennis. It'll be fun. Come on Vera, let's go upstairs to your room.'

They were clearly going to enjoy each other's company. Anne was reading chemistry at Manchester. She had completed her first year successfully and had spent the summer with her parents in Oslo. As the summer waned, war engaged and uncertainty mounted. Anne was anxious to return to her studies. Little had been heard of naval engagements, but she felt they would soon start and that might jeopardise her return by sea. She told Vera so and that became an anxiety for Vera too.

'I feel I have escaped from war, but it is on my tail. I will not be at ease until I have reached home.'

'Oh, I am sure it won't be long.'

They entered the guest's room and Vera noticed her case was on the floor, opened. It was empty.

'I should explain,' said Anne. 'Your clothes were in need of some attention. They are being washed and ironed. Expect you'll get them back very soon.'

'Oh dear. They were really in a very bad way. How kind.'

Susan arrived with a collection of summer clothes for tennis. 'Now I think we should leave you to try some of these things on. See how they fit. We'll fit you for shoes downstairs. So, perhaps a short rest and we'll gather in our tennis togs in half an hour.'

Suitably decked, Vera took to the court, wearing a large white brimmed hat to shade her eyes from the sun as its rays pierced the trees from the south-west. After a few practice serves and rallies, Anne's parents arrived and doubles commenced. Anne and Vera took on Ian and Susan. In an erratic match, Anne and Vera won 1-6; 6-4; 6-1. Vera enjoyed the game very much. So did her opponents.

Saturday 15th August 1914.

The following morning, after breakfast of porridge and waffles, Vera strolled in the embassy grounds for a few moments, to be with her thoughts. While she was walking on the lawn, a car entered the driveway and stopped at the front door. A military man got out and entered the building. Anne wandered down to join Vera, to announce that she was required in the attaché's office. 'It sounds exciting. I wish I was a fly on the wall,' she exclaimed.

Vera sat in the hall awaiting her appointment. She gazed up at the portraits and wondered how greatness was achieved. Were they born or made great? Were they also great in family life, or was that a necessary sacrifice to achieve public acclaim? Why were these paintings here? Were they part of a grand collection distributed throughout British Embassies, or were they the Ambassador's own collection? Perhaps she would ask Anne later.

A middle-aged officer approached her. 'Miss Caldwell? Please follow me.' He led her to the rear of the building, along a corridor that echoed to the sound of angry competing typewriters. The door, through which they entered, displayed a name-plate bearing the name of Colonel A.R. Barbour.

First Lord of the Admiralty, Winston Churchill, warned Fleet commanders on 12th August 1914 that: *"Extraordinary silence and inertia of the enemy may prelude to serious enterprises or possibly a landing on a large scale.*" He suggested that the British Grand Fleet move down nearer to the theatre of decisive action. Meanwhile Lord Jellico continued his remote and fruitless patrol in the grey waste of waters between the north of Scotland and the Norwegian coast.

Between August 14th and 18th meanwhile, no fewer than 137 separate Channel crossings of the British Expeditionary Forces took place.

On the mainland, most of the Belgian forts had remained initially intact. The German assault had an inauspicious start. Von Emmich's troops suffered heavily on 5th August. On 7th August Ludendorff took personal charge and penetrated between forts to enter Liège. Thereafter progress was maintained and the Belgian forces, having waited in vain for French and British reinforcements, gave way to the advancing General Paul von Hindenberg. Wearing blue tunics and red trousers, the French Armies of Dubail and de Castelnau were picked off at Morange and Sarrebourg. They were the first to realise that the offensive spirit was insufficient and would not overcome the modern artillery and well positioned machine guns. Suffering enormous casualties, the horrors of the enemy's efficiency was realised. Colonel Barbour was privy to this information.

The colonel asked Vera where and when she had seen troops after the war was declared. He asked what colour of uniforms they had, what type of caps did they wear, were there any cap badges she remembered? What was their demeanour, their tunic button arrangement, and their footwear like? What weapons did each soldier carry? Did they look like regular soldiers? Were there any reservists? How young did they look? How many horses did she see?

He asked about the state of roads in Germany, how wide they were, what design of bridges did she recall? What sort of artillery had she seen? Was it carried by troops, by horsepower or machinery? What was a normal family diet like? What level of church attendance had she observed? Had she seen any aeroplanes? What did they look like? How many were on board? Did they have fixed weapons? The questions kept coming.

Vera was surprised the questions unlocked so many details from her memory. The colonel never stopped her flow and in fact encouraged her responses by asking supplementary questions, until she indicated no further recall.

'We'll take a break now. I think lunch will be ready soon. Vera you have done very well. We'll continue at 2pm.'

Vera enjoyed an open sandwich lunch with Anne. They drank some juice in the garden and Vera told her how surprised she was that she could remember so many details. 'The colonel kept finding questions to ask. I felt sorry for the shorthand secretary. She was writing all the time.'

'I'm not surprised, Vera. You have been through a difficult time with German mobilisation all around you. It must be really important information you are providing.'

The afternoon session was equally intensive but by 4.30pm both the Colonel and Vera knew, she had nothing left to tell. The Colonel stood up. He thanked Vera for being so patient and providing the sort of information that would be invaluable in a number of situations. He had much to forward in his report to his superiors.

Vera looked puzzled. 'Really?'

'Oh indeed. It is important that field commanders can recognise the enemy they are facing and know the enemy they capture. It is equally important to know what life is like in the country. It is a matter of time before we will have had some of our own soldiers captured and, if any escape, your information will be crucial. I don't think you realise just how valuable your knowledge has been, Vera. You gave some very precise details. My superiors will be pleased.'

The clouds had thickened in the afternoon and the temperature dropped accordingly. It was not long before the sound of rain was heard on the window in her bedroom. A knock on her door followed.

'May I come in, Vera?'

'Of course, Anne.'

'Tennis is off. It's wet outside. Never mind. There is a table tennis board in the attic. Interested?'

The two young women set off up the second floor flight of

stairs to the attic which seemed to have the floor space of the entire house. At one end lay a snooker table. At the other, a table tennis table. Vera looked out of the skylight window, through the raindrops beyond the city, to the sea.

'I heard one of our naval patrols was out this way. Lord Jellico I believe.' Anne felt her information might interest Vera. 'Wonder if he could call into Oslo and take you home?'

'That would be ideal. A whole ship to myself!'

After a meaningless and endless practice rally, they agreed to play. Anne delivered a top spin drive then a forehand attack. Vera defended, without making an impact. The backhand attack followed, then Anne's forehand spin-drive won the point. Vera knew this was Anne's game. 'You are too good at this, Anne.'

'I suppose that's because I play at University. I should be honest with you. I play quite a bit. In fact I'm the team captain.'

'Never mind, by playing the best, I can only improve.' In fact, Vera soon gained the rhythm of the game and gave Anne a good contest. She never won a game, but her scores crept up 21-8, 21-14, 21-16, 21- 17, 21-17. Dinner was called.

At table that evening, Ian gave the news that Vera was waiting for and wanting.

'I had hoped that a British naval craft could approach the Norwegian shore and take you on board, but that will no longer be possible. We are unsure where the German fleet is at present and anyway the Navy would not necessarily wish to provide such individual service! So we have come up with a different plan. It will mean some cross-country travel for you in Norway, to the port at Stavanger. This is the port where several Scottish trawlers visit, after fishing on the north-west coast off Alesund. They offload their catch, then chase the haddock shoals across the North Sea to their ports at Fraserburgh, Peterhead or Arbroath. Our consul in Bergen will make the arrangements, but as there are not so many frequent boats now that the Navy needs men, he tells me that you should come straight away. He has prepared to meet you in Stavanger tomorrow evening.'

'That's wonderful. Only I have some reservations about rough weather in a trawler. I had a recent experience you'll remember!'

'Vera, believe me, I did mention this matter to Mr Stockdale, our consul in Bergen. He replied that whereas you had little control over which day you left Germany, we have the benefit of choosing a promising crossing, after consulting the weather forecast. You will not be locked up in the hold either. It's bound to be more comfortable.'

'If you are ready to go tomorrow, there is a train from Oslo at 11.30am. It gets to Stavanger at 1.15pm. Mr Stockdale will meet you there.'

'Thank you so much. I will certainly be on it.'

'Oh, and there's one extra bit of good news. We have sent a telegram to the Police at Forres, to tell them you are safe and in Oslo, on your way home. They will inform your parents.'

'Oh, thank you very, very much. They will be so relieved. Thank you.'

Sunday 16th August 1914

Anne saw Vera off on the train at 11.30am Once more a packed lunch accompanied her and this time her German suitcase contained freshly ironed clean clothes. The train journey was not eventful but was spectacular. The coastal route took her through Porsgrunn and Kristian where she saw in each town families wearing their very best on their way to the Lutheran kirks. Their peeling bells overcame the hissing train sounds and brought peaceful harmony to her ears as she travelled. There was no naval interest on the sea, by this neutral country, but some small-sailed boats and some yachts had taken to the water. The train made its way through mountains and along valleys to the colourful port. The smell of the sea and a nearby fish market, although not trading on this day, pervaded the railway station.

Mr Stockdale met her on the platform and took her to a guest house overlooking the bay. He had been busy on her behalf and was satisfied with his efforts. He had arranged with the skipper of the Harvest Morn, to take her across to Scotland. The boat intended landing at the port of Lybster in the north of Scotland. It would be a day's journey and the weather was not thought to be too unsettled. The captain would be sailing at 1pm the following day. There were no sailings on the Sabbath. Vera would be required to be at the harbour by noon.

She spent the afternoon walking round the curved harbour, admiring the Hanseatic port within its tall coloured houses on the sea front, from both ends. The fish market had been washed down the previous evening. Now there was little evidence of the busy fish stalls that were at the heart of the local economy. Norwegian families strolled along the sea front wearing their bright and smart Sunday best attire. The men wore traditional white shirts and black felt hats. The women wore bonnets with ribbons matching the colours of their flouncing red, blue, green and yellow long skirts. The atmosphere was congenial. Vera felt that at this northern European outpost, the ripples of strife in continental Europe were yet to impact.

Vera returned to her guest house where that evening she was served with herring lightly grilled in oatmeal, a plate she regularly enjoyed at home. Her herring was served with new potatoes freckled with finely chopped parsley and two slices of tomatoes. She retired to her room where she repacked her belongings with care, before spending a further half hour playing with her hosts' young children. Before ending the day she enjoyed hot waffles with syrup and dollops of fresh cream, with a mug of hot milk by the log fire. Inevitably, she slept soundly in her wooden bed, with a brightly coloured patchwork bedspread covering her excited but tired frame.

Monday 17th August 1914.

At the agreed time, Vera arrived at the harbour and made her way towards the fishing trawlers. Some were Norwegian while others had English names. The ones that caught her eye had PD, FR or AB on their bows representing their home ports of Peterhead, Fraserburgh or Aberdeen. FR178 Harvest Morn, was a maroon trawler with gold lines and flourishes painted around its girth. It looked new as it reflected the late summer sun on to the calm port water. It lay on the end of three other boats.

'Is that you, Miss Vera?' a voice called from the midst of creels and rigging.

'Yes. Are you the skipper of the Harvest Morn?'

'Indeed I am. Skipper Rory Fraser. Wait there. I'll give you a hand down.'

Rory was a bearded man of around fifty years of age. The weather of the North Sea had aged him considerably but he had two sons to assist him in the family business. Two heads appeared from below deck. They were his sons, Angus and Colin.

Vera made her way gingerly down the metal rungs of the harbour. Rory carried her case and took her hand as she crossed the oily ropes on the decks of the adjacent boats. 'Mind your feet. Looks like a German case to me. Hope you are not a spy!' Rory laughed.

As she crossed over to the final boat, Rory welcomed her aboard. 'Come down to the galley and meet my sons. You realise we are breaking with tradition on this crossing. There is an unwritten rule that we don't take clergymen or ladies on our boats. Well it seems to me that it is an unwritten rule. An' it seems to me you are not a clergyman and you'll have to wear fisherman's oilskins on this trip, so you won't look like a lady anyway!' Rory laughed. 'Truth is two trawlers turned you down because you are a woman.'

Angus and Colin were happy with the arrangement. It would make the trip more interesting. As brothers they lived together with their parents, worked together with their father, so it was good to have an outsider for a change, even although she was a woman, an attractive woman too.

Vera was given wellington boots, a sou'wester hat, a warm woollen jersey, oilskin trousers and top. She was left in the galley to change. A kettle was put on to boil and mugs of sickly tea were soon produced. At 1 o'clock, the ropes were released and the trawler eased itself from the neighbouring boat, the quay, and from Norway.

The Harvest Morn made its way out of the sheltered harbour, past the headland at Randaberg, beyond the final small island of Mosteroy and out into the North Sea. It left on its own with no boat in its wake and none ahead. Only two seagulls accompanied them briefly. There was a slight but noticeable breeze. The trawler gracefully rode the tender waves. A regular rhythm took them out to sea and slowly the Norwegian coastline diminished. Then it disappeared. Daylight was with them for a little while after that enabling seals to be seen bobbing up ahead of the boat.

An hour before dusk a warship loomed on the horizon. Then Vera saw another and yet another. All were sailing south. That was significant and reassuring, but Rory had never seen such a convoy before. Yes, three ships. Probably part of a larger convoy. Their collective interest in a trawler should have been negligible but their paths would bring them much closer. To change course suddenly might arouse suspicion as would any slowing down and so Harvest Morn sailed on, with four pairs of eyes focussing on the procession.

Colin thought two were cruisers. The third was most impressive. One of the Dreadnoughts perhaps. Through his binoculars, he could make out the nearest cruiser was the Defence, a 140,000 ton, 9.2-inch gun. Then he saw the identical cruiser was its sister ship, Black Prince. The Dreadnought with its 12 inch guns and a speed of 21 knots could outrange and outpace any other type of battleship. What were they doing, where could they be going? Why so few if they were in earnest?

Six hundred and seventy German merchant steamers were holed up in neutral ports or at rest in home ports. Only a few were left plying the Baltic. The raiders Emden and Königsberg in the Indian Ocean, Admiral von Spee's squadron in the Pacific, and the German Navy had retired from the surface of the oceans before August was over. Even by 14th August the Admiralty could report that 'the passage across the Atlantic is safe. British Trade is running as usual.'

At this time, neutral countries like Sweden, Denmark and Norway were free to trade with Germany. But what good was it to deny use of the seas to the enemy, if neutrals were allowed to supply him with all his needs? The Dreadnought and its two cruisers were heading to make their presence known to the recalcitrant neutral countries. Then on 20th August 1914, the Cabinet issued an order in Council, declaring that henceforth Britain would regard conditional contraband as subject to capture if it was consigned to the enemy or an 'agent of the enemy' or if its ultimate destination was hostile.

As the Harvest Morn approached, the three British vessels slipped by without any acknowledgement. The swell of these sleek ships caused a sudden commotion for the trawler. They knew this was not a North Sea storm, but as the boat rolled and crashed over the crests of waves, it displayed signs of its vulnerability. Vera clung to the central rail in the galley, till the swelling subsided. Then she bedded herself into one of the four sleeping compartments, gathered up the quilt to her chin and tried to sleep.

Several hours later, while it was still pitch dark, she heard voices. She got up and went on deck. There was a gentle breeze, but no significant swell. The crew had hauled their nets over board some time ago and now it was time to reel them in.

'Make yourself useful, Vera. When the net rolls in, use that wooden plank, to stop fish rolling down back into the sea. You'll soon get the hang of it.' Colin had placed his confidence in her.

Vera steadied herself and found little force was required to direct the slippery wayward fish on to the deck. Cod and haddock were the main catch, but dogfish, mackerel and ling came in good numbers. It took all three crew to turn the wrench latterly.

When all the net was in, Angus took Vera down to the bow and below deck to where empty wooden boxes lay stacked.

'Now, what I want you to do, Vera, is stand at the bottom of this chute. Place a box here in front of you and then lift the sliding door of the chute to let the fish come down. Be careful you do not cut the fish in half! I'll take each box when it's full and store them and get you out another empty box, ready for the next load. Understand?'

'Yes, I think so.'

Vera soon got into the swing of it. Box…chute…close…box.. chute…close. She was not aware of how time was passing. She was impressed with the way Angus lifted these heavy boxes and stacked them. She felt surprisingly able to do this 'man's work' and a little surprised she had been asked to do so much. Yet, the Norwegian women had gained the vote and, with that, they gained their independence. She wondered what Britain's womanhood could do for the war effort and whether it would be rewarded with political emancipation. The Norwegians had shown it was possible after all.

Eventually, all the fish had been delivered down the hatch into boxes and she climbed back on to the deck and joined the crew round the central table in the galley. The ubiquitous sickly tea was being brewed once more. Vera asked for tea with no milk this time.

'That was hard work, but fun,' Vera admitted.

'You probably did not think it was polite to ask you to help us. It's even a bit smelly. But you see you have been busy and that takes your mind off the motion on the boat. That's what prevents sickness.'

Rory's explanation pleased Vera. 'I wonder what women will be able to do to help in the war effort? That might, even lead to us having the vote!' Vera ventured.

'Oh, I don't know about that,' said Rory. 'Remember, this has been a quiet crossing. It can get very rough.'

Vera smiled. 'Oh, I've been in a much wilder sea, in a smaller boat quite recently. I admit it was a frightening experience. You're right, I don't think I could do this often.'

'Can I ask where you are from?' said Angus.

'Forres, between Nairn and Elgin.'

'Nice part that. Inland of course.'

' Well yes, but near the sea. And where are you from?'

'Lybster, just south of Wick, but we have a room in Fraserburgh where the Harvest Morn was registered. That's where the big port and the money is. We've had her three years now. She's a good boat. She's been kind to us. We treat her well and she does the same to us. In fact, my wife can not understand how we can keep a boat clean, but not a house tidy! Strange isn't it? I've not got the answer to that yet.' said Rory. 'We've been away for six weeks now. Since before the war started. Catching fish up the Norwegian coast. That's where you find them. It's a ready market too. Norwegians can not get enough fish. Any fish. This, here, is a small catch. So we'll take the catch to Lybster for the town and the rest to Wick. That's why we'll have to drop you there, but I guess you are used to travel. It won't take you long to get down to Inverness and along to Forres. Bet there will be a celebration when you arrive home.'

'I'm not sure what to expect. Of course my parents will be glad to see me, my sisters too, but I am still very worried about my aunt, left in Germany. I hope she will survive the war.'

The Harvest Morn entered the Moray Firth. Three hours later dawn broke on 18th August.

Tuesday 18th August 1914.

The German 47th Infantry Regiment, part of the 10th Division in Crown Prince Wilhelm's Fifth Army, advanced unopposed across fields in north-eastern France. Two miles behind was the Schleswig Holstein division, which Vera had watched parade in their finery in Hamburg. Meanwhile, having waited in vain behind Gette for the French and British, the Belgian Army withdrew to the fortress of Antwerp. Two days later, the German Army entered Brussels.

Two hours later, Vera entered the harbour at Lybster. She had settled herself on the capstan on the trawler's bow, for the last hour. As the minutes passed, the haze of the coastal grasses became clearer, the row of cottages became individual homes and the shoelace glint of yellow, expanded into a ribbon of golden sand. Some sleek black rocks covered with kelp and seawrack lay off shore. Vera was pleased to see her native shores so near but it seemed that if she wound back her last few days and broke down each journey, Germany was not that far away. And if it was not that far away from Lybster, how much nearer was it from the shores and cliffs of the south of England? Would war reach our islands?

Why had she not insisted on Fleur coming with her? Germany was no place to be until the war was over. She had been a fine hostess to her. What lay before her? Vera wondered. Fleur was a remarkable and loyal woman. An aunt to be proud of. Vera wondered if she would ever see her again.

Sanderlings and oyster catchers patrolled the water's edge, as if to welcome home the Harvest Morn. A woman was on the pier waving. Colin and Rory waved back. This was Mrs Sadie Fraser, who always kept an eye out for the returning trawler. She knew if it did not return she would be mourning not just the skipper, but her entire family and its livelihood. She never missed their return, loyally standing on the harbour wall in all conditions. Today, it was bathed in sunshine and the maroon and gold livery of the Harvest Morn, was a sight to enjoy as it entered the harbour.

As the trawler drew alongside the pier, Colin leapt off and secured the boat, before giving his mother a brief hug.

'I see you have caught a mermaid, Colin!' laughed Sadie.

'Aye, you could say that, but she's also our new crew member! She was working the fish boxes a few hours ago. Made a good job of it.'

Vera was helped ashore and Colin passed her brown case to Rory. 'Come to the house Vera, and we'll find our land legs.'

Vera lowered her head to enter the white cottage. A strong smell of cooking came from the kitchen in the rear of the building. The table was set for four. Mrs Fraser quickly moved in another place setting and then returned to her stove. She reappeared from the kitchen with her hands full.

'It's a wee treat we always have when the boys return. A hot bowl of pease-brose, their favourite meal.'

'That's when we know we are home all right,' announced Rory.

The Wick to Inverness omnibus stopped by the post office at Lybster to collect Vera at 12.20pm It would take her to Inverness. It was an uneventful journey, but one which Vera enjoyed. It called at Helmsdale, then Golspie, where she had a good view of Dunrobin Castle. The bus detoured to collect passengers at Dornoch, before arriving at Dingwall. In no time, they were across the Black Isle and entering Inverness. Vera made her way to Inverness station and bought a single ticket to Forres. She wondered how her parents would react to her arrival.

While sitting in the waiting room at Inverness, a young man approached and asked if she was Miss Vera Caldwell. Quite taken aback, but without being rude, she enquired why he was asking.

'Well, when the war broke out, the local paper reported you were still in Germany. The story speculated that you would be arrested as an alien, and in the worst case scenario, you may be tried as a spy and shot. Everyone was talking about it. We published a photo of you in the paper. That's how I knew it was you. Do you mind if I take a picture of you holding your suitcase? It's for the Inverness paper.'

'Well, I suppose so.'

'Turn to your right, Miss Caldwell. Don't look at the camera. That's lovely. Now let me take a close up.... excellent. Thank you very much.'

Some passers-by looked to see what was happening. In a reserved manner, they looked at Vera, smiled but said nothing. Vera was glad to board the train for the relatively short journey to Forres. She had never been the public focus of attention before. Little did she know that the picture taken at Inverness was already making its way to the broadsheets down south.

The train slowed down and stopped abruptly. Forres at last, her destination. Vera descended, gave her ticket to the ticket collector and crossed through the station forecourt to the main street. She turned right and started to walk to her grandparent's hotel. She looked up and saw it, hastening her approach. She also noticed it was decked in flowers. She thought there may have been a wedding recently. Then she noticed red, white and blue ribbons too. As her steps took her closer, she began to focus on the writing on one of the banners. WECOME HOME VERA. She smiled and a tear came to her eye.

She crossed the road and mounted the steps leading to the hotel entrance. Tam, the porter, took her case. 'Miss Caldwell, welcome home. We are so happy to see you again.' His remark aroused those in the reception area.

Not only was her mother, Ada, in the hall waiting to greet her but her grandmother too was there. Her father, William Caldwell, was called from the bank to join them in this happy reunion. Edith and Hilda arrived excitedly and the three daughters embraced. It was an emotional greeting. Tears ran like raindrops, sobbing, laughter, hugging. The commotion was not lost on the hotel staff. Then the neighbours and the Forres townsfolk arrived to show their delight at Vera's safe return. On 2nd September 1914 the Forres, Elgin & Nairn Gazette recorded her adventure, modestly under the heading "Forres Young Lady's Experience." Vera read the article and was relieved that the paper had not published the name or address of Fleur.

After the celebrations died down, Ada took Vera aside and asked of Fleur, her sister. Their anxieties now turned to her.

Troon 27th December 1991.

Vera was surprised she had been able to recall the traumatic events of August 1914 so clearly and pleased that she had imparted a part of history to the next generation. Fiona had enjoyed her story so much, that she wanted to know even more. She invited Vera to tell her what happened to Fleur.

'Well, Fiona, I was never to see Fleur again. She only visited Scotland briefly in 1939. But her story surpasses my adventures. She had been a friendly hostess to me in Hamburg but she became a very troubled and different type of hostess many years later.'

'Please tell me more,' begged Fiona.

'Not tonight darling. Let me sleep on Fleur's life and I will be able to remember much more tomorrow. I'll even take some notes, to aid my memory.'

'Promise you won't forget?'

'No darling, I promise. Anyway, Fiona I enjoyed telling you the first part of the story. I'm sure I will want to complete the saga, but not tonight. We've still to finish the Trivial Pursuit!'

Part 2

CHAPTER SEVEN

Foreign and Commonwealth Office
London
Room E026 West African Section

London 5th March 1939.

Fleur sat by the reception desk awaiting her interview. She was forty-nine years old. Too old for interviews in her mind, but she would not have been given an appointment, had the authorities considered her application unsuitable. Nor would they have paid her travel expenses from Forres and given her quality hotel accommodation in Russell Square, had they not been serious about her suitability, she reasoned.

'Mrs Richter? Good afternoon.' A smart young man in a dark grey double-breasted suit approached her. His college tie was Oxbridge. So was his clipped accent. 'I am Sir Anthony's secretary. He is ready to see you now. Please follow me.'

They proceeded along a marble-floored corridor. Their heels involuntarily performed a latin tempo. They entered a lift that took them to the fourth floor, where their footsteps were hushed by the plush patterned carpet. They stopped outside an oak door. The secretary opened it and invited Fleur through. Sir Anthony Pitt-Stevenson rose from his desk at the end of the room, beneath a portrait of King George VI.

'Sir Anthony, ….Mrs Richter.' The secretary withdrew.

'Good afternoon Mrs Richter. How kind of you to come down from Forres.' They shook hands. 'I enjoyed a round of golf at Nairn last Easter. It's a delightful part of the country. Pity it's so far away. I gather it's not been your home for many years. In fact, yours was the most interesting application for the post we have in mind.'

'I wondered if I'd even be considered! I am only just under fifty years of age.'

'Fluent in German, confident in French and just the right age. Why ever not?'

'I have been honest in my application. I have seen the way in which Germany has chosen to avenge its defeat in the First World War and I had no intention of becoming an enemy alien once more. Germany will be at war soon. Of that I have no doubt. The Führer is building his empire. I wish to serve mine now, now that I am a widow.'

'Yes, tell me about your family in Germany.'

'My husband, Dr Willy Richter died suddenly of a heart attack in 1935. We had one son, Otto. Otto Bruce Richter. Otto is eighteen years of age. In December 1936, the Hitler Youth Law made membership compulsory for youth aged ten to eighteen. Otto joined with his friends. He craved for its ideals and it gave him constant promotion. Can you believe it? Between the ages of ten and fourteen, he went through the ranks from Pimpf all the way to Jungbannführer. Then between fourteen and eighteen from Hitlerjunge, then Kammeraldschaftsführer and Scharführer, and now he is Obergebeitsführer. No wonder this uniformed organisation attracts them.'

'Tell me how they are organised.'

'Well the smallest unit is the Kameradschaft, with ten to fifteen boys. Then there is the Schar, the Gefolgschaft and the Unterbann. It's a massive organisation of the youth. More than seven million boys belong. It's the army's breeding ground. Even the girls have a similar structure.'

'But, you say your son is eighteen years old? What will happen to him?'

'Yes, Otto will always be my son, but I know the Party has him now. Hear him reciting his motto: "Live Faithfully, Fight Bravely and Die Laughing. We were born to die for Germany. You are nothing – your Volk is everything". I despair. Even his pledge has no place for his parents. "I promise to do my duty in love and loyalty to the Führer and our flag." Yet, it was not easy to reach the decision I have made. He knows he is German but I am Scottish. He bears me no ill will. I think he forgets I was under house arrest during the First World War, despite my marriage. I do not want to be in that situation again. Otto now stays with his Uncle Karl and Aunt Renate in Hamburg. He will be nineteen next month. These are difficult times. I would not have abandoned him had he been a year or two younger, but he is his own future now and his extended family will support him. I know they will. They supported me in the past. So I decided to come home. After two months living with my mother and visiting my relatives I knew that I could make myself more useful. Then I read your interesting, while enigmatic entry in the appointments page of the Times. It was both vague and yet specific. You seemed to be looking for a linguist who was required to travel extensively, yet undertake domestic duties. It seemed an odd combination, but I replied with the intention of finding out more about the offer. I was very surprised with the promptness of your reply.'

Sir Anthony was in no hurry to provide details of the mission.

'Your father, Colonel James Bruce. Tell me about him.'

'Since retiring from the Army some years ago, he and my mother have been running the Union Hotel in Forres.'

'I mean, about his Army days.' Sir Anthony's sharp reminder focussed Fleur's mind.

'He was with the Scots Guards. He served in the Sudan and fought at Omdurman with Lord Kitchener. They defeated the Dervishes and destroyed the Khalifa's power. He was then sent to West Africa to sort out the Ashanti troubles, in the Gold Coast Colony. So Africa was his main field of service.'

'Did he like Africa?'

'Very much so. He often tells me stories of his adventures and about his time in Africa. He was very fond of the people of the Gold Coast in particular. He even wanted to go back one day, possibly if he was widowed. But I think it would be too late now. He is getting too old to travel.'

'Now, you said you wanted to make yourself more useful.'

'As I was saying, I read in the paper that the Foreign and Commonwealth Office was looking for women, with language skills, to be employed in a number of fields abroad. The advert was not specific, yet I felt that this was a last chance for me to play my part in serving my country. Although my family is in Scotland, it has been so long since I lived there. I feel I would settle just as easily abroad.'

Sir Anthony began to reveal his intentions for Fleur. 'Women have been employed in the Foreign Office since its creation in 1782. We do not however, appoint them as diplomats of course. This creates opportunities for a number of administrative or social posts from time to time. The advert was placed to see which individuals might consider the service and your application stood out. It was impressive.'

'I am surprised.'

'Why no! Experience comes with age and, if I may say so, you look young for your years. Tell me, would you consider working in West Africa? Is your health up to it, in the White Man's Grave?'

'I had not been thinking where you were considering I might be sent, but West Africa would certainly meet my approval and I feel I am as fit as I should be at my age. I loved hearing stories about Africa from my father. I am sure I will like it. Where in West Africa?'

'In a moment. Let me describe the post first. What we have in mind, is a position of Hostess to the Governor General. The Governor in question is single and there will be many social occasions when he may wish to call on you to accompany him. That is one part of the job. The second is more cerebral, taking account that you are a fluent German speaker. I am not sure how much you know about German influences in West Africa. Suffice it to say for the moment, there may be a need to have a ready interpreter and some travel will be involved on behalf of the Governor. Would I be correct in thinking this work would interest you?'

'I think the two aspects which you mention interest me greatly and I think I now see why you noticed my application.'

'Then may I assume it appropriate for me to make further arrangements, for you to undergo a medical examination and a preparatory course at London University's School of Oriental and African Studies?'

'Certainly. I would be delighted to start my preparation as soon as possible.'

'One of our diplomatic orientation courses, for West Africa, will take place at SOAS in April. It lasts for four weeks. We will pay your fees and living expenses, naturally. So, Mrs Richter, my congratulations to you are in order. You have a week's leave to make your arrangements. Be back the following week so that we can start your inoculations. The Foreign Office is now responsible for you and your health. You are in their employment. My secretary will make the necessary arrangements.'

Fleur made her exit walking on a cloud of air, bathed in warm sunshine. This moment exceeded her remotest dreams.

She spent the four week course in a mixed company of

students. Some were career diplomats about to start their careers. Others were in the process of being transferred from one cultural post to another. These courses were designed primarily for academics, embassy staff and a miscellany of students interested in administration, geography, culture or economic aspects of foreign lands in Asia or Africa. Consequently, courses on Colonial expansion, Christian missions, Islamic conclaves, traditional African religions and commercial development beyond the coast, crowded her mind. On one drizzling morning the class moved to Kew Gardens' tropical glass house, where the humidity was deemed similar to some of the more equatorial postings. Fleur learned that the White Man's Grave was not so much the fault of the mosquito, as it first seemed. Daily quinine medication was now prescribed and readily available. Instead, the habit of colonial families growing addicted to the gin they mixed with the quinine water was leading to many cases of cirrhosis of the liver.

Four weeks had never flown by so quickly. Fleur had enjoyed the company of the students and the tutors. To conclude the course, the Colonial Secretary Lord Harlech gave a valedictory address to the students, wishing each and every one well in their postings. He reminded them that in whatever sphere of work they were engaged it was on behalf of the King and in the service of the people of Great Britain and Northern Ireland. It was an honour to serve in this manner. He then intimated that the Foreign Office postings were now in place, pinned to the board in the corridor outside. The ceremony concluded and an orderly procession filed out to see what the future had in store for each of them.

Fleur looked down the typed list until she found her name:

No 9. Mrs Fleur Richter (née Bruce) Hostess to His Majesty's Governor General to the Gold Coast, Sir Ronald Murray at Accra.

In retrospect, Fleur realised how her interview had progressed to West Africa without indicating the locus. She remembered what Sir Anthony had said about the dual responsibilities of being a Hostess and engaging in unofficial diplomatic work. She wondered what the balance would be. She hoped she could work amiably with Sir Ronald.

It was time to purchase tropical attire, gather ample medical supplies and as many personal effects as the permitted seven metal trunks could contain. Having sufficient and manageable hand luggage for the voyage created her most demanding domestic challenge. She found a strap to secure her robust oboe case to her suitcase. She decided an opportunity to play on deck at sea would be rewarding and would be thwarted if her instrument travelled in the ship's hold. If her fellow passengers objected to her playing, then she was sure to find solitude down by the engine room. Yes, her oboe had earned its right to travel in her cabin.

The Royal Palm, flagship of the Elder Dempster Line, would sail from Glasgow Broomilaw, on 12th May 1939. She had a last opportunity to go home and bid her farewells to her family in Forres. She also wrote and told of her appointment to Otto care of Karl and Renate in Hamburg.

CHAPTER EIGHT

Fleur had been given a port window cabin on the Royal Palm. It had a modern shower, a writing table and a chest of drawers. She had a double bed to herself and storage room for her case and hand luggage. This was a more than an adequate environment for five weeks sailing, she thought. Her metal cases were securely stored in the ship's hold. No access to them was possible during the voyage.

As the ship eased itself from the Broomilaw, guided by two Clydeside tugs, the dull morning gave way to a bright sky, inundated with soft white clouds and a gentle breeze. Glasgow and the Clyde were looking their best.

The voyage would take the Royal Palm across the Bay of Biscay, past the Portuguese coast and down the West African coastline, to Bathurst in the British Protectorate of The Gambia. Then it would call at Freetown in Sierra Leone, before docking at Takoradi in the Gold Coast, where Fleur would disembark. The Royal Palm would then proceed to Lagos and then Port Harcourt in the colony of Nigeria, where it would arrive at its destination. In an accompanying note with her ticket, it showed that the five-week sailing to Takoradi was subject to any delays in the cargo handling that might occur at Bathurst or Freetown. Fleur rather enjoyed the feeling that she had no definite date of arrival. She was going to enjoy the voyage.

The Royal Palm was restricted in speed as it passed down the upper reaches of the Clyde. Once before, Fleur had sailed this stretch of water. That was on a day trip, from the same quay, many years before on a summer family outing. The Benmore paddle steamer plied this route faithfully each summer, bringing downtrodden city families from the clustered tenements into the fresh air, the sea air, the beauty of the countryside amid isles and kyles. There too, on board, were the more wealthy families, enjoying the same sensations in harmony. The children had the freedom of the boat and were often to be found together in the engine room, mesmerised by the large pistons driving the cogs that rotated the paddles. She recalled the blind violinist and his son, who played the accordion on deck. Passengers lingered around their performances, tapping feet and clapping hands when the slow airs changed to jigs and reels. Medleys of *Leaving Glen Urquart*,

The Hills of Moffat and the *Glendaruel Highlanders* gave way to *Shifting Bobbins* and the *Bonnie Wells O'Wearie*. After a short break they would move to a sheltered position by the funnel and then entertain with a selection of Johann Strauss II waltzes. Fleur recalled first hearing *The Blue Danube* on board the Benmore. That thought, took her momentarily to the outdoor summer concerts in Hamburg, where the city orchestra played Strauss's *Wiener Blut*, *Gross-Wein* and *Du und Du* as she held on to Willy's arm. If only Willy could have shared this moment with her now on the Royal Palm. In her mind, he was ever present. He would remain a solid comfort for Fleur throughout her life.

She remembered passing the Dumbarton Rock, calling at Gourock, then crossing over to Dunoon before turning round Toward Point into the Kyles of Bute and arriving at Tighnabruaich. The Royal Palm would not be taking such a scenic route on the Clyde. As it turned round the tail of the bank at Gourock, the ship picked up speed and sailed due south past the Great Cumbrae Island, into the Firth of Clyde which was peppered with many yachts at outrageous angles, combating a stiff sou'westerly.

From the confines of the ship's lounge, Fleur saw Ailsa Craig approach. This granite rock served both as the quarry from which curling stones were hewn and as a friendly reminder to Irish travellers, that they had reached Paddy's Milestone. There would be no more milestones before docking in Bathurst. Twenty minutes later with Ailsa Craig slowly diminishing in the distance behind, a passenger took to the starboard deck with a glass in his hand. He leaned on the rail with his eyes fixed on the coastline. Then he raised the amber fluid to the rich Ayrshire farmland passing by. 'Tae Balkissock an' Glen Tig,' he toasted the view in a broad Ayrshire accent. He drank with slow precision.

The captain approached quietly to let him savour the moment. 'The sun's beneath the main sail then!' The man slowly turned round to face the captain, clearly mystified with his oration. 'A naval term, you know, announcing the time to open the rum! When the sun sinks beneath the main sail, work is over as it were. You are entitled to it sir. Toasting the old country?'

'Naw. Ma farm at Balkissock. I've a nephew looking aefter eet while I'm awa'. Nae sayin' how he'll cope. Onyway, I've niver seen it fae this view a'fore. An it makes me hame seek alreedy!'

‘I know the feeling, Mr Barr. I’ve already passed my home village at Bishopton, further up the Clyde. But it’s always there when I come back and that will be the same for you. I’ll leave you to your thoughts and see you later, at dinner.’

The Royal Palm was primarily a cargo ship, but there were twelve cabins for paying passengers. They were soon to be acquainted with each other, but it could be seen that a vicar and his wife were among them. Presumably there would be representations of those engaged in mining and forestry ensuring gold, cocoa and hard timber was ravished from the African soil to find its way to colonial coffers. Colonial administrators must be represented she thought, but she felt uncomfortable to count herself amongst them. ‘Hostess’ seemed such a superficial title for an administrative post. Still, there was time to get to know them all. There really was no hurry.

She retired to her cabin, sat before the dressing-table mirror and stared at herself. How significant voyages were, she thought. A crossing of the North Sea, some twenty-seven years before had led to marriage. Where would this one lead? She leaned forward, rested her two elbows on the table, cradling her face in her clenched fists. Her face lacked its youthful charms, but retained its indelible dimples, which had seen few enjoyable expressions in recent months. Worry had gnawed at her thoughts as she had prepared to leave Germany and they were there as she embarked on her first steps of her future life. Her beliefs had been tested in the face of raw nationalism and there was guilt at leaving her son in Hamburg. Fortunately, her face was not reflecting these internal anxieties. Though she could not be sure it would show.

She turned to the black box, which lay by her bedside. It had the power to change her emotions instantly. She opened it carefully and took the bell out and inserted it into the bottom joint. She inserted the bottom joint to the top joint and with a slight twisting action at each joint, aligned the keys of her oboe. From a recess within the purple padded velvet box, she selected one of a number of reeds that she would need. She placed it in her mouth to dampen and soften the hard dry reed. She took her handkerchief and wedged it into the bell to mute the instrument’s volume and began to play.

She played the hauntingly beautiful *Dolly Berceuse*, by Fauré, note perfect. The music wafted its way around the cabin and beyond the window into the Irish Sea. Feeling content, she lay down for a nap. She was woken by knocking on her door at 4pm. As she rose to open it, she heard a voice announce that tea was being served in the dining room. She took a warm facecloth to her face, combed her hair and set off for afternoon tea.

'Darjeeling, Assam, Earl Grey or Lipton's Ma'am?' asked the waiter.

'Darjeeling please.'

'I shall bring it to where you choose to sit,' he responded.

'Thank you very much'.

Fleur took a seat at the top end of the dining room, giving her a view from the starboard windows. Her fellow passengers had grouped themselves in twos and threes, at distances that precluded conversation between tables. They awaited their assorted teas to arrive. The waiter approached in his white starched jacket with immaculately creased trousers and bent forward to lay a silver tray, with all its accoutrements, on the table before Fleur. He asked her to let the tea brew for a further minute before serving herself. Fleur secured a cube of sugar by the silver tongs and placed it at the base of her cup, poured a little milk over it and after counting slowly to twenty, let the golden stream of Rangdoo Darjeeling tea flow freely towards the rim of her cup. Fleur enjoyed a first sip of the elixir from the china teacup, bearing the Elder Dempster's livery. As she returned cup to saucer, a flaxen-haired woman of a similar age approached Fleur.

'Good afternoon. May I ask if you occupy cabin number 6?'

Fleur wondered if she was about to become the subject of a complaint and answered with a degree of anxious concern. 'Yes, I do.'

'Then am I right to conclude that you were playing the oboe so beautifully?'

'Thank you. I hope I did not disturb you.'

'Disturb us! Not at all I assure you. You would not have disturbed us, even if you were playing in the middle of the night. We, that being my daughter and I are next door as it were, in cabin number 8. We listened to every note and when you finished we wished for more. Would you care to join us for tea?'

Fleur prepared to gather her handbag and tea cup to join her newly acquainted fellow passenger, but the waiter had anticipated the move and took her cup from her, to her new table at which the lady's daughter was already seated.

'I'm Madge Hall and this is my daughter Joan.'

'Fleur Richter'. They shook hands.

Madge informed Fleur that they were sailing out to join her husband for three months at Kumasi where he was the General Manager of the Ashanti Timber Company. 'Are you joining your husband in West Africa?' enquired Madge.

'No, I am now a widow. I am taking up a post in Accra at the Governor's office.'

'Ah, with Sir Ronald?'

'Indeed, ... you know him?' Fleur was surprised.

'Sir Ronald travels around the country from time to time and when he stays in Kumasi, he sometimes visits my husband, David. Oh yes, Sir Ronald, a delightful man indeed. A great historian too.'

'Oh, then he does a lot of travel?' enquired Fleur.

'Not really. He's a bachelor you know. A great reader, very knowledgeable and I think quite sporty for his years. A good chap anyway. You will enjoy working with him.'

'That's good to hear. I have not met him yet, though I will be working closely with him. This is my first overseas posting.'

That information did not particularly surprise Madge in view of her being a recent widow, but she chose not to follow up that line of questioning. Instead she indicated that Joan had her violin in her hand luggage and wondered if they might consider playing something together at some point in the voyage.

Joan felt a little awkward. She had completed grade 5 in her violin lessons, a stage that gave her some confidence, but most of her music books were in a trunk out of reach in the ship's hold.

'I'm sure we could practice a few tunes, Joan. I remember being asked to play when I was your age and I can sympathise. I'm sure we can have some musical fun anyway.'

'Yes, then we'll meet sometime,' agreed Joan.

'After breakfast tomorrow might be a good time,' suggested Madge.

Fleur felt it best to change the subject and save Joan any further discomfort. 'Have you met any of the other passengers?'

'Not all yet, Fleur. The vicar is Reverend Simon Fisher and his wife is Lillian. Quite easily recognised, of course. I can not imagine him without his clerical collar. They are headed for Port

Harcourt in eastern Nigeria. You'll find them a perfectly pleasant Methodist couple but don't forget to wait for grace if you join them at the table and don't invite them for a card game! I wonder if he will be asked to take a service on Sunday.'

'Probably not, unless you ask him to, Mum,' Joan said indignantly.

'The Fishers are in cabin number 4.'

'Oh dear. Next cabin to mine! I had better be careful with my musical selection. You know one of my favourite pieces has such a riotous reputation. *The Stripper*! It's a raucous jazz piece, which sounds terrific on the oboe.' The ensemble had a good laugh at the thought of the Fishers tapping their feet to *the Stripper*.

'I suspect Captain Alastair Cameron may introduce all of us at dinner this evening. It's a bit of a maritime tradition on the first night. We'll see if he does. Then we will know everyone. But I am interested to know who the two men are in cabins 5 and 7, or if I might say, in 5 or 7!' Madge raised her eyebrow as she said this.

'Oh I see. In Germany, homosexuality used to be a little more established in some Berlin night clubs but Hitler has crushed them now. The lucky ones are in hiding, or have gone to Amsterdam or Paris. Hitler will deal with the others in his own way. That's the way of it. If you are not to the party's liking then there is no place for you. It's quite terrible.'

'You know a lot about Germany and Hitler then?'

'Yes, I lived in Germany for twenty-seven years. It is not a place for me to live in now. There will be war soon. Germany is fully armed. Not just the Army, but the Navy and the Luftwaffe are too. Hitler will not stop. He still wants a place in the sun and he wants to ensure a pure German identity is established. That has caused too many disappearances over the last few years. Yet the people are fanatically behind him, the saviour of the German people they call him. If you do not fit into his society, then you are expendable. When my husband died, I chose to leave. But I did so with a heavy heart. My son, Otto is still there.'

'Oh, how dreadful. You are Scottish though aren't you?'

Fleur smiled. 'Only six months ago, I would say I was German. I must be British now, otherwise the Foreign Office would not have appointed me! Yes, from Forres. And you?'

'Cardonald, Glasgow. Grew up in Govan, not three miles away. I've never lived very far from the Clyde. I always knew the shipping companies by their funnels. Yellow with four red rings for the China Line, green palm tree of the Elder Dempster. There were so many from South America, Asia and North America. Never did I think I'd be sailing on one. David was in the Forestry Department you know. After wet summers, cold winters and restricted promotion, he got a chance to manage the hard woods of West Africa. Can you blame us for the move? This will be his third tour. David loves it in Kumasi.'

'No, I think I would have done the same if I were in his shoes.'

Dinner was at 8pm. Captain Alastair Cameron along with Angus Rae, the Chief Engineer, formed a welcoming party. As the passengers arrived, he announced them and invited them to the sherry reception.

'Mr Edward, Mrs Sally and Miss Ann Philips from Kirriemuir, Angus. Passengers to Bathurst, British Protectorate of the Gambia.'

'The Reverend Mr Simon Fisher and his wife Mrs Lillian Fisher from Newcastle, passengers to Port Harcourt, Colony of Nigeria.'

'Mrs Madge Hall and her charming daughter Miss Joan Hall from Glasgow, passengers to Takoradi, Colony of the Gold Coast.'

'Mrs Fleur Richter from Forres, passenger to Takoradi, Colony of the Gold Coast.

'Mr Hugh Patterson and Mr Ted Mathers from Manchester, passengers to Lagos, Colony of Nigeria.'

'Mr Andrew Barr from Ballantrae, passenger to Lagos, Colony of Nigeria.'

'Mr Donald and Mrs Mary McLeod from Aberdeen, passengers to Port Harcourt, Colony of Nigeria.'

The passengers formed an arc leaving the Captain and his Chief Engineer facing them to address them further.

'Ladies and gentlemen, good evening. I welcome you on the Royal Palm's voyage to West Africa. We are sailing at a relatively settled time of year and so I am not expecting a rough passage. You should enjoy this trip and, having met most of you, I am sure you will enjoy each other's company too. After all, we are prisoners for the next five weeks! Our Chief Engineer is Mr Angus Rae on my left here and not only does he ensure we make good progress, he is also our qualified medical orderly. By that, I do not mean he is a doctor. But having performed an appendectomy on me two years ago and brought premature identical twin girls into the world last year, I assure you he has your good health in mind and he does scrub his oily hands before he operates!' This comment caused much laughter and eased the reservations that this first get-together inevitably generated.

'Bodies and engines are very much the same thing. Love to keep them in good working order,' further joked the Chief Engineer.

'Our two circular tables are bolted to the floor, but in relatively close proximity. On this occasion, our first meal together, the Chief Engineer and I will host separate tables. In a moment, I will ask you to join one of the tables. With all future meals, please make your own seating arrangements.

Now, Chief Engineer Mr Rae will host Reverend and Mrs Fisher, Mr and Mrs McLeod, and Mrs Hall and Miss Hall. On my table I invite Mrs Richter, Mr Patterson and Mr Mathers, Mr and Mrs Philips and their delightful daughter Miss Ann Philips and Mr Andy Barr. Please take your seats. I now call upon Mr Fisher to say grace.'

Mr Philips had been a modern language teacher at Webster's Seminary High School in Kirriemuir. German and French were his languages and Fleur learned of this through Madge, but he was taken aback when in fun, Fleur addressed him in vernacular German. That led to many informal discussions in French and German, during the voyage before the Philips disembarked at Bathurst where he would be head of languages at the Ridge High School, while his wife would teach physics in the same school. Ann would start Secondary school stage 2 at the Ridge High School where there was a good mix of European and African pupils. Meanwhile Fleur enjoyed the opportunity to speak German freely again with Ann's father. When overheard, it did lead to covert innuendoes by the crew, but none that ever came to her ears.

Hugh Patterson and Ted Mathers on the other hand were highly animated listening to Fleur and Edward speaking 'continental' as they said. Hugh and Ted ran a chain of barbers' shops in Manchester and had decided to spend a month in Lagos, on the suggestion of a Nigerian customer, learning to cut African hair.

They wanted to run a fully comprehensive barbers' service, at which all kinds of hair could be cut. They had been given addresses of Nigerians in Lagos and they had taken the whole venture on a spur of the moment extravaganza. They were going to make the most of their month in Lagos and return to launch into their African hairdressing boutique, having recognised a growing market. They hoped to sail to Japan the following year, to gain experience with very straight black hair.

'But you could find straight hair in Manchester surely!' exclaimed Fleur.

'Oh, straight yes, but the Japanese hair is not just straight, it's thick. Quite different, isn't it Ted?'

'You are not putting us off a trip to Japan are you?' he teased. Fleur smiled. 'Have you brought your trade tools with you on board?'

'Ah! My customer, Hugh, but if I may say, I would not touch your hair now. Let the sea spray get to it as well as the sun's rising temperatures. Perhaps the day before you disembark, come and see me. I'll freshen you up.'

'That would be much appreciated.' Fleur made sure her eye contact with him sealed the deal.

Ted smiled and nodded. They seemed such a refreshingly comical and obliging couple. Mr Barr did not seem to take to them so readily.

He was from near Ballantrae on the Ayrshire coast. He was going to visit his brother and sister-in-law in Lagos. They had been there for more than twenty years. Andy was quite unlike his brother. He had laboured on the Ayrshire family farm as the younger son and his tanned leathery skin unkindly aged him. His brother was a surgeon in a teaching hospital in Nigeria. His sister-in-law was a nurse in the same institution. They had felt sorry for him, not having ever left the Ayrshire coast and it was their gift to bring him out to Lagos to see a wider horizon. It was a social experience as much as a cultural one, in his brother's eyes. The holiday might give him greater social confidence back home. It was a horizon that would be a challenge but one that was felt to be in his best interests. In truth, he was not looking forward to the holiday. In an effort to ease the destination from his mind, he followed one whisky after another even before his first meal on board. At dinner, he was consequently quiet and his eyes made little social contact. By the time the coffee was being served, he was fast asleep. The captain had him removed to his cabin.

The passengers retired to their rooms around 10pm after learning that their position was south of the Solway, in alignment with Barrow-in-Furness on the Westmorland coast. Fleur fell asleep promptly, but stirred momentarily around 3am, her senses disturbed. Not enough to waken her, but there had been a shout, a scream and a disturbance. The murmur of the ship's engines dispelled any meaning to the commotion. She slept on.

At breakfast the following morning, all assembled except Hugh. When Fleur enquired if Ted had seen Hugh, Ted turned white and said nothing. Fleur did not enquire any further. Ted kept himself to himself at breakfast and toyed with his meal. He left his table abruptly without speaking.

Fleur turned to Madge. 'What do you think has come over Ted?'

Madge smiled with mischief. 'Lovers' tiff!'

'Oh really, Madge. They were good company last night. Perhaps Hugh is under the weather and Ted had a bad night. No more than that.'

They changed the subject. 'I think you and Joan could practise a few pieces and if I can ascertain whether there is more latent musical talent on board, we might be able to have a concert. What do you think?'

'Do you think the Captain will agree to it?'

'I don't see why not. He might be a pianist, but if not, perhaps an amateur magician!' They laughed at the thought.

'And what about the McLeods?' asked Fleur.

'I could see Donald play a fiddle and perhaps his wife could sing. I think we should make discreet enquiries, don't you?'

Suddenly a bell sounded and the foghorn blared. 'Man overboard! Launch the lifeboat!' The ship's propellers were put into neutral. Fleur saw the lifeboat containing three crew members being lowered into the sea. While the ship was still proceeding, the lifeboat was released causing a considerable splash as it reached the water. The crew rowed smartly away from the ship and headed for a bobbing head in the heaving water.

'Oh I think it's Ted. What an accident! He must have lost his balance. Poor fellow,' said Fleur.

'I can't see how he could have fallen over, Fleur. That must have been an attempt to kill himself. End his life. Goodness knows why.' Madge then turned to Fleur with an anguished expression on her face. 'Fleur, he was not himself at breakfast, was he? No. You asked if he had seen Hugh and he did not reply. I suspect something is not right. Let's go to Hugh's cabin and check, to see why he's not come for breakfast.'

They left the dining room. Crew members rushed past informing everyone to stay calm. Madge and Fleur entered the cabin corridor.

'Which cabin does Hugh have?' asked Madge.

'Number 5, opposite my cabin.'

They stood in the corridor. Madge knocked twice. 'Hugh, are you coming to......Fleur...look!'

Her eyes lowered to focus on the door handle. It was smeared with blood.

'Quick let's inform the Captain.'

They set off to the bridge, passing the chain that demarcated crew from passengers. Madge shouted for Captain Cameron. He came from the Bridge. 'Its all right Mrs Hall, the rowing boat has picked up Mr Mathers. I am writing a report on the incident. I'll have to speak to him.'

'I think you should come to cabin number 5. Hugh has not come for breakfast and there is blood on the door handle.'

The captain suddenly realised his report was premature. Was he hearing that a passenger had been injured last night?

'Right, please return to the lounge and keep everyone calm there.'

The news of blood on the door handle and the man overboard was beginning to look very suspicious. Captain Cameron called for the Bursar to get a master key for cabin number 5. Together they entered the cabin. Hugh was apparently asleep in his bed, but blood was smeared around the room. The porthole was open. The Captain approached Hugh and rolled back the covers. He was covered in stab wounds with blood everywhere. Mr Hugh Patterson was certainly dead. A murder investigation was now underway.

The captain made arrangements for Ted to be arrested immediately he came on board and had him locked in the cell next to his own. He tucked handcuffs into his tunic pocket and went on deck to see what progress the rowing boat was making. It took a further quarter of an hour for the boat to come alongside. When it did, he saw that the crew had already tied Ted's hands together, behind his back. They seemed to have reached their own conclusion or was it to prevent him jumping over again? Nevertheless an investigation would have to take place. The lifeboat was raised and brought on board. Ted was arrested by the captain on suspicion of murdering Mr Hugh Patterson in cabin number 5. Ted looked through tearful eyes at the Captain.

'Why did you save me? Why, why, why did you save me?' he asked pitifully.

The captain took his tie and his belt from him and locked him in the ship's cell, from where the sound of sobbing was heard for more than an hour. The Reverend Mr Fisher sought the captain's permission to sit with him. A crewman sat in with them both. Only the minister was left, after the bent-over silent prisoner fell asleep though exhaustion. Captain Cameron ordered that the ship be put on a course to stand off St David's Head and he sent a telegram to the police station at Milford Haven in the Carmarthenshire Constabulary, to inform them of the incident.

The crew sealed off cabin number 5 under the instruction of the captain. Meanwhile, Fleur felt pity for both the victim and the accused. After all, she had enjoyed the company of both of them at dinner, only hours before. She took her oboe to the corridor leading to the captain's quarters and played the hymn *The Lord is my Shepherd.* From within the cell, Reverend Mr Fisher quietly sang each verse to her music.

Two hours later, a pilot boat was sighted approaching the Royal Palm. Two detectives were aboard. The captain was pleased. This would expedite the removal of the suspect, let them clear up the cabin and get underway sooner. The officers were not working to a similar timetable. When they boarded, they took the names of everyone and informed them that statements would be taken shortly. The police asked that the Royal Palm be securely anchored off shore, from where the murder investigation would be conducted.

Captain Cameron indicated that the ship was two miles off shore, with Ramsey Island and St David's Head in full view. But, showing his disappointment with the constabulary's pedantic investigation, said dryly, 'We have a body with stab wounds, the victim's travelling companion jumped ship but was rescued. Since his arrest, he has been inconsolable. Officer, the case is open and shut to me.'

'Seems so, Captain,' agreed the older of the two detectives, a man in his mid forties with a rounded welsh accent and the figure of a rugby front row prop who had seen many a derby confrontation. 'Nevertheless, we need statements to back the case. A man's life is at stake. About that you must agree.'

'Very well. Please let me know if you require any assistance. The sooner this is finished the better.'

Fleur gave her statement to the second detective who was younger than his colleague and much fitter looking. It did not amount to much. She may have heard something in the night, but she was not sure and she certainly did not wake or recognise any voices. Madge gave a similar account. The Fishers had heard nothing, but all had said that Hugh and Ted had seemed in a good mood last night. The rest of the crew were then asked to give their evidence. Judging by the time they spent with the officers, they had not seen or heard anything either.

Andy Barr was then interviewed. He admitted he had drunk quite a considerable amount with his meal and found himself in his bed. He could not remember how he got there. A police officer prompted him. 'The Captain took you back, I believe. You must have had a lot to drink.' Andy reached up to comb his fingers through his hair as he recalled the night, revealing dried blood on his cuff.

'Mr Barr, when you went to bed, did the captain prepare you for bed?'

'No, I slept in these clothes.'

'So you did not take them off all night?'

'Aye, that's right. I've nae even shaved this morn. Can't ye see?'

'Have you been to see Mr Patterson's body then?'

'I certainly have not. I jist heard he had been killed.'

'Then how do you account for the dried blood on your shirt cuff, Mr Barr?'

Andy shook his head, but no words came out.

'What do you think of homosexual men, Mr Barr?'

'Nae much, why?'

'I think we will close this interview now, unless you can remember any other detail, Mr Barr.'

'No, I don't think I can help ye ony further. Can I go noo?'

'Yes, for the moment sir.'

The detectives went to the cell where Ted had woken, but was still quite shaken.

'Mr Mathers, tell me exactly what happened last night.'

Ted looked up and saw the officers poised over their writing pads. The anguish had subsided. He was once more in dry clothes and he had eaten some tea and toast. His senses were returning to him.

'It was a pleasant dinner last night and we retired at 10.30pm We had each had a couple of glasses of wine with our meal, but we were not drunk. I went to Hugh's cabin and we had a night cap, a small whisky each, just one, honestly. About 11.20pm Hugh said he wanted to go to bed and I got up to go. He followed me to the door and as I left, ...well, ...we kissed each other goodnight. I suddenly heard a noise from the end of the corridor and saw a man turn around. It was Mr Barr's jacket. I recognised it. I suspect he had seen me and I was worried that he might report what he had seen.'

'What happened next?'

'I went to my cabin – number 7 and slept. I slept soundly. After I got dressed this morning, I went to Hugh's door to see if he was ready for breakfast. I knocked three times. Harder each time. I tried the door but it was locked. Just as I was leaving, heading for breakfast in the dining room, I noticed some blood smeared on the door handle. I was terrified. I feared the worst. I felt if I reported what I had discovered, I would be the prime suspect. So I went off to breakfast very worried and feeling low. I did not want to speak to anyone. I had difficulty putting my thoughts together, deciding what to do, what to eat. Then Fleur asked if I had seen Hugh. Well I panicked. She had not seen him that morning either. Words failed me. I was scared. Hugh should have been at breakfast by then, but he wasn't. I left abruptly. I went to his cabin door and knocked. Still there was no answer. I knew something had happened or Hugh would have opened the door. But then the blood was on my hand! I knew something dreadful had happened. I would be held responsible and a charge would be forthcoming, especially after Andy saw me kiss Hugh goodnight. I went on deck then. I looked overboard at the passing sea. It seemed it was inviting me. It looked near and I could not resist its pull. I was filled with remorse and the sea begged me to jump overboard. It really did and.... I did just that. I remember I wanted to jump overboard, but I do not recall wanting to die. The water was much warmer than I feared. Nevertheless, the drop almost knocked me unconscious. I thought I might be able to swim ashore eventually, but the crew was very quick to lower the lifeboat. When they approached, I was strangely relieved. They had come to rescue me. They did not have to. Yes, they came for me!'

Ted's face was crushed with wrinkled tension. Tears welled up inside, then silently trickled down each cheek from glassy eyes. The younger detective then looked Ted straight in his eyes and with gravity confronted him.

'Mr Mathers, this is an important question. Listen carefully.' He paused momentarily. 'Did YOU kill Hugh Patterson?'

Hugh straightened himself and focussed on the face of his questioner. He was now fully compos mentis and eager to reply.

'No officer, I did not kill Hugh, I DID NOT kill Hugh.'

'One final question, Mr Mathers. How do you find Mr Andy Barr?'

'Officer, were you ever a cub or a scout or a team player? You know the feeling, one that gives you a feeling of loyalty, of friendship, and trust. That's how it was with Hugh and me. I could depend on him. We ran a joint business. We trusted each other in every way. It's a successful business. I loved him. That becomes a source of envy to some. It seems Mr Barr did not like our relationship. He did not speak to us and he was a heavy drinker, a heavy lone drinker. I told you, he saw us part last night. That would have disgusted him. Other than that, I do not know the man.'

'Thank you. Mr Mathers, I am not going to arrest you. What I would ask you to do for the time being, is stay here until I have completed my enquiries. It will be safer for you. Do you understand?'

The two police officers retired to consider their notes. Then they asked the captain to arrange to interview Mr Barr once more.

Mr Andy Barr was sober, bitter and unforgiving. The pressure of an ambivalent voyage, mixed with undesirable homosexual company, brought to the surface his prejudices, in a nightmare and a night of frenzied aggression. He slowly began to reveal the night of horror to the officers, sparing no detail.

He visited Hugh's room a few minutes after Ted had left and knocked quietly. Hugh had assumed Ted had left something behind and opened the cabin door without making any inquiry. The door flew open hitting Hugh's head and trapping his toes under the door. Andy threw his left hand over Hugh's mouth to stifle his howls and with a swift movement of his other knife bearing hand, plunged his penknife deep into his chest. The force brought him down on the bed, where Andy repeated his frenzied attack, later counted as twenty-two stabbings, to Hugh's upper body, neck and arms. He then opened the porthole and threw the knife into the sea. He had no remorse. The officers were astounded by his attention to detail. Here was a man pleading for the services of the hangman. Nevertheless, the questioning had to be thorough.

'Do you know where the key to Hugh's cabin is?' the detective asked.

'Aye. I locked his room when I left. Then I jist threw his key overboard after that.'

The officers took down his statement and read it back to him.

'Yes, that's how it was. That's how it is.'

An examination of cabin number 2 found traces of blood around the sink, where Andy Barr had washed his hands after the deed. He had not noticed the blood on his cuff however.

'Mr Barr, I am placing you under arrest, for the murder of Mr Hugh Patterson on 13th May 1939 onboard the Royal Palm at some point in the Irish Sea. You repeatedly stabbed Mr Patterson within his cabin, cabin number 5, by the use of a knife or other similar weapon as yet unknown and you did kill Mr Patterson. You are not required to say anything but, if you do so, it may be recorded and used against you at any forthcoming trial. Do you understand?' He simply nodded in reply.

The Royal Palm lay still, at anchor. Mr Andy Barr was taken in handcuffs ashore. Mr Ted Mathers was released from the captain's cell, but was deemed to be medically unfit to resume the voyage. He was taken ashore to a hospital in Carmarthen for a psychological assessment. The police did not consider any other charges against Ted Mathers. The Royal Palm's pertinent cabin and corridor were given a thorough clean and on May 15th, the captain announced that the Royal Palm would lift anchor and resume its voyage the following morning at 8am.

The feared Bay of Biscay was as relaxed as the drooping

ensign on the stern of the ship. Most of the remaining passengers admitted that the Bay had been the anxious part of the voyage. No doubt as it slumbered, it was renewing its vigour and would undoubtedly give trouble to ships passing another day. On this voyage the Royal Palm respected its inertia. The Royal Palm would be returning again and again and would meet its different moods. However, such was the calm that day that the captain arranged an impromptu game of badminton on deck, leaving the well-used quoits for another day when less favourable weather conditions determined.

Reverend Simon Fraser had command of the court with a deft service enticing a fateful step forward, only to find the shuttle fly over and past to win point after point. His wife had obviously tuned to his game and was easily his match. When doubles were played, teams were never keen to have the Frasers together as opponents. The McLeods were enthusiastic to play as were the Philips. Soon a league was established. It was the antidote they needed after the traumatic events in the Irish Sea. In the breathless calm, the shuttle flew true and no shuttlecock met with an untimely dousing.

The league brought the passengers together and each slowly divulged enough personal information for mutual satisfaction. It transpired that Donald McLeod was a master joiner. He was alighting, with his wife at Port Harcourt, but from there they would travel northwards to the town of Owerri. It was a Presbyterian Mission station, where he would teach local craftsmen. His wife was a domestic science teacher and the classes she would lead were in house management, cookery and nutrition. Joan found out he had with him an accordion and indeed Mary McLeod was a talented singer.

Joan concentrated on drafting a musical entertainment and when she put her suggestion to the captain, he readily agreed to have an evening concert. He himself, wished to give a recitation and he asked that a crew-member, Eddy, be given a turn. His work rota would have to be considered first and Captain Cameron asked Joan to bring the draft programme to him for final venue, timing and, of course, printing of programmes. Joan relished this undertaking, giving her some authority amongst her elders.

Joan first approached the Fishers.

'Yes, certainly, my dear. Now Simon, what could we do for the concert?'

'We sang at a South Shields concert last November. It was a gospel evening. We sang many hymns, but we had lighter moments too. Lillian played the piano. I think there is a piano in the dining room…'

'Yes there is,' clarified Joan.

'Then we need not require too much practice. We will sing *The Holy City.'*

'And another piece perhaps?'

'Well, maybe *Jeanie with the Light Brown Hair*, a Stephen Foster song.'

'That will do very nicely thank you. Let me know if you need any extra practice time.'

'And what will you be doing, Joan?'

'I'll play some pieces on the violin. Then Mrs Richter and I will play a duet.'

'That sounds delightful. I look forward to that very much, Joan.'

Joan began to compile a list of performances and performers and soon the programme was ready. She took it to the captain, who gave his approval for a Royal Palm Evening Concert to take place on Saturday 19th May 1939.

ROYAL PALM CONCERT

Saturday 19th May 1939
8pm in the Dining Room

On board the Royal Palm
(Off the Portuguese Coast near Oporto)

Introduction by Captain Cameron

The Programme

G.F. Handel- *Air from the Water Music* by Joan Hall (violin)
Eddy - the Juggler
A Borodin – *Nocturne* by Fleur Richter (oboe)

Recitations by the Captain:

The King's Breakfast by A.A. Milne
To a Mouse by Robert Burns

Duets by Joan and Fleur:

Sarasate: *Carmen Fantasy*
The Entertainer by Scott Joplin

The Interval

Songs by Rev Simon accompanied by Mrs Lillian Fisher (piano):

The Holy City by Stephen Adams
Jeanie With The Light Brown Hair by Stephen Foster

Eddy - the Ventriloquist

Mr Donald McLeod (accordion):

A Selection of Scottish Airs and Jigs

Ed Philips (mouth organ):

The Arrival of The Queen of Sheba by G F Handel

The Grand Finale

A medley of community songs to the accompaniment of all the instrumentalists:

Comin Through the Rye
She'll be coming Round the Mountain
Little Brown Jug
The Man on the Flying Trapeze
My Bonnie Lies Over The Ocean.

The concert was a great success ranging from the spiritual singing of the pastor and his wife, to the ventriloquist doll dressed as a one-eyed pirate, who took delight in mocking the captain. The concert concluded at 10.15pm after the captain had given a vote of thanks, hoping that in the last song, those who were unattached might find their 'bonnie' over the seas by courtesy of the Palm Line! Then the ship's cook arrived with a plate full of sandwiches, hot drinks and cakes. The passengers were at ease with each other once again. The Royal Palm was steadily progressing through the

Atlantic, with Madeira and the Canary Islands slipping by on the port side, just out of sight.

On 22nd May, the Royal Palm lay off the port at Bathurst. The Philips family said their farewells and they were ferried ashore with their cases. The ship took on additional supplies and some additional cargo marked for Lagos. On 26th May, the Royal Palm's engines spurted into life and the ship continued round the curved West African Coast.

On 31st May the ship set anchor off Freetown, where a fleet of cut out log canoes, launched their way through the angry surf to service the ship. The canoes were painted colourfully, with emblems and biblical quotations on their hulls, which pleased Reverend Fisher. 'If only we had buses and vans in Britain declaring the Lord's work,' he proclaimed loudly.

Awed by the pounding surf, Fleur wondered how much of the coastline had been eroded in recent years. She wondered how many lives such powerful surf had claimed, and how much cargo lay at the bottom of the sea as it was transferred from ship to land, lost in transit. Would this be her misfortune at Takoradi? Time would tell, but the omens did not look good. The Royal Palm had to lie half a mile beyond the breaking waves. When the canoes arrived, the paddlers looked tired. Many of them engaged in this work were non-swimmers. The dangerous undercurrents of the West African coastline made swimming impossible to learn and drowning was not uncommon. Yet this was lucrative work. Sometimes sailors would give them inconsequential European gifts, in exchange for wooden carvings from the interior or African grey parrots or pet monkeys. Novelty exchanges were common. Africa's charms were eagerly traded with mutual satisfaction at each port of call. Fresh fruit and water was essential and the stevedores worked hard in teams to bring them to the ships, returning with the oil drums, crates and cases destined for the hinterland.

The cargo manoeuvring took time. Work started as dawn broke at 6am and finished promptly at dusk at 6pm. During the day it grew hotter and hotter. A mid day siesta was essential and loosely clad passengers sought the balmy shade of the decks while by night, ankles and wrists were covered to deter the ubiquitous mosquito. 'I'm not sure how, but the Scottish midge must be related to these mosquitoes. The bites itch something dreadful,'

Donald announced.

'I'd rather have the midge any day,' replied Mary. 'At least it brings no malaria.'

'They won't like my pipe smoke, so I hope I'll not attract them. They are the curse of West Africa – the white man's grave.'

'Only indirectly, Donald,' Fleur interjected. 'It was the amount of gin consumed with quinine tonic water, which caused so much cirrhosis of the liver that accounted for many deaths. The gin companies have to answer for that.'

'Are you sure?'

'Yes, you will see if you analyse the number of colonial deaths in West Africa. By comparing the deaths with the percentage of mission staff who did not drink alcohol, but died of malaria, you will see it is the liver damage and not always malaria which gave this region its reputation as the white man's grave.' Donald reflected on this assertion.

On 9th June the Royal Palm rounded the Liberian coast and passed by the French West African colony of Ivory Coast. On 11th June 1939 the ship dropped anchor off the Gold Coast at Takoradi. An hour later a pilot boat guided the Royal Palm to quay No 1. Fleur had reached her port. Later that morning, all her seven cases were gathered and eased from the ship's hold, by a mammoth crane on the dockside. There, they were loaded on to a lorry. She walked down the gangway after parting with the ship's company, felt the heat of the morning sun, saw the smiling faces of the natives below and placed her foot on dry land. Her traumatic voyage was over. She had been at sea for six weeks. She looked at her watch. It was approaching midday. Midday in Takoradi, midday in London. They were the same. She was pleased to be still in the same time zone, very close to the Greenwich Meridian.

CHAPTER NINE

Takoradi's deep-water harbour had been built in eight years. It was officially opened on 3rd April 1928. The town was connected to Sekondi by a double line of railway track, two miles long. The municipality of Sekondi-Takoradi was connected by road and rail to Kumasi, in the heart of the Ashanti region and by road to Accra via Cape Coast. Consequently, the colony's gold fields, hard wood and cocoa made their way to this exporting deep-water harbour. These advantages attracted considerable trade and commercial firms. No fewer than sixty-two Gold Coast tribal divisions, were represented in town and so English was the universal first language.

A smiling young man approached Fleur. 'Mrs Richter? I am Seth, your driver to the Governor in Accra, Sir Ronald. Please, sit in the shade here until I have loaded all your cases.'

Fleur was shown to a wooden bench, across the quay that lay against a whitewashed store. Before allowing her to sit down, Seth took his handkerchief and vigorously cleaned the bench, though no dirt, dust or offending matter seemed to exist. 'Thank you Seth. How long will the drive take to Accra?'

'Please, it takes five hours so we will leave as soon as I secure your cases on the lorry.'

Seth ran back to the lorry and sought the assistance of some young boys, looking for casual employment's multifarious opportunities. He shouted at them to take care of the boxes and got them on board the lorry, to stack them and tie them down. Much of his authoritative instructions convinced Fleur that he was trying to impress her of his dedication and thoroughness. The boys were certainly not cowed by his commands.

An orange-headed lizard approached Fleur as she sat. She drew herself up. It was about five or six inches long with a tail half that length again. It moved in an arc round her, eyeing her all the time. Its head rocked up and down as if contemplating who would strike first. It skittered back to where she first saw it. Fleur was frozen to the spot.

'Ah Mrs Richter, don't worry it will not harm you. It's giving you a welcome,' Seth joked. He clapped his hands. 'Kiteri.'

'What was that you said to it?'

'Oh, I called its name, it's a lizard. We call that kiteri.' Fleur repeated the word.

'It's like the noise it makes while skittering around the ground.'

'Yes, that's why we call it kiteri.'

Fleur realised it was an onomatopoeic word. 'Do you have any more names like that?'

Seth smiled. He could claim to be her teacher now. 'Yes. Let's see if you understand them.'

'Oh, I don't think I will.'

'Well, there is akawkaw. Can you understand that one?'

'A Kaw Kaw, sounds like a cockerel to me!'

'Nearly! It is a chicken, Mrs Richter! Now what about daboudabou?'

'Daboudabou...daboudabou ....would that be..... a dabbling duck?'

'Yes, a duck. I think you will be speaking Akan Twi very soon. It is good you learn, Mrs Richter. Now come, the lorry is ready and comfortable.'

Fleur sat in the lorry passenger's seat and wound down the window. The road ahead was constructed of a red laterite surface that had many potholes for the lorry to contend with. Seth seemed to know where the worst ones were and he drove around them without braking. They passed the red baked mud homes of villagers set amid high grasses of various shades. She saw bananas clinging to one set of bound leaves for the first time. They were small green fingers. Their riper predecessors sat on the heads of walking street sellers and at their stalls. Seth stopped the lorry to buy some together with a small paper twist of roasted groundnuts. 'Try these Mrs Richter, they taste good together.'

And so they did. Fleur realised that this was a land of plenty and if she ever got to travel, she would be sure of finding food to eat, food she enjoyed eating.

The lorry passed by Cape Coast where the Dutch built a lodge as long ago as 1630, on an abandoned site built on earlier by the Portuguese. This main slavery castle brought a note of condolences from Fleur.

'We were just as bad,' said Seth. 'After all, we often brought the slaves to the castles for the white men.'

Fleur knew that trading slaves was a dark period of history, one that still caused resentment, but Seth's comment made her realise the complexity of native dealings. This was what she had also seen perhaps in Takoradi, with so many different traders.

'Who were the boys who helped you with my boxes? Did you know them?'

'They are the pilot boys, Mrs Richter. We used to call them street boys, but because of the port, we call them pilot boys in Takoradi. They are always looking for work. So they are ready to do anything. They fend for themselves by stealing, gambling, acting as guides to sightseers or directing European sailors and soldiers to prostitutes. Most do not have real homes. They sleep in market stalls, on lorries and on the bench you sat on, when the lorry was being packed. Many are in league with particular prostitutes to whom they "pilot" customers. When the ships are not in the harbour, they unload manganese from train wagons, into dry bays in the covered barn, while younger ones prowl about the railway station, the tennis courts and golf course to caddy and earn a few coins. They are good at scoring in tennis and golf. They often have cheeky smiles and the younger ones get extra payment. But sometimes they gang together and go for more lucrative prizes. That's when the law catches up on them.'

'What happens then?'

'They go to court, where they find out about the boys' background and might place him with a relative. If not, and in serious or repeated cases, they are sent to the Boys' Industrial School at Agona Swedru, or His Majesty's Industrial Institution at Maamobi in Accra.'

'Do you know of any of these boys well?'

'Oh yes, when I get them to work for me, I always get the same boys. Once I knew Kofi. He was seventeen. He was born at a town called Swedru and lived with his father and mother, till he was eight. His father's work was transferred to Takoradi, but he died the next year. His mother then died three years later. So Kofi had to live with his aunt and continue at school. But his aunt was not good like his mother. Kofi complained that he was not getting enough to eat and his clothes were worn out and his school fees were always in arrears. The aunt said she could do no more and other family members were not helping, so he joined the pilot boys at Takoradi. These pilot boys are strongly attached to one another. Sometimes the gangs fight, but within each gang of pilot boys, there is intense loyalty. So the youngest member is always given the easiest jobs and gets as much to eat as the older boys. Theft and delinquency offer adventure and livelihood while the comradeship of delinquent companions, compensates for the neglect which they have suffered at home.'

'But do the authorities not do something about this?'

'Sometimes. But if they take them all off the streets, they will soon fill up with new pilot boys. I know the Industrial school at Swedru has 130 boys in residence. It's bigger in Maamobi.'

'What's the Industrial Institution like, Seth?'

'It's built on a House System. There are two, the Wilberforce, which is Red and the Howard is Yellow. Wilberforce has all the boys from Sekondi-Takoradi, Kumasi and Elmina and the west while Howard has all the boys from Accra, Keta, Tamale and Ada in the east. Each house has a separate dining and recreation room. But, there is keen inter-house competition in work and play. Each inmate is granted his first brown bar on reception. The second brown bar is sewn on his tunic when an inmate earns it at the end of each term. On reaching a third brown bar, an inmate may be promoted by the House Board to the Blue stage. The House Board meets monthly to approve promotion or otherwise. They get training in carpentry, tailoring, farming and have classes in English and Mathematics and Religious Instruction. An inmate becomes eligible for release on licence after he has served six months of his term of detention. But in fact many enjoy the structure of classes and want to learn more. So some of the churches provide homes and some money to keep them at school. Is it like that in England?'

'Seth, I don't know.'

'But, Mrs Richter, you have children?'

'Yes, I have a son, Otto.'

'That's fine. I have a friend called Otto.'

'Really! But that's a German name!' Fleur said in surprise.

'Oh yes, very much so. But there are lots of German names in the Gold Coast. When you hear of Wilhelm, Otto or Karl, then you know they are Presbyterians.'

'Really, I am a Presbyterian too,' Fleur remarked.

'I'm a Wesleyan, a Methodist, like most Fante people. The Presbyterian missionaries set up schools and hospitals and theological colleges. They were either from Scotland or from the Basel Mission, or sometimes the Bremen Mission. We often call our children after the white people we meet. We also have many Gold Coast families, with European surnames like Bannerman, Vander-Puye, Casley-Hayford, and Blankson. You will meet such names soon. But it would be wrong to think we accept everything from the colonial powers.'

'What do you mean by that?'

'Two years ago, there was a cocoa hold up when the farmers refused to sell their cocoa at a low price to the colonial traders. They asked their local chiefs to take the matter up. So two more Africans were appointed to the civil service. But that does not mean we are ready to take over our country. We want to be treated fairly, that's all.'

The lorry was by now approaching Obutu. 'We will be in Accra in three-quarters of an hour. Let's stop here to buy some oranges. They will slice the top off and you squeeze them to drink the juice. Let's have some.'

As they proceeded along the last stretch of road to Accra, Fleur asked Seth to give her some Akan Twi sentences to remember and so by the time they reached Accra, Fleur could introduce herself. '*Yefre me Fleur. Me firi Scotland.*'

'You must remember that and greet your house boy with those words.'

'Do you know him?'

'His name is Luke. Luke Ahiabu. He is an Ewe from the Volta region, but he speaks Akan Twi too. You will like him. He will cook for you and keep your quarters clean.'

The lorry entered the outskirts of Accra at 5.15pm. It was a little cooler at this time in the afternoon, but Fleur felt the red laterite roads must have deposited a film of dust on her complexion. She was not feeling her best and certainly not suitable to be presented to the Governor.

The lorry swung into the Cantonments driveway and proceeded between two empress palms, giving way to a border of deep flouring bougainvillaea, frangipani bushes and coloured zinnia beds. The lorry rounded the Governor's residence and entered a narrow driveway leading to a white bungalow.

'Mrs Richter, this is your home.'

'It's beautiful Seth, really beautiful. I know I will be very happy here.'

Fleur met Sir Ronald Murray briefly on the evening of her arrival and they conversed in a polite manner, exploring their experiences and backgrounds without intruding too much into each other's lives. Sir Ronald made no effort to indicate what Fleur's day to day activities might be. Rather he wished her to settle in, and get the feel of the Colony, have a period of local orientation and pursue her interest in the local language. He had been impressed when she introduced herself that night. '*Ye fre me Awuraa Fleur Richter. Me firi Forres!'*

'You have a flair for languages. Perhaps Seth can take you around town and keep up the language instruction. Let me make an appointment for you in two weeks time. You'll soon get to know the staff around the compound and the wives of my staff. Now off you go and enjoy yourself.' Fleur departed with a strange feeling of both excitement and disappointment. Glad to have an opportunity to mix freely in Accra, but after the voyage she had been eager to start work in her new post and she was still unsure what that work would involve.

The next two weeks passed with social, cultural and culinary delights occurring daily. She met the Governor's staff wives and played tennis with Sarah, Caroline and Ruth. She attended a durbar at the village of Kotobabi with Seth at which colourful attire preceded drums and dancing. Fleur's eyes were transfixed as a man in a white cloth opened a bottle of schnapps and poured its contents to the ground. She learned that he was a fetish priest pouring a libation for the spirits. She toured the market and saw such a variety of fruit and vegetables. Yam, cassava, maize, bananas, rice, peppers, garden eggs, onions, tomatoes, avocado pears, oranges and pineapples were in good supply. So were pulses, okra, beans and groundnuts. The rearing of livestock was prevalent too. Live chicken, goats, ducks and snails abounded. Being so near the seas, there were fresh red snapper, barracuda and lobster as well as dried fish, which was heading for the inland towns north of the coast. Luke, her cook-steward, purchased a variety of produce each day and prepared traditional African meals for Fleur. Sarah was a little surprised that Fleur was throwing herself into the culture so much. One evening she called to visit Fleur.

'How are you settling in, Fleur?'

'I am thoroughly enjoying being here, Sarah. Although I wish I had a clearer understanding of my role.'

'We understand you are to be Sir Ronald's Hostess. Is that not so?'

'Yes, but the Foreign and Colonial Office prepared me to have a much wider role and, anyway, if Sir Ronald merely needed formal social company, surely you or Ruth or someone would have obliged happily?'

'We have in the past, Fleur. That is why we are not really sure why Sir Ronald asked for you.....I mean without any disrespect. ....I hear you speak German well?'

Fleur realised she was being interrogated. Honesty being the best recourse for her, she explained her past. Then she asked what Sarah's husband did?' 'He is the Military Attaché to the Governor. He is a Colonel.'

'Would I be right to think that he was not sure why a German speaker, with a German surname has been appointed to Accra? Would it not be too impolite for me to suggest that you were sent to clear this up?' Fleur smiled as she placed Sarah on the spot.

'If it makes it any easier for you, then please remember I am British, I hate Nazism and I too am not yet sure what my role is. When I meet with Sir Ronald, I will ask that he considers how I am seen. I need not mention our discussion. I understand why you feel uneasy. I agree, it does seem a strange posting.'

Fleur's meeting with Sir Ronald was much more formal. It was held in his spacious office beneath a purring electric ceiling fan.

'I hear you have been enjoying the sights and sounds of Accra. You have been sampling the local cuisine and engaging in durbars and funerals. Great stuff. The Africans admire your involvement and respect for their culture. You know we are simply the latest colonial power in this country. Portuguese, Danish, Dutch and in the past German powers, have laid a veneer on the Gold Coast character. The Ashantis have a soft spot for the Dutch, the Fantis for the English and the Akwapim area for the Scots. Some Africans have even taken the names of whites. Some out of respect, others out of fatherhood.' He rose from his seat in the oval room, lit his pipe and gazed down the steps to the lawn and garden before him.

'Fleur. These are troubled times. Hitler's troops entered Prague in March. They forced the Czech government to agree to the imposition of a German Protectorate over the country. I am hearing of preparations for a German – Russian, non-aggression pact and the stage is too familiar. A Second World War is looming. Do you agree?'

'I have held that view for more than four years. Governor, I need not remind you, that I have lived in Hitler's Germany. I have made a personal sacrifice as you are aware, but I am both surprised and delighted that this has led me to the Gold Coast.'

'Let me explain. But first, I must take you back in time. I hope you don't mind a history lesson. I assure you, it is pertinent to your post.'

Sir Ronald went to the mantelpiece and lifted his pipe. He looked into its dark bowl and seemed to frown. He tapped the stale tobacco embers into an ashtray, scrapping it clean with his silver penknife. He took a strip of St. Bruno's Best Flake from his black leather tobacco pouch and rubbed the dark material in the palm of his hand. As he refilled his pipe, relishing the tutor-pupil relationship in which he was about to engage, he began his lecture.

'Let me start as far back as 1727 when the reconstitution of the Moravian Brethren, under the leadership of Graf von Zinzendorf, had made Herrnhut in Saxony a hive of mission activity. This spread within Europe, but also Moravian missionaries were sent to difficult places on earth, not least to the Gold Coast, where they had made two unsuccessful attempts to preach the Gospel earlier. Similarly, the zeal for missions at the Pietistic centre of Halle, had produced no fewer than sixty foreign missionaries in the same period. Many went to Danish territories in India. The Pietism, which characterised the Basel Mission was of the Württemberg variety, a combination of religious emotion and deep thought, of individual conversion and strong Christian fellowship, its life rooted in a profound reverence for the Bible. Within the Lutheran churches of south Germany, Pietism had shifted the emphasis, from concern with the arid dogma and from a rationalistic, deistic outlook, to the personal relationship of the saved sinner to his Lord, to the responsibility for saving souls and for spreading the Kingdom of God on earth.'

Sir Ronald considered his introduction and how to develop its theme by lighting his pipe, drawing heavily to ignite the initial fire. Fleur knew not to disturb his thought process during this ritual. Taking the pipe from his mouth he continued his lecture.

'The Basel Mission had retained these early characteristics. For example, the Director of the Mission was always an ordained Württemberg Pietist from Germany. At any one time, approximately half of its missionaries were from Württemberg. The remainder was Basel missionaries from Switzerland, of whom eighty percent had been trained in Württemberg in Germany. From the outset, the Basel Mission showed a biblical, evangelical, ecumenical and international character that it has not lost to this date.'

'You know a lot about the Church missionaries of the Gold Coast.'

Fleur required a brief break in this history lesson. Her mind wandered to the Royal Palm, where Madge had told her how much Sir Ronald enjoyed his history. She had been right in her assessment. Sir Ronald detected her momentary lapse in concentration and the need to make his history lesson relevant.

'It is my work to understand the workings in this colony, influence them when I can and be wary if they conflict with the aims of Britain. At times like now, it is important to ensure the Africans stay loyal to us. We may need to rely on them if a conflict becomes world wide. Let me bring the history more up to date.'

Sir Ronald told of how Basel missionaries had established a foothold on the nearby Akwapim ridge. In 1851 Simon Suss soon mastered the Twi language and adopted a popular independent approach to the African, taking a group of youths wholly into his house, living communally with them, working, teaching and praying with them day by day. His idea was to share his life so completely with them that in all the circumstances of daily life they might come to see that Christianity was not only a faith to be believed, but also a life to be lived and that idleness and Christianity were incompatible. He worked out a rational system of farming, clearing an area of forest, digging, manuring and planting. He reared goats for milk. From sunrise to sunset he worked on the farm. Then his young men went to school till 8pm after which there was Twi conversation, discussion and prayers. Suss was convinced that the evangelical task and the raising of material standards of life belonged together. His colleagues thought him restless and feared for his health, but Suss felt the time was ripe for advance and for new methods.

'You see many Africans have much reason to thank the

German missionaries.'

'But the Swiss Basel missionaries, would surely stress their independence, not so?' Fleur enquired.

'Indeed they would. But they spoke German, thought as Germans and, to the Africans, were no different. Forgive me, if you think I am being hard on them. They did a lot of fine work. Their work in agriculture, schools and medical fields have stood the test of time and of course many suffered too.

At Anum, a town on the foothills on the east bank of the Volta river, there was tribal quarrelling ongoing. The Ashantis burned the mission house to the ground in 1869 and Reverend and Mrs Ramseyer and Reverend Kuhne were taken prisoners at Kumasi.

Meanwhile, Christaller devoted himself to the Twi language and in 1859 published the four gospels and the Acts. This was pioneering work of the highest calibre. How do I know this?

R.S. Rattray, the greatest anthropologist to study the Ashanti people, refers continuously to Christaller in his volumes, and J.B. Danquah notes "....but for Christaller's foresight, in recording in permanent form, the scattered elements of the beliefs, hopes and fears of the Akan people at this particular juncture... the Akan people of the Gold Coast in West Africa, would have failed to bring their indigenous contribution to the spiritual achievements of mankind."

Fleur's religion was simple but she recognised the numerous biblical quotations in conversation with many Africans she had met.

'In summary, the Africans saw Christaller's work achieve three things. It raised the Twi language to a literary level and provided the basis of all later work in the language, it gave the first real insight into Akan religious, social and moral ideas and it welded the expression of Akan Christian worship to the native tongue.

There was some initial suspicion against the white man's schooling, which came with his religion, usually out of ignorance, but as the value of literacy came to be realised, there was generally no shortage of children in the Basel Mission schools. Children attended either the German named Erziehungsanstalten boarding school or the Gemeindeschulen day school. Furthermore, since 1856, the education of girls was a marked feature of the Basel Mission. Wilhelmina Maurer, Katerina Rudi and Anna Furrer were the first female boarding school teachers appointed.'

A knock on the door stopped Sir Ronald's flow. A house girl entered and enquired when Sir Ronald would be taking lunch.

'Lunch for two at 1pm. If it is manageable, let's eat on the veranda. Thank you.'

Fleur wondered if this would become a regular duty. Surely taking meals with the Governor was not what the Foreign Office had intended. Sir Ronald continued his history of political mission developments.

'Meanwhile, the British government ensured the Moslem faith was recognised and protected which led to Moslem proselytising, particularly in the southern Fanti country.' Fleur recalled many night watchmen were Moslems in Accra. But it was the Basel Mission that interested Sir Ronald.

'When Huppenbauer and Buck visited Kumasi in 1881, to seek permission of the Asantehene king to begin mission work, it was clear that the Ashanti were still in a very troubled state. There were party struggles for power, defections of confederacy tribes and consequent outbreaks of fighting and stool disputes. Major General Sir Garnet Wolsey became increasingly exasperated by the Ashanti forces. In September news reached Switzerland of the detention of Basel missionaries in Kumasi by the Ashantis and representation was made to the British Foreign Office, through the Swiss Consul in London, concerning these captives. This elicited the reply that, as the missionaries had been taken in territory outside British protection, the British government could not assume any responsibility in the matter. On all the mission stations, preparations were made for a hurried flight to the coast. As the British government took so long to reach a decision on the Ashanti question, it seemed to the church committee in Basel, that the entire thirty years' work of the Mission was at stake, not to speak of the lives of fifty-one missionaries then in the field. Relations between the Basel Mission and the British government were very poor at that time.

I trust I am not being too pedantic. You see relations between the British and the Swiss have not always gone smoothly in Africa. I feel we need to understand history to understand why people have formed their allegiances.'

'I quite agree. I hope you do not mind me taking notes of this conversation.'

'Not at all, it is quite a history lesson I am giving you, but one which will come alive for you in due course.' Sir Ronald emptied the contents of his pipe into a large conical shell and began to clean it.

'During 1871 and 1872 efforts to procure their release from prison in Kumasi failed. The King proposed to free the captives, against a ransom payment of 1,800 ounces of gold (about £6,500). Ramseyer and Kuhne counselled against accepting this proposal, lest it should arouse a desire among the Ashantis, to capture further Europeans. I can not stress how fine a man Ramseyer was.'

Lunch was served on the veranda. Portions of boiled yam, ripe plantain and a fish stew, set on leafy kontomere, the leaves of the cocoyam, were enjoyed.

'Do you often eat African meals, Sir Ronald?'

'Almost every time. It's the official functions and the invitations I attend that serve me European food but the native food is very wholesome. To be honest, I prefer it, though I take African meals less hot, than the Africans.'

'I could not agree more. It's a very healthy diet. But let's not let this break detract from the history I am enjoying.'

'I'll continue then.' Sir Ronald took a moment to chew his yam while gathering his thoughts.

'It seemed that the British would never take action against the ever-threatening Ashantis. During the dry season of 1872-3, the Ashantis mounted another attack against the coastal tribes. The Fanti army was defeated at Junkwa and thousands of refugees thronged the streets of Cape Coast. British Marines held Elmina and Cape Coast, resulting in the Ashanti retreating to the river Pra. At this point, the British government realised, only an invasion of the Ashanti territory itself, could put a stop to these repeated attacks upon the tribes of the Protectorate. So in 1873, Major-General Sir Garnet Wolseley was given full authority to deal with the situation. He had 2,500 British troops at his disposal. Few African soldiers backed them, as their chiefs were reluctant to take up arms against such a redoubtable foe as the Ashanti. The main attack was led by Sir Garnet. He followed the main Cape Coast – Kumasi route through Prasu. After a relatively short campaign the Ashanti army was driven back and on 4th February 1874, the British forces entered Kumasi and released the prisoners. The town was then shamefully burned to the ground.

The ensuing treaty of Fomena, by which the Asantehene had to pay a large indemnity in gold, give up his claim to Elmina, Assin, Akim, Adansi and Denkyera, keep the trade routes open and to stop human sacrifice, brought the so-called Sagrenti War to an end.'

'Why the Sagrenti War?' asked Fleur who had not recalled mention of this town. Sir Ronald laughed. 'Ah, a good question. It was difficult for the Twi speakers to pronounce Sir Garnet. So they called him Sa-grenti!'

Sir Ronald lay down his pipe in the ashtray on the mantelpiece and looked straight into Fleur's eyes. 'I need not remind you how Germany felt after the Treaty of Versailles. They had to pay for their defeat, give up their claims to significant parts of Africa and disarm. Likewise, the Ashanti felt a grievance. They would bide their time. Yet to the British, this was a period of calm and prosperity. Ashanti was quiet and during the ensuing twenty years, there was a new feeling of liberation and security everywhere. In September 1874, the Gold Coast was raised to the status of a colony; two months later, laws were passed forbidding slave trading, freeing all domestic slaves and establishing the nucleus of a police force and a proper civil service administration. Ashanti, however, still remained independent.

From the Ashanti perspective, the British government had left their people alone and refused to become involved in their internal affairs and progress.

Between 1875 and 1896 was therefore an era during which the Ashantis tried to reassert their dominion over those tribes which desired to break away from the Confederacy. Agyeman Prempeh (Kwaku Dua III) was elected Asantehene (King of the Ashantis) in 1888, in a time of great strain. After years of war and fighting, the Ashanti were weary. The sub chiefs only continued their loyalty to Kumasi, fearing the British government might attack the Ashanti. The Asantehene did not trust the British government, which officially professed a policy of non-interference in Ashanti affairs, but in reality had received Kwahu into the colony and at different times protected Adansi, Kokofu and Juaben refugees from the Asantehene. At length, in 1894, the Asantehene by now fully convinced that the Accra government was not treating him fairly, decided to send a deputation directly to Queen Victoria.'

'Queen Victoria! That was quite inspirational,' exclaimed

Fleur.

'Well, yes and no. After all, the King of the Ashanti would have a right to bypass the colonial power and go straight to the Queen of England. That's proper protocol,' Sir Ronald asserted.

'However in September that year, events moved to a climax. The Governor sent a letter to the Asantehene, in which he accused him of breaching the Treaty of Formena. He declared that henceforth, a British officer would live in Kumasi as adviser to the Asantehene, that any Ashanti tribe wishing to come under British rule, could do so and that the indemnity of 50,000 ounces of gold still owing for the war, must be paid. The letter complained that the road from Kumasi to the river Pra had not been kept open, that human sacrifices had not stopped and that the Asantehene had done nothing to foster proper trade

The government asked for a reply by 31st October. The Asantehene replied that he must wait until his envoys returned from England in December. Then he decided however to accede to the Governor's demands, but it was then too late as the British had already resolved to send an army into Ashanti. On hearing this news, the Asantehene dispatched three messengers to Reverend Ramseyer in Abetifi, asking him to use his good offices with the Governor, as he was ready to accept the conditions. He would agree to come under the white man's rule.

Meanwhile, on 17th January 1896, the vanguard of the British troops reached Kumasi.'

'I know,' said Fleur. 'Sir Ronald, this may come as a surprise to you, but my father was part of that vanguard. He was a captain at the time, seconded from the Scots Guards. He was there at Kumasi.'

CHAPTER TEN

On 1st January 1896 the troop ship SS Glencoe docked at Takoradi and volunteer, Captain James Bruce set foot on Gold Coast soil. His detachment made their way to the Castle at Cape Coast where they acclimatised, prepared provisions and studied the terrain ahead, in anticipation of the instructions of the Governor. They set off on 10th January, proceeding north on the Cape Coast – Kumasi road.

Their first night took them as far as Fanti Nyankumasi where the Africans gave them fresh water and fruit. The Pipe Major played the pipes for their interest, fear and amusement. The pipes could be heard for miles. This was to the detachment's considerable advantage. No other instrument could muster up such resolve and enhance the likelihood of victory. Word would soon be reaching Kumasi that a great force was on its way. In the morning, the contingent tightened their puttees round their legs and ankles to prevent water borne bugs and mosquitoes attacking. At night they slept under mosquito nets. A campfire burned all night with damp leaves constantly dousing the flames, creating smoke to minimise mosquito activity.

It was a hard march through rich vegetation. But it was a well-trodden trading route and they made steady progress. They marched at 5.30am as first light appeared. They stopped to eat at 12 noon and rested in the shade for two hours before marching again until 6pm when dusk fell. Wax candles and paraffin lamps lit the villages and they were treated with respect and curiosity. Edubiasi was their third stop. In this village they heard the singing of hymns for the first time and the soldiers joined in. The natives sang in Fante. The tunes were familiar and the Scots sang in English but the words and music scanned and they always finished on the same note. A soldier's mouth organ joined in the music, swelling their voices to its plaintive and often fulsome chords. A fraternal bond was struck in these circumstances and they felt very much at ease with the villagers.

Next day when they crossed the River Pra, they were no longer in the Fanti lands but in the outlying Ashanti territory. This was not instantly noticeable. The Africans still came out at the call of the pipes and were keen to bring fresh water and foodstuffs for the troops.

Smiling black faces speaking excellent English and singing familiar hymn tunes, hardly seemed willing to oppose this military expedition. At nights there was increasing fraternisation. Captain Bruce reprimanded some of his soldiers for going off into the dark with young native women. The likelihood of them meeting their deaths was remote but they could be lured into sexual activity making them unfit for service, or worse still, creating unwanted fatherless children of mixed race.

The troop proceeded through the hills around Brofoyedru and Fomena, then on to Bekwai. They made good progress. Then two soldiers fell ill and it was decided that they should not proceed beyond Bekwai. Captain Bruce sought the local catechist and gave him some money to care for and treat his Christian brothers. This caused no resentment for the catechist and both soldiers responded to the traditional medical remedies offered. The skins of the pawpaw fruit were placed on their fevered foreheads and they felt the heat diminish from their bodies. A drink made from an areca nut, pounded then mashed into a paste with mango gave them sustenance and in a matter of six days, they successfully joined the rest of the troop, by then stationed in Kumasi. The sight of these two soldiers returning in good health, gave Captain Bruce much encouragement and considerable trust in the Africans he was amidst. Native medicine was reverentially welcomed. Two soldiers had cause to swear by its effectiveness.

It was 17th January 1896 when the vanguard of the British forces reached Kumasi. Then on 20th, the Asantehene knelt before the Governor, without wearing his sandals or his golden circlet and agreed to submit to British demands, promising to pay 680 ounces of gold immediately and the rest in instalments. The Governor refused to accept this offer and took the Asantehene, the Queen Mother and a number of important chiefs in custody, to the coast as security for the payment of the indemnity. The Ashantis were utterly taken aback by this unexpected turn of events but they could do nothing except protest vigorously. Their protests were not heeded.

The British built a fort in Kumasi on the raised ground at a junction, then named as Stewart Avenue and Harper Road in memory of the two ill soldiers, brought back to full health in the Odum district. Captain Bruce was promoted to Major and became the officer in command at the fort. A council of chiefs was appointed, headed by Major James Bruce. He had the fetish groves destroyed by fire and the chief's burial ground at Bantama, the scene of so many human sacrifices, destroyed.

James wrote to the Ramseyers concluding his letter with the words: 'Kumasi will henceforth be open to missionaries and should you yourselves arrive in Kumasi before I leave, it would give me pleasure to meet you.'

Twenty-nine days later, twenty-two years exactly, after the day of his release from imprisonment, Ramseyer re-entered Kumasi. He wrote on his arrival:

It is no longer a dream; I am again in Kumasi and can now say Kumasi is a Basel Mission Station. Here I stand as a free missionary and the entire country is open to me. This is not simply a hopeful expression; no, in fact all the towns are open to our approach, as far as Nkoranza. In Ashanti a real change has taken place such as I never would have imagined.

Bruce contemplated how satisfactory his efforts had been. He now enjoyed the early morning pipes played rousingly at the coolest part of the day. He followed the Africans in having a quiet time between noon and three in the afternoon. About 6.15pm as the sun went down, he prepared to eat groundnut soup, with chicken or snails. Tasty bean stew with yam or rice was another favourite meal and fresh fruit was always readily available. Pawpaw, pineapples, oranges, limes but never apples. They would not grow in this hot climate. At night the pipes called for lights out. The community slept soundly.

The mission was allocated a piece of land between Kumasi and Bantaman. A catechist started to build a temporary house. In June that year, Major Bruce arrived at the mission with a number of slave women and children from the interior of whom nineteen died of their previous privations, but the rest prospered in the care of the mission. Major Bruce chose to stay on in Kumasi, extending the fort and ensuring hostilities were minimised. An open day at the fort was held to encourage families both young and old and to see how the white soldiers lived. The pipers played marches and airs, the drummers gave rattling solos that attracted considerable interest and once more the harmonica played spontaneously. An impromptu choir sang in harmony, when it recognised the tunes. Soon the fort doors were left open during the day as a sign of peace and traders freely entered. This was a period of mutual trust that Bruce had nurtured with pride. Little could he have anticipated what the Governor had in mind.

In December 1899 Major Bruce informed the Governor, Sir Frederick Hodgeson, of the alleged whereabouts of the legendary Golden Stool of the Ashanti Kingdom. The Governor decided it would be a good strategy to obtain it. The British authorities had no idea of the sacred and social function of the Stool that embodied, in a sense, the 'soul' of the Ashanti nation. They thought it would be simply a sign of power that it would be good to possess, to show that the British were now masters. At a durbar in Kumasi the following March, the assembled Ashanti chiefs were told by the Governor never to expect the return of exiled Asanthene Prempeh and an annual tribute of around £64,000 (the interest on the indemnity imposed at Formena) was demanded from them.

Finally, Sir Frederick foolishly demanded the surrender of the Golden Stool on the grounds that this emblem of power now belonged to the Queen of England. There was great indignation among the Kumasi chiefs. They met immediately after the meeting and began to make instantaneous preparations for war. The Queen Mother of Ejisu was chosen as their head and the ensuing fighting became known by her name, the Yaa Asantewa War. Bruce's hard work at reassuring the Africans of his good intentions was now being undermined.

On 31st March, Major Bruce led a party of soldiers to try to find the Golden Stool and they had to fight their way back into Kumasi. The Governor and Lady Hodgson, the mission personnel and other Europeans took refuge in the fort as the hostilities grew. Meantime, the Ashantis blocked every road leading out of Kumasi to Accra, to Cape Coast and to the north. The fort was besieged from 15th May to 15th July. On 23rd June, all the European civilians in the fort, in the company of two soldiers, left the garrison making a successful breakout at four in the morning and set out along the path to Manso Nkwanta. Although they were attacked three times during the day, they finally reached the village of Trebuom, where the famished and exhausted party rested under improvised shelters against heavy seasonal rain. The chief of Manso Nkwanta led them the next day to comparative safety but the survivors still had a journey full of hardships before them until they reached Cape Coast. Near Fosu, a black cobra was disturbed on the march south and a soldier was bitten on his leg. The snake's jaws clung on to his leg, while a rifle butt was showered down on its head. The man's screams could be heard for miles around. The snake released the soldier and with remarkable speed and stealth slipped into the grassy embankment and was gone to recover from its wounds. A tourniquet was administered tightly round the soldier's thigh. His rising temperature was first assuaged by a cloth dipped in the nearby stream and then by stripping him and waving palm leaves over his sweating body. Within an hour he had lost consciousness and moments later the life of Corporal Kenneth McKay, came to its premature and unforeseen end. He was buried in a marked grave by the roadside opposite a crop of cassava, three miles south of Asin Bereku with full military honours and a fitting service conducted by the remaining soldier, Corporal William Duff.

Duff then saw Karl Weller die on this journey. His body was wrapped in banana leaves and bound by strips of palms and taken to the mission at Christiansborg in Accra. Thus the end of a valuable mission life was recorded for posterity.

Heading the other way, British troops led by Colonel Willcocks, with several Twi speaking Basel Mission volunteers from Akim, reached Fomena on 20th May. They were on their way to relieve the garrison. They feigned an attack on Kokofu and when the section of the Ashanti forces was withdrawn from Kumasi, to defend Kokofu, they moved swiftly through Pekyi to Kumasi. After a short fight, those still besieged in the fort were relieved but this was not until 15th July and a number had meanwhile died of hunger.

Major Bruce lost eighteen pounds in weight but survived, was mentally alert and was promoted to full colonel. He kept the spirits of the troops up and had negotiated the supply of fresh water from the Moslems, who took shelter against the fort's walls. With the end of the siege, the Moslems began to provide a multitude of complementary services including leatherwork, pottery requirements and supplies of various market stall items at African prices.

Until the end of the year there were still isolated campaigns in various parts of Ashanti. Some of the captured chiefs were sent to the Seychelle Islands and others were imprisoned for shorter terms in Elmina Castle. The indemnity sum however, was never paid.

On 13th December 1901 Ramseyer stood in front of the ruined mission station in Kumasi with a heavy heart but still hopeful for the future. Some Christians came back and on Christmas Day there were five baptisms. Slowly the Basel Mission revived in Kumasi. By 1914, there were twenty-one Basel Mission congregations in Kumasi, eight hundred converts and seventeen schools. Many other government schools were being opened in the colony at this time and at the opening of the Sunyani Government School, the traditional beliefs and customs were enhanced when the Headmaster declared: 'The instruction given by the Government does not necessitate any religious change as is the case in Mission Schools; boys and girls can attend school....and still remain loyal to the beliefs, customs and traditions of their ancestors.' The Church and State reserved their educational and cultural rights amicably.

In 1902, Colonel James Bruce's tour of duty came to an end. He returned to barracks at Inverness and engaged in peaceful duties until he retired from the Army in 1908. From that date, he and his wife had run the Forres Central Commercial Hotel.

Reverend Edmund Perregaux relieved Reverend Ramseyer in 1904. Ramseyer died the following year. Andreas Baur literally wore himself out in three years of evangelical work in Ashanti. In that time, he visited over eight hundred towns and villages preaching the Gospel. He died in 1909 at Nsuta, of black-water fever. There was no shortage of Basel missionaries to the Gold Coast. The pioneering work had to be consolidated. Missionaries from Switzerland and southern Germany were constantly in demand and in supply.

CHAPTER ELEVEN

'These were hard times, Fleur. But of course there was still one further crisis looming a few years later. I am sure you can see where it came from.'

'I presume you are referring to the German influence and presence during the First World War in the colony?' Fleur ventured.

'Exactly. Indeed it was not an easy time. There are points to learn from this as we are fast approaching a Second World War with Germany.'

Fleur wondered how her German background might be useful in the coming months. She was wondering how to question the Governor about this when he stood up.

Sir Ronald invited Fleur down the steps into the garden. Amadou, the night watchman and gardener, was watering the flowerbeds and lawn. Sir Ronald greeted him and complimented him on his hard work. The garden was looking well. Amadou smiled, revealing the most beautiful smile enhanced by two rows of strong white teeth.

'He looks after his teeth very well,' Fleur commented.

'It's these chewing sticks they gnaw on all day and perhaps the cola nut too. It's clearly very effective.'

Amadou turned off the hose and swept his prayer mat clean. They reached the end of the lawn and sat on wicker cane garden chairs under a bower of bougainvillaea and Indian lilac.

'1914 was an eventful year for me,' Fleur ventured. 'I was by then married to Dr Willy Richter, a wonderful, cultured man. We had invited my niece Vera to Germany, for a holiday, but the war began and we had to somehow get her home.'

'Did you succeed?'

'Oh yes, thank goodness we did. But it was not easy.'

Fleur gave a full account of how Vera had escaped and how she had practically been under house arrest during the whole of the First World War, in Hamburg. Sir Ronald was intrigued by the detail and Fleur answered his every inquisitive question.

'But what happened here, to the Basel Mission and the German missionaries during the First World War?' she enquired.

Sir Ronald informed Fleur that Government records were kept at his office and he had read them thoroughly. He explained that at the outbreak of war in 1914, French and British troops advanced across neighbouring German Togoland and, after a short campaign, took over the administration of that territory. The German missionaries at Yendi were restricted to their work in the immediate area of their station. They continued under increasing difficulties. There was considerable anti-German feeling. The small mission school was closed. Only the medical and language work was allowed to continue. In March 1916, at the height of the dry season, a fire destroyed more than half the station, resulting in the loss of valuable documents, books and personal effects. It was never established how the fire began but foul play was suspected. Then quite unexpectedly in August 1916, the missionaries were informed by British Authorities that they should leave Yendi and settle near the coast.

On 22nd June 1916 the British Ambassador in Berne informed the Inspector of African Missions in Basel, that the British government desired in future that all missionaries sent to the Gold Coast should be native born Swiss citizens. To this, the Mission Board responded that it could not promise adherence to such a request as it would mean a break with its history and a denial of its character as an international Mission Society.

In reaction to this, the British Foreign Office took a firmer line. A note was handed to the Swiss Embassy in London in October 1916. Its tone was austere. His Majesty's government had arrived at the conclusion, that the Basel Mission, as at present constituted, was so German in sympathy, that it could not be allowed to operate any longer in a British dependency. As regards the Basel Mission Trading Society, His Majesty's Government regarded it as ancillary to the mission and could only allow it to continue its operations under purely Swiss control and with purely Swiss representation and personnel.

Although the trading company then took active steps to effect a definite break with the mission and although it had already given an assurance that its German connections had been severed, this did not prevent the eventual liquidation by the British government. At the end of 1916, preparations had been made for the eventual cessation of the entire work of the Basel Mission in the Gold Coast. In December that year the Swiss Superintendent of the Basel Mission in Accra received a letter from Reverend A.W. Wilkie, Secretary of the United Free Church of Scotland Mission

Council in Calabar, Nigeria, intimating that along with his wife, he would land in Accra the following January.

The Home Board had not informed the Secretary of the Basel Mission of this appointment but the visitors were cordially received. Meanwhile rumours had spread that German missionaries had sent messages by torch from the high ridge at Akwapim, some twenty-four miles north-east of Accra, to the Gulf of Guinea where German naval vessels had received their coded messages. Concern was also found in two vernacular history readers. The objection was based on the chapter on the Franco-German War of 1870 that emphasised the German victory. Then the Cape Coast newspaper, the Gold Coast Leader, published an article in May 1917 alleging that the missionaries were seeking to persuade the people of the inevitability of a German victory, a quite unfounded report that caused much distress in mission circles.

In the second week of December 1917, all German missionaries were brought to Accra and on the 16th they left by ship. The men were bound for an internment camp in the Isle of Man and the women and children for London, from whence, eight weeks later, they were repatriated to Germany.

That left eight, non-German, Basel missionaries. It initially seemed they would be left to carry on their work but an Order of Council of 12th January 1918 forbade any European alien to remain on the Akwapim ridge. Two Swiss missionaries applied to be transferred up country but this request was resolved by force majeure when on 2nd February all the remaining missionaries were ordered home by the next steamer, in consequence of instructions from the Secretary of State in London, to the Governor:

I consider that in view of the German sympathies....all the Europeans must be regarded as suspects. Your Government can not afford to take risks and the public safety must be the first consideration. You should therefore deport the remaining members of the Mission and Trading Society as soon as possible.

Sir Ronald brought the bound record to the table for Fleur to see for herself. 'See, Fleur, here it is,' *...Legislative Council Debate 4th February 1918,...while introducing the Bill, the Colonial Secretary A.R..Slater, remarked: 'I have no startling disclosures to make of any overt acts of enmity, hostility or disloyalty. The members of the Basel Mission have, outwardly,* *observed the neutrality they were required to observe. But although there has been an absence of openly expressed enmity, there has been a notorious persistent covert unfriendliness...'*

Fleur had one thought floating in her mind. She put it to Sir Ronald. 'What led the British authorities to take action against the Germans at such a late stage in the war?'

'Remember Fleur that the closing months of 1917 were a very dark period in the war for Britain. We had just experienced the third Battle of Ypres, the failure of the Nivelle offensive, the French mutinies and, of course, the life claiming mud at Passchendaele. Yes, a most sombre year. There was a natural tendency to feel suspicious of all Germans. While the Basel Mission was officially a neutral international missionary society, at least two thirds of its personnel in the Gold Coast at any time had been German nationals who were naturally, if not openly, in sympathy with the German cause. Many Swiss missionaries had been trained in Germany. The refusal of the Basel Mission in 1916 to send only native-born Swiss citizens to the Gold Coast confirmed the Government's view that it was in sympathy with Germany. At the same time there was no evidence on the part of the Basel Mission, of any open act of hostility or their failure to strictly observe their neutrality. The Governor's attitude was clear when he said, *"Since 1915, I have personally held that the interests of this Colony were not well served by having in our midst, persons of enemy association whose influence cannot but be harmful to loyal British subjects."* Had Sir George Gugguisberg, with his keen appreciation and fuller understanding of the work of the Basel Mission and the Scots Mission been in his shoes at that moment of history, a less dramatic course of action might have been taken.'

'Do you really think so?'

Sir Ronald opened a glass window of his bookcase. He selected a second large leather-bound book from the shelf. He carefully opened it. 'Come, Fleur read what Sir Gugguisberg had to say':

First and foremost among the Missions, as regards quality of education and character training, was the Basel Mission; and their removal from this country during the war of 1914 – 1919 was the greatest blow which education in this country has ever received. The removal of some staff was necessary, for no country that is fighting for its existence can afford to retain in it enemy subjects. Nevertheless the blow was a great one. However there were recompenses, for it resulted in the arrival in this country of that devoted and efficient band of missionaries – the Scottish Mission. It is no exaggeration to say that the Reverend A.W. Wilkie and his people saved the situation.

'Fleur, now that you are aware of the political background in which we find ourselves today, I wish to ask you to undertake a special mission for me. Not just for me, of course. Are you ready to undertake work on behalf of His Majesty King George VI and the Foreign Office?'

Fleur felt the solemnity of the moment but had no idea what she was about to be asked or whether in her fiftieth year she would be fit enough to endure the challenge. She found herself nodding agreement and with a suddenly dry voice she uttered, 'Yes, I am.'

'I wish you to live at the Ramseyer Centre at Abetifi on the Basel Mission station, on the Kwahu ridge. There you will stay and mix freely with the Basel missionaries, while during the day you will travel to the neighbouring village called Nkwatia. You will learn the Twi language from a teacher called Kofi Frempong. Your cover is that you are an anthropologist, who has just arrived in the Gold Coast and you wish to study the Twi language before you set about your anthropological study of Obuasi in the Adansi area. You have no connection with the Foreign Office or myself. You must state, if asked, that you have never been to this residence. What you will do, is get to know the missionaries and find out about their allegiances to Germany. Find out what messages may be coming from Germany, through their letters and conversation or any other avenues of communication. Find out how strong their support of the Axis powers are and what influence they have on the local people. You will be given a Post Box at Nkwatia where we can write to you and send you money. You must destroy your letters from us. Make sure nobody is aware that you are working for the British government. Do you understand what I am asking of you?'

'Yes, I do. I understand. Am I free to talk about my life in Germany, my son Otto and my knowledge of Germany?'

'Yes, by all means and retain your Richter surname. Let them feel you have sympathies for Germany. That way, they may open up to you. But do not rush. It takes time to be accepted and trusted in the present circumstances. I will call this work on which you are now engaged, Operation Oboe.'

'Operation Oboe! Well, how perceptive! I will not forget that!'

'You need not refer to it. It is our way of identifying your activities to my superiors. I think it sounds like the right note for you. My staff will see to your arrangements. If it suits you, I hope you can start on Monday. Your Twi classes are to begin next Wednesday, at St Peter's School in Nkwatia. These have been arranged already.'

Suddenly, Fleur felt the jigsaw was complete. This must have been in Sir Anthony Pitt-Stevenson's mind all along. That day at the Foreign and Commonwealth Office seemed a long time ago. To confirm her thoughts, she asked Sir Ronald, 'Do you know Sir Anthony Pitt-Stevenson?'

'I know him well. I went to see him in January this year, when I was in London.' He paused a moment then looked Fleur straight in the eye. 'Fleur, he made the right decision!'

She smiled. Hostess indeed, she mused!

Sir Ronald looked at his watch. 'The sun's beneath the main sail, Fleur. Please join me for a drink, to wish you well in your appointment. A port perhaps?' Fleur recalled the captain of the Royal Palm use the same nautical expression.

'That would be delightful and most appropriate in the circumstances. Thank you.'

Sir Ronald poured two glasses of port. The glasses clinked. 'To success in your mission, Operation Oboe.'

Raising her glass she replied, 'Operation Oboe and success in the war.'

CHAPTER TWELVE

Fleur had enjoyed staying in the Governor's compound at Cantonments but fortunately had not established herself there. Her departure from her houseboy Luke, would have deserved more warmth but for the clandestine task she was about to undertake. She did not wish to keep in correspondence with either Luke or Amadou. Her anonymity was paramount in her mind. The sooner she cut off links in Accra, the better.

At 10.20am on Monday morning, a car arrived to take her as far as Nkawkaw. Seth was the driver once more. 'Good morning Mrs Richter. How are you?'

'Very well, Seth. And you?'

'I am fine but my wife is not well so I am late because I had to get some medicine for her.'

'I'm sorry to hear that. Can you get someone else to drive then?'

'No, but it will be all right. I know it will. Anyway, I'll be back in five hours.'

As they left the Governor's compound, heading north on the Kumasi road, Fleur enquired further about Seth's wife. 'There is a story Mrs Richter. It's about a sick wife. Can I tell you it?'

'Please do, I'm interested.'

'One day in the village of Afransi long ago, a young wife called Amma went off one day to visit a friend in the next village. When she returned home that evening, she felt very ill. Could it be that her circulation had stopped she wondered. Her husband, of only one year, was alarmed. Her clothes were loosened. Her face was bathed in cold water. Her husband, Yaw, dissolved into tears. Then he decided to send immediately for a physician. The physician appeared and sat by Amma's bed and assumed an expression as much as to say he had precisely the right remedy.

Yaw asked him what was the matter with his wife. "You ask me what is the matter? There really is no need to tell you that. You know, it's a very good sign when wives fret and complain!" At this news the husband was overjoyed. She was not seriously ill.

The night passed. The patient drank the physician's potion but it had no effect on her. Another physician had to be summonsed. Patience! At last they were about to discover what ailed his wife. The second physician was in no doubt at all. She was coming down with smallpox! At this news Yaw shouted, "Say no more. Prescribe nothing more. For at least one of you physicians is entirely in the wrong. Rather, leave her in the hands of nature and the mercies of her own comfortable bed. No matter how dangerous the disease, it is not half as dangerous as the doctors' cures I am hearing. Perhaps she will recover soon."

Her good husband never left Amma's side. He constantly asked how she was feeling, but her replies got weaker and weaker. It was easy to see by her speech that the pain was increasing. Alas, poor woman! Death seemed at hand. Then someone arrived at the door. "Who's there?" It was the village tailor, bringing a dress. Ha, he comes at a good time, thought Yaw.

"Is it," asks Amma, "my funeral dress? Alas, I will look quite ill in it. It is such a beautiful dress. Had heaven permitted me to live, I would have ordered a dress just like this one, of the same kind of material as the one my friend whom I visited just yesterday. She wore it then. Ah, how short life is."

"Take courage grief stricken husband. You hear that your wife can at last speak with ease? Do not lose hope. The breath has not left her body."

The tailor left the room and the husband went with him. The two spoke secretly together, behind the closed door. The tailor swore mighty oaths and went off to do what he had promised. He returned before evening and went in to see Amma who, still in bed, thanked him heartily for coming. What did the tailor bring with him?

He proceeded at once to unroll something that was wrapped in cloth. What a wonderful sight to behold! The self same cloth, the rich and marvellous dress! But what was it doing there? Surely the young wife could not hope to wear it. "My dearest angel," said Yaw, "I would give everything I possess to see you well again and wearing this dress!"

"Oh, I am so ill," began his wife, "I am not even strong enough to deny you anything. I will get up from this bed, so that you may see this very day how the dress suits me."

The tailor and the husband left the poor woman alone for a few moments. Although she had lain this last week as weak as though she had lain in bed a whole year, she got up. After she was completely dressed out in her finery, her husband and the tailor returned. They gave her cocoa. She sat down and drank. At last, there was no trace of any illness.

A dress was what had ailed her and a dress was the only effective remedy. A tailor had cured what no physicians could so much as diagnose.' Seth turned to Fleur and smiled.

'You see that is why man has to work so hard to keep a wife. I mean think how much the dress cost and which husband can tell when his wife is going to be ill? That is why traditional medicine is as important as the white man's medicine.'

'Seth, that is a lovely story. Perhaps you should bring a dress back from Nkawkaw?'

'What! oh no, my wife is not that ill!' They laughed heartily.

'The story I have just told you, it is a story that once was told by a German missionary. He said it was a fable by the son of a Saxon clergyman, called Christian Gellert. You see what you hear is not always true. Likewise, medicine is not always from a bottle. For us Africans, the word medicine has a lot of meanings. Traditional medicine is used for many purposes. One is to put things right and to counter the forces of mystical evil. So you will meet African friends engaged in the positive use of mystical forces. They help to stabilise society with their knowledge, skills and religious activities like prayers and rituals and sacrifices. They channel good fortune, fertility, peace and welfare. For that reason, they are true friends of society and a public asset.'

'Are there traditional priests in every town?'

'Of course, they will pray for you as a new person in their community and you will see the priests and priestesses perform their ritual dancing. It's part of village life.'

'I am told I have to drop you off at Nkawkaw in the town centre at the lorry park. Do you know where you are going from there?'

'Oh yes, it's all arranged for me.'

Nkawkaw was a busy market town at the foot of the Kwahu ridge, on the Accra-Kumasi road. It was an ideal dropping off point for there had to be no possible connection with her arrival in Abetifi and the Governor's office. From here she would join a local transport lorry and ascend the ridge to the hill top towns and to the Ramseyer Centre at Abetifi. She would have two days to settle before starting her Twi classes at Nkwatia. Seth wished her luck and hoped to see her again soon.

Fleur boarded the back of the lorry on which wooden benches

had been bolted to the floor. Her baggage was unceremoniously thrown on to the soft roof, then tied down with all the other baggage under a tarpaulin that was strapped to the sides by taut ropes. Her remaining metal trunks would be following within a week after the painted address of the Governor General had been removed from each trunk and her new address painted on.

For three miles they travelled along a very flat piece of land noticing the Kwahu ridge in front rise more and more steeply before their eyes. The lorry changed down to second gear as with the first bend, the gradient made its presence felt.

Fleur noticed the gradual drop in temperature keenly in the open backed lorry as it gained height. It felt like an almost European climate. Hanging above the road were the dark broad leaves of so many trees that daylight was obscured from view. The clicking of crickets and the hissing of other insects grew louder as the passengers concentrated on the lorry's lethargic progress. Looking to her left, Fleur was pleased that the lorry was moving slowly. One wrong move and it would tumble over the laterite precipice to the plain below. From the looks on the fellow travellers' faces, this was a journey that was never enjoyed. The constant chatting at the start of the journey had dwindled into the occasional expressions of anguish, as the lorry lurched left before accelerating up a right hand bend. It was a stressful and anxious journey. After fifteen minutes of sheer tension, the lorry found more straight lengths of road and more gentle bends, until it reached a plateau at Mpraeso. 'Not yet, Miss. You stay on the lorry,' instructed the driver.

More people joined at Mpraeso. They clambered aboard, then noticed Fleur. She felt it better to welcome them on board as if they were entering her house. 'Akwabaa' she announced her greeting.

There were great cries of '*Oboruni o te Twi kasa.*' (The white lady speaks Twi!)

'I am coming to Kwahu to learn Twi,' she explained.

'Oh fine, you will do well.'

'Remember, *Kakra. Kakra, akoko benum nsuo.* It is a Twi proverb meaning, little by little, the hen drinks water. Do you understand? You see the hen does not drink like the dog. Instead it takes a very little water at a time and then throws its head back to swallow. Likewise you will learn Twi that way. Each day you will learn a little more.'

Fleur practised the proverb over and over until her captive audience felt she had the right intonation. It had been a good way to get the word around that the middle-aged white lady in their midst had come to learn Twi.

The lorry proceeded along the ridge to the outskirts of Abetifi. Some passengers left at the start of the village, bidding Fleur farewell. Others alighted at the crossroads in the centre of the town. Again the lorry driver asked her to stay on board. As the last passenger Fleur noticed the lorry found it easier to respond to the fractured road surface. Then it turned right at the crossroads and found itself on a particularly rough patch of ground. Great fissures in the road had been created when torrential rains had fallen, washing the red laterite away. It was a slow job to fill in the cracks and a thankless task too. No sooner had the potholes been filled, than the rain returned to wash the earth away. The lorry was driven with great care. Fleur held on to the side tightly as it was rocked by the driver's attempts to find good ground. Then after turning sharply to the right, the Ramseyer Centre came into view.

As the vehicle drove into the compound, Fleur took an instant delight at what she saw. It was a two-storied Swiss building with wooden balconies surrounding its walls on the first floor. The covered rusting aluminium roof sheltered the veranda walkways and the whole structure was set on a solid stone foundation. The wood was nourished by a rich soft dark brown colour. The walls had been freshly painted light cream. At right angles to the main building was an administrative building, smaller, but in the same Swiss style. As the driver unpacked Fleur's possessions, she made her way to the administrative block, where she was greeted by the matron.

'You are welcome, Mrs Richter,' announced Mercy. 'I hope you had a good trip.'

'Thank you. I enjoyed the trip, but my heart was in my mouth when we came up the Kwahu ridge.'

'Ah, it has the same effect on me. But there are not many accidents on that road.'

'I'm glad we did not meet any traffic coming down the road.'

Mercy laughed 'Not possible, Mrs Richter. The road would be too dangerous if it were two-way.'

'But I thought....part of my worry was the fear of meeting

traffic.'

'Oh, no no, there is one way up and another way down! It's an entirely different road down!'

'I wish I had known that before I left Nkawkaw!' They laughed heartily once more.

'Do please call me Fleur, if you prefer.'

'Certainly, Fleur, and call me Mercy then.'

Fleur was taken to her quarters. She was led up the wooden staircase at the side of the main building on to the first floor. From there they walked the length of the building and turned left at its end. In front of them was a building set slightly lower on the ground. It was reached by descending six more steps. It too had its veranda. Mercy produced a key and opened the door. It led into a square room dominated by a large four poster bed. Mosquito netting hung from the posts. Mercy showed Fleur how easy it was to release the net at night and tuck it into the mattress. She showed her how to roll it up in the morning.

'Mosquitoes are more active at dusk, as I am sure you will know. The generator that provides light will shut down at 9pm. At 8.45pm there will be a flicker, to remind you the generator is switched off at 9pm. That gives you enough time to get into bed. But first, we will let you unpack. A meal will be ready for you in about an hour. Please let me know if you need anything else.'

Fleur thanked Mercy. She unpacked her possessions onto the dressing table and placed them in the cupboard. Then she explored the bathroom. It had a pulley system and a bucket with perforations in its base. A line marked the height at which hot water must not be exceeded. A further line indicated the amount of cold water that would be sufficiently comfortable for a warm shower. She felt she would soon master this challenge.

She stood outside on the veranda, closed her eyes, breathed deeply and felt she was in Bavaria on a summer's evening. She turned left around the corner of her room and walked along the short distance to the end of the wooden rail. She turned and looked over the garden before her. There was some movement on the flowering hibiscus. She focussed to see the antics of a hovering olive-bellied sunbird, extracting the pollen from the flower's trumpet. It suspended itself in mid air as it fed. Beyond the flowering hibiscus bush at the corner of the compound, both the yellow-crowned bishop and the sparrow weaver, fought noisily to feed on the insect colony of the flamboyant's sprawling branches. As they fed, Fleur's meal was announced. She was called over to the communal dining room.

She arrived to find a table occupied by six Europeans and four Africans, with an empty set place to which she was invited. After grace was said in Twi by the native pastor at the top of the table, Fleur was made welcomed by one and all. She introduced herself as Frau Richter. Inevitably, this interested the assembled group, who learned that she was a widow and had a son in Germany. Her anthropologist status was not queried. Her Twi language course, which would necessitate her going to the neighbouring village each day, was highly recommended by the table. She felt she had revealed sufficient for the first day, so then made her inquiries of those around her.

Reverend Emmanuel Okine, who had said grace, was the Centre's Bursar. He organsied the pastoral training centre and his wife Comfort assisted his work. Mr Daniel Tetteh was the lay preachers' organiser and catechist. And of course Mercy Appiah, the Matron, who had welcomed Fleur to the Mission Centre, sat at the table too.

Reverend Jurg Fendler and his wife, Martha, were from Liestal, around twenty miles south east of Basel. They had been missionaries with the Basel Mission since 1920. After years in various parts of the southern Gold Coast, they had come to Abetifi for their last few remaining years of service devising contemporary theological courses for aspiring African pastors. Martha prepared all the women's courses.

Reverend Andreas Schmidt was an evangelical pastor who had always longed for a pastoral mission with the farmers and hunters of the area. In a way he was the rural industrial missioner at a time when the urban industrial mission concept was taking hold in mission thinking. Andreas was from Brugg in northern Switzerland. His wife, Gisela, came from a town thirty miles away, called Schopfheim.

Hans Winkler was an agricultural adviser. The Basel Mission had overseen several agricultural developments over many years, and Hans was its latest servant. He came from the shores of Lake Constance, the Bodensee, at Romanshorn. Every day in his home town, he looked out towards Lake Constance and saw Germany. He worked on nearby mission land with views towards the Volta river.

Dr Dieter Hoch was the oldest mission member. He was a charming grey haired and bearded medical man, from Weisshorn under the towering Matterhorn. The ideals of the Basel Mission suited his philosophy of life. He was an internationalist, pacifist, humanitarian, whose medical manner and expertise was worshipped locally. He had overseen the work of twelve local clinics on the Kwahu ridge over the past fifteen years and was always ready to absorb native medicine in his treatment, when appropriate or fortuitous.

Two days later Fleur, who had been given a bicycle by Dr Hoch to enable her to cycle the four miles to Nkwatia each day, began her studies. Her teacher, Kofi Frempong, walked her around St Peter's Secondary School and introduced her to his method of teaching.

'Mrs Richter, do you know on which day of the week you were born?'

Fleur thought long and hard. 'I think it was a Tuesday.'

'Then Tuesday it is. From now on, you will be called Abena in my class. This means a woman born on a Tuesday. You see, when a child is born then the family has to be notified and a naming ceremony is arranged a week after the birth, when the mother and child are at home with the family. So everyone has a day name. Some keep their day name. Others do not. But Abena, it is a genuine African name for you. I was born on a Friday. All Friday born men are known as Kofi and the Friday women are called Afua. You will hear these names often. Listen out for them.'

'Kofi, I hear the word Osofo a lot. What does it mean?'

Kofi smiled. 'You are living with many of them at Abetifi. It means Reverend in our language. It is for any ordained preacher of any church. Whenever you hear a man called Osofo, then you know he is a man of God.'

'That explains why I have heard it so much. I thought it was a popular Christian name!'

They walked around the school grounds and came across two large cages. They contained two primates. 'They are quite tame. The pupils give them oranges and bananas regularly but, be careful, if the gorilla caught your arm he would hurt you. He is strong.'

Fleur kept her distance. They proceeded down the path to two semicircular concrete pens. Each contained a crocodile. Fleur was sad to see the condition in which they survived. ‘They’ve no room to move Kofi. That is cruel.’

‘Oh, not so cruel Abena, they are very dangerous. They get watered daily and fed by the students. Its part of their studies.’

Fleur understood what Kofi was saying but she felt desperately sorry for them in that restricted condition.

Kofi then took her to a room at the end of the school compound where he had been given a classroom for Fleur’s instruction. It was a plain rectangular room. A blackboard and several desks were scattered around. It was not a classroom in general use. On two sides of the room, the two longer sides, there were eight windows with each window supporting eight glass louvers. Within each window was a wooden framed mosquito net. Beyond the rear window lay an open farming area where stalks of cassava stood close and erect.

He then announced, quite dramatically Fleur thought, that he was about to utter his last sentence in English! Henceforth, Fleur would learn to speak Twi as if she was a newly born baby, acquiring the language. There was to be no translation from English into Twi. Instead, by exaggerated movement and repetition, he would teach Fleur his language just as a young child learns. At lunchtime, he would accompany her to the village where she would learn to buy her food. The stall sellers would always have time to speak to her and encourage her. This was the only way to learn. Fleur agreed. She took a deep breath and for the next three months never spoke English again, in class, in front of Kofi.

After class on her first day, she cycled to the Nkwatia post office and introduced herself. She was asked why she was not seeking an Abetifi Post Box number, as she lived in that town. She merely replied that she was studying in Nkwatia daily and it would be very convenient to collect her mail before cycling home. On that basis, no further questions were asked and Fleur became the key holder of P.O.Box No 37 Nkwatia, Kwahu. She went to the front of the post office building and located her box. It was sited conveniently on the third row down from the top, giving her eyes full view of the box’s contents when opened. She had no mail for a week but the following Tuesday three letters awaited her. She gathered them, locked her box and placed her key in her purse.

She slid her correspondence into her jotter and placed the jotter in a kente woven shoulder bag that she slung round her neck. She mounted her bicycle and started to ride back to Abetifi.

She approached a small clearing by the side of the road on which a large boulder was situated. She rode over to this tranquil spot and rested her bike against the shaded side of the stone. She examined the boulder and found by climbing it from the back, she could gain access to a relatively comfortable sitting position. At least it would be for as long as it took to read her letters.

The first letter she opened was from her parents. It had been re-addressed from the Governor's office. Fleur did not think it significant that the letter was written by her mother, nor that it was written in broad black ink but, in retrospect, she saw the significance. She had known she might not see her parents again but for the death of her father to come so soon after her departure, gave her a feeling of slight guilt. Had she contributed to his death by setting off so far away? Surely he would have been pleased if not envious of her being in the Gold Coast where he once served? Would this guilt constantly return to haunt her? But there again he had been in his 89th year. He was born on 6th October 1850 and died on 6th August 1939, peacefully at home. Her mother gave an account of the funeral at Forres on 11th August. The town paid its respects to a worthy son and the cortege retired to the town's cemetery, where Fleur would be able to visit his grave one day. She shed a tear remembering the happy days in his company. She was grateful to him for giving her the adventurous spirit that had led her to this quiet peaceful copse in the country where he had once served. She folded the letter carefully and returned it to her bag.

The second letter was from Sir Ronald. It was dated 3rd September 1939. It notified Fleur that Neville Chamberlain had made a statement to the House of Commons declaring that Britain was at War with Germany. His words could not help but reflect the nation's growing despondency, defeatism and uncertainty about its war aims. Sir Ronald stressed Fleur's need to keep her cover secure and cautiously eke out any information which the Basel missionaries might divulge. Finally, he reminded her to ensure this communication was destroyed. This second letter for the time being was returned to her bag. With anxiety she opened the third letter. It was from Germany. It was from Otto.

Otto greeted his mother affectionately. He wrote that Renate and Karl had looked after him well. However he had been undertaking much training in recent weeks and not spent much time with them. He was no longer part of the Hitler Youth, having reached the rank of Oberbannführer at the age of eighteen. Otto proudly claimed that he was now with the SS-Stanadarte Germania, a Hamburg based motorised infantry regiment commanded by SS-Standardenführer Carl-Maria Demelhüber. He had enjoyed the sports training at Bad Tölz and was good at fencing. This was part of his officer training. He was sorry he could not give any information about his duties or whereabouts, but he was confident about three things. One was that Germany would create a new harmonious Europe. Secondly, he would survive the war, which was about to start and thirdly, he would meet his mother in happier times in the years to come. He concluded the letter, expressing his love for his mother and his country. It was signed SS –Untersturmführer Otto Bruce Richter.

Fleur took out the three letters from her bag and cried quietly. Never before had she received three personal letters in one day, let alone three with such significant and perturbing news. She felt very alone and sad. Through her tears she noticed she suddenly had company. A beautiful, predominantly blue butterfly had landed on the rock. Its wings were outstretched. Its colour was so vivid yet so vulnerable in such a tropical location. Who was its enemy? Fleur focussed on its fragile wing markings and had to clear the tears from her eyes to see its beauty clearly. What could she take from this moment of solitude? She noted the markings were symmetrical but not geometrically shaped. What attracted it to this location? Why did it want to share this moment with her? Was it the colour of her dress? Or was it the warmth of the stone? Was it part of an even greater plan beyond human understanding? Comfort it gave Fleur and she did not move before it finally fluttered its wings and made for the cover of the grasses. Fleur gathered her books and bag, mounted her bicycle and set off for the security of her room in Abetifi.

On reaching her room, she took off her shoes and lay on her bed to consider the impact of her letters once more. The exertions of her cycling, her day of tuition and the contents of her letters overcame her and she fell into a self-pitying sleep.

'Agooo, agooo, Fleur.' Fleur remembered this salutation. There was someone at the door. Knocking was not traditional as it could be interpreted as a goat kicking at the door making the noise. Hence the call '*agoo.*' It was the Matron, Mercy.

'Fleur, have you heard the news? Britain is at war with Germany!' Fleur remembered that she had received this news only from Sir Ronald. 'What!' she exclaimed.

'Yes it's true, for the second time Britain and Germany are at war. Oh Fleur, I hope this will not mean we lose the Basel missionaries again. You know we lost them during the First World War.'

'Yes, I read about that before I came here,' she lied. 'But they are all Swiss missionaries so I don't think its going to be so bad for them,' Fleur suggested, bringing an interesting response.

'I think Frau Gisela Schmidt is not Swiss. Her husband is, but she is not. Hans Winkler is Swiss, but some of his family are in Germany and I know he has been talking about how well Hitler has been doing to get Germany to be a proud nation again.' Fleur listened to every word carefully then shared her grief as the need was paramount within her.

'Dear Mercy, I had sad news today. I learned that my father died recently. You know, he loved his time in the Gold Coast.'

'Oh, I am sorry.... You mean he was in our country before?'

'Oh yes, he was a soldier who came to quieten the Ashanti rebellion. He helped to build and extend the fort at Kumasi and became its camp commandant. He loved the native people though. It was his influence that made me a bit of a traveller and to think I am now in the country which he served. Well, it gives me some comfort at this time.'

'My dear Fleur, you will be in my prayers tonight.' Mercy left closing the door behind her. Fleur looked through her Twi lecture notes. She was determined to make a go of this language. Not just because she had been posted here but because she felt at peace with the people and, at her age, she wished to prove to herself that she was not too old to learn a new language and lead a useful life. She wanted to serve as well as her father had, follow his footsteps as it were.

As light was beginning to fade and the generator rumbled into action, footsteps were heard on the wooden stair leading to her room. They grew louder until they stopped outside. 'Agoo,' a deep voice sounded. Fleur went to the door and opened it to find Dr Dieter Hoch standing before her.

'Frau Richter, I am so very sorry to hear of your sad bereavement. May I come in?'

'Yes, please do. Yes, I learned today that my father had died. He was 89 and had a very full life so I am grateful for that. It was sudden, I suppose, but my mother was able to tell me about the funeral service. I will write to her this evening.'

'Yes, your mother would welcome a letter, I am sure. Not just to let her know you have received her sad news but it will be a comfort to her too. Now, I will leave this bottle of pills. You may not wish to use them, but if you do, take two with water last thing at night and they will ensure you get a good sleep.'

As Dr Hoch made his way towards the door, Fleur followed him and asked to accompany him across the compound for a breath of fresh air. He was delighted for her to do so.

'Dr Hoch, you have heard the news that we are at war again?'

'Yes, a sad day for us all. Why can't we all be Swiss and stay neutral long enough to sort out the world's difficulties?' he said rhetorically.

'Do you think the colonial powers will send the Basel missionaries home this time?'

'I hope not. We are no threat to the British. A few years ago there were many more German missionaries, but they returned. Now we are all Swiss. But there will be hardships ahead. Supplies from Europe are sure to be affected. Especially my medical supplies. Let's hope the guns of Europe will not be heard on Africa's soil.'

That was a comforting thought and a satisfying note on which to terminate her conversation. She bade Dr Hoch farewell and made her way back, following the perimeter pathway. Her senses were attracted to a courtyard at the corner of the compound.

Fleur smelled charcoal burning. She approached and saw a large black pot suspended over a fire. Water was boiling. She found she had Sir Ronald's letter in her pocket. She went down to the cooking area and enquired what was being cooked. It was explained that three other cooking areas were being lit and the water from this large fire would be used for cooking rice and palmnut soup. Fermented dough, wrapped in a casing of corn leaves, was laid in a pile by the other two fires.

When no one was looking, Fleur laid Sir Ronald's letter on the fire and watched it curl up in the heat, catch light then dwindle. She took a stick to break up the burnt pages, then placed a small log over the debris. She hoped that she would not have to rely on this method too often. It was a cumbersome process. Surely Sir Ronald did not expect her to go to such lengths to destroy his letters on every occasion. She hoped his letters would be few and far between.

The evening communal meal was the one time everyone met each day. Osofo Emmanuel Okine always enquired how each of them had been that day and inevitably it led to everyone sharing their experiences, their concerns and their achievements. It was equally important to know who had met whom for Osofo Okine and Daniel Tetteh. They kept abreast, not only with the European contingent, but they were also part of the African Abetifi community. The words and actions of the Basel mission staff would often leave the evening table and be shared in the native community in a matter of hours or less. This was an appropriate process and a natural one. It was not forced nor over inquisitive. It ensured the Africans were comfortable with what was happening in their midst and made for a more accepting environment. That did not of course mean that all Africans flocked to the Christian tradition however.

Hans Winkler was the exception to the group. Fleur realised he had been the newcomer until she arrived. She made this her opening remark to engage him after the meal at which he had said very little.

'Now that I have arrived you are no longer the new arrival, not so?'

Hans spoke in heavy guttural English, 'Ah, so you know about me?'

Fleur was a little taken aback. Her approach had not been sensitive enough. 'Herr Winkler, I know only that you have not been here very long and I have arrived after you. I know nothing of what you do, or your personal circumstances.'

'Frau Richer, you trouble me somewhat.' Fleur looked puzzled. 'Really Herr Winkler?'

'You are different things to me. You are German and you are English. You are old enough to be my mother, yet you are in West Africa learning Twi and not at home where your family need you at a time of war. If I was you, whether German or English then I would be helping the war effort from the safety of home.'

Fleur paused before replying. Before her, was a man indeed young enough to be her son. He was Swiss. Yet he talked as though he was a German, and he was certainly confused by meeting her. She spoke to him in German and told of how she had married a German doctor who had died four years ago. They had a son in Hamburg. Her explanation of why she left Germany was couched in regret. It was her work as an anthropologist that had led to her posting in the Gold Coast. She was not running away or seeking a safe haven. She hoped she had said enough to reassure Hans.

He listened carefully. He now had a greater understanding of the woman before him and was confident enough to explain his situation. He had had an unhappy childhood. His father was very strict and he had taken refuge in the great outdoors, on the shores of Lake Constance. From that he knew the outdoor life was for him. He grew up trapping wildlife, skiing and shooting, harvesting wild berries and introducing new strains of cereals. He had worked with Paul Müller, the scientist who had recently discovered the pesticide DDT, which Hans saw as the solution to kill disease-carrying insects like mosquitoes. Such was his interest in farming matters over his early years that he decided to study at the famed Agricultural College at Innsbruck in Austria. He graduated in 1938. He returned home but was unhappy. The Basel Mission gave him an opportunity to experiment with new cereals and crops in a different climate while, at the same time, developing traditional farming methods in the mission farms. He jumped at the chance. His faith, was not however, nearly as sure as those with whom he lived, but it had satisfied the selection board at his interview. He looked up at Fleur, his face serious 'My one regret was not being born German,' he declared. 'You have a greater claim than me.'

Seizing the opportunity, Fleur went into her handbag and brought out the letter from Otto. 'Here read this.' She handed him the letter. The letter was of course, in German. In silence, he read about Fleur's son, Otto, and his progress through the Hitler Youth. He smiled as he reached the second page, on which reference was made to his training course.

'You must be proud of him, Frau Richter. I wish, I was serving with him.' On that damning statement, Fleur returned the letter to her handbag. Before bidding farewell, Hans had one more disclosure to concern Fleur.

'If you count yourself and me as sympathetic to the German cause, then that's three of us out here, when we should be back home playing our part for the Fatherland.'

'Three, Hans?' asked Fleur casually without showing too much obvious interest in his remark. Hans hesitated. He had said more than he had intended. He merely smiled and nodded.

CHAPTER THIRTEEN

Fleur's classes proceeded at a steady rate. Eventually she was no longer confined to the classroom. She made regular sorties to Nkwatia town with Kofi who oversaw her greetings and purchases. He took occasional notes, more frequently basking in his own achievement of instructing the white woman in his language. Meanwhile she learned many proverbs that she managed to fit into her conversations. This was sheer delight to the market traders' ears and gave Fleur a greater insight into the beauty of the Twi language. When complimented on her efforts to speak Twi, she responded with the proverb: *Bad dancing does not harm the ground.* In other words there was no harm in trying anything sincerely. But one proverb, which brought her mind to the present, was that, *The white man's guns in Europe shook the palms of Africa.* Shortages began to appear in the wayside stores. Hoarding was becoming common. When sugar appeared it was sold within hours. Yet whatever deprivations were being experienced on mainland Europe, here, Fleur rationalised there was still a rich supply of fruit, yams and cassava and various meats and fish.

By April 1940, her competence in the Twi language had reached a plateau. Kofi agreed to concentrate more on written Twi and gave her exercises to complete at her leisure. They kept her busy for days in Abetifi, not requiring her daily cycle to Nkwatia. It was fortunate that her progress coincided with the rainy season. It announced itself cautiously.

While Fleur was working hard on her exercises one morning, she began to feel a chill. She rose to get a cardigan and noticed the sky darkening. That observation led her on to the veranda where Reverend Jurg and Martha Fendler were already standing enjoying the cool breezes.

'Good day, Fleur. We are about to see the beauty of a tropical storm announcing the rainy season. Have you seen this before?' Jurg enquired.

'No, just a few drops of rain on my arrival at Takoradi.'

'It's quite beautiful and frightening at the same time. Nothing like your English summer drizzle!' declared Martha.

'Have you experienced our British drizzle?'

'Yes, Martha and I visited Hampshire not long after we were married. We spent a month in southern England in the summer of

1898. That was a long time ago. Elephants never forget! I remember that was one of your sayings! It was wet most of the time, I think. Not heavy showers. Just long grey days with drizzle,' recalled Jurg.

'This will be over in an hour or so and the sun will come through again. It's beautiful when it does. The dust on the vegetation is washed away and the colours become so vivid,' remarked Martha. 'The roads are a mess for a while after though. The laterite runs like the Red Sea!'

The dark sky approached. The wind bent the trees and circled the threesome. Then the first rain drops were felt. They preceded a heavier shower and then, with a crashing clatter, heavy rain struck the mission building's aluminium roof. Inside the noise was deafening and quite unbearable. In seconds the rain made its way to the edge of the roof and fell like a sheet of smoked glass, obscuring all before them. It became impossible to be heard so making gestures of farewell, they agreed to part and make their way along the veranda in different directions, to their rooms. There they would lie on top of their beds with pillows over their heads to dull the noise of the storm. Gallons of rain fell for half an hour. Thunder and lightning broke the monotony of the deluge. Then the light increased slowly but the dripping rain continued to roll off the roof and splatter mud on the concrete pathway around each building. Beyond that, all pathways were a running river of red laterite and the grass struggled to breathe through the bubbling soil. This was also uncomfortable for animal life of all sorts and it was not long before a cry of 'Snake' was heard. A black mamba had had its crevice inundated by the rain and was moving to higher ground. Fleur followed the cries and approached the pastor's residence where there was a gathering. She arrived to see the snake some seven feet in length make for the gap beneath the front door step of the manse. Osofo Okine was anxious that the snake did not take up residence in the manse compound. From inside the compound, the front door was closed. Then it was decided to set light to the entrance of the gap to produce enough smoke to force the snake to retreat to safer land.

Comfort Okine shepherded the children who had come to see the commotion so that they did not obstruct an exit route for the snake. A long wooden pole lit at its end was inserted into the gap amongst some paper. It took some few minutes before the snake's head appeared and sized up its options. Scrub land lay round the side of the manse and that was the shortest route of escape. The children became more excited. Having seen where its head was, Osofo Okine prodded the stick through the gap on the other side and that made the snake make its dart for cover. Fleur noticed the Black Mamba was more a variety of grey shades than pure black as it sped its way along the open grass to the scrub. Once it saw its cover, it moved swiftly and made off as quickly as a ship's trailing rope leaves the quayside on its departure.

The excitement over, the relief was shared amongst the gathered group. Fleur was told just how dangerous the situation had been. The Black Mamba was the largest African poisonous snake. It strikes quickly and its venom is potent. It hides in rocks and the old haunts of animals, usually near water. There were many snakes in Kwahu as the Volta river was nearby but the Black Mambo was the most feared of all.

Needless to say, the excitement of the snake's appearance was discussed at the evening meal. The table noticed Hans had not arrived to eat. His absence was not a source of concern though as he must have been caught in the rain with his agricultural force and there was probably much clearing up to do which would have delayed him. His meal was covered for him to eat later.

A car was heard to approach the compound. Reverend Fendler looked out of the window. 'A police car! Three policemen...and Hans!'

'Really, what's happening?' asked Gisela

'They are taking Hans up to his room. One of the policemen is heading towards Osofo Okine's office. Perhaps it's best not to interfere at this stage'

Reverend Fendler's expression was one of concern and anxiety. 'Oh... look... Comfort is coming over.'

Reverend Fendler opened the door for Comfort Okine. 'Oh God, please God, have mercy, have mercy,' she screamed. Gisela held her arms and tried to calm her. 'Comfort, what's wrong?'

'Oh! Frau Schmidt, ...it's Hans. His gun went off in the fields and one of his workers, Kwasi Amissah, is dead. Shot in the head. Oh God, have mercy, mercy.'

'But how did it happen?' Gisela asked.

'I don't really know yet. The police think it is an accident, but they are checking his room to see if Kwasi may have been there and to take away any firearms.'

'Hans will have ammunition in his room, but he never used his gun in the compound. It was for farming, for safety surely.'

Numbness descended over the compound. Was it an accident? Had Hans lost his temper? What were the other workers saying? Eventually the police car was heard to leave. Just as the assembled group were considering whether to go up to Hans' room, the door of his room opened revealing a shaft of light. He descended the wooden staircase and was heading towards the dining room. The group tried to look relaxed, taking up positions of strained comfort in the room. The door opened. A tearful Hans staggered in. Reverend Schmidt came to comfort him. 'Tell us, Hans. What happened?'

Hans was still sobbing. He sat down, bent forward and clasped his hands with his arms resting on his knees. 'You know I have weapons. I always have them when I work. The Africans have their cutlasses but I have a field sport rifle and a revolver. We had cultivated a square area of ground two days ago. We planted young corn plants this morning and covered them with a thin sheet to protect the shoots for the first month. Then the rain fell. Kwasi helped me to lay more stones around the perimeter. When the rains began, he and I took cover under the tamarind tree nearby.' He then resumed sobbing and Gisela handed him a handkerchief.

'It rained for almost an hour, but during that time a gust of wind forcibly removed the corner stones and the wind got under the cover. It blew up and we both ran to capture it.'

'Where were the other farm hands?' asked Osofo Okine.

'They had all gone home when the rains began. It was only Kwasi and I left. We gathered the sheet and bundled it together as the rain and wind were too strong. But part of it was torn off. It was perhaps a piece no longer than my height and square. I returned to the tree for some shelter and I did not see Kwasi after that. I thought he must have gone home.'

Fleur asked if he had heard him say he was going home.

'He may have done. But I did not hear him. It was very stormy and wet. Some time passed, I can't be sure how long. Then I saw a commotion behind a shrub. It was about twenty metres away. I feared what it might be. I took out my pistol. I strained to see through the driving rain but I got no sight of what it was. I decided to frighten it off anyway.'

At the memory of the next thought he again sobbed loudly. 'I just fired once.....only once. Then I heard a human cry. I realised it was not an animal. I walked quickly over to the shrub and lying there in a foetal position clinging on to that loose piece of cloth, was Kwasi. I called his name, but he did not respond. I knelt down and turned him over. His face was covered with blood. I realised I had shot him. I had shot him between his eyes. He must have been killed instantly.'

Osofo Okine called the group to prayer and prayed in English to start with, then he continued in Twi. Fleur thought deeply about his prayer. When he prayed seeking forgiveness, he spoke of our troubles today stemming out of deviation from traditional ways of life. Was this a reference to Hans' firearms in the fields? Then a touching thought when his prayer turned to Kwasi. He asked if it was not only right that a bedfellow in sowing the seed should be a partner in the harvesting? Kwasi would enjoy a rich harvest now. And he gave thanks to God for the business of farming, which must go on. To trade, he said, is good but farming is business. His final thought in prayer struck a poignant note. We forgive, he prayed, however grave the offence. He concluded with a benediction in English. Then in German, Reverend Jurg Fendler took up the prayer for a further four minutes.

Hans thanked him also for his prayers. Yet he had understood he had been prayed for too, as the culprit. He wanted to lay that thought to rest promptly so tried to show he could have done no more in the tragic circumstances.

'I went straight to the police to inform them of what had occurred and I took them to the spot. They rightly questioned me why the gunshot was so accurate between his eyes. But I could not explain other than to tell the truth. It was a shot in the rain, in the wind, in fear. It was not a shot aimed to kill. Not the shot of a marksman or a criminal.'

Osofo Okine offered to take Hans to the Amissah household. 'Is this wise?' he replied.

'But why not, Hans? The police were satisfied you had committed no offence. You explained the circumstances to their satisfaction. The family will be mourning. They will expect you to have consideration for their loss.'

'Then I will come to the wake. Also, I must pay for the funeral.'

'That would be appreciated.'

The following evening at 7pm Hans, Fleur, the Schmidts, the Fendlers, and Dr Hoch accompanied Reverend and Mrs Okine, Daniel Tetteh and Mercy Appiah, on a solemn walk down the hill from the compound, through the town to the courtyard of the Amissah home. For some distance before reaching the wake, the constant ticking of the crickets was heard accompanying the quiet singing of hymns and loud wailing of souls.

They entered the courtyard and saw the body of Kwasi lying in an open coffin, mounted on cases covered in a black cloth. He lay on a layer of starched white cotton with his head on a pillow. A black cloth lay over his face revealing only his nose and mouth. The bullet's accuracy lay hidden from view. A solemn procession circled round the coffin. They greeted Kwasi's mother and father, then his brothers and sisters. Fleur listened to the rich sayings of the gathered bereaved. *One cannot weep and meditate at the same time*. The most comforting thought to reach her ears came last. *If death could be tasted, everyone would be more willing to try it.*

They were given seats facing the corpse and served with orange juice. Hans held his head in shame and let the tears flow down his cheeks. The wake would continue till dawn the next day. At noon, Kwasi would be buried in his family grave, inside the church walls at the top of the hill. The grave-diggers had already prepared his final resting place. Impromptu prayers were said to which the gathering gave its appropriate responses. Moved by the occasion, after a moment of quiet contemplation, Fleur began her own public prayer in English and then as if filled with the Holy Spirit, confidently turned her prayer into Twi. The mourners silently listened to her every word and when she concluded with a quiet Amen, the mourners in unison repeated 'AMEN'. Osofo Okine gave his prayer and so too did Reverend Schmidt. Hans sat silently throughout the night knowing his deed was known to all present, yet no eyes lingered on him and no blame was heard to pass his way. Midnight came quickly and some mourners sought permission to return home. At half past midnight, the mission staff sought the family's permission to leave and duly departed taking a last look at the young Kwasi, whose life had been so cruelly cut short on that foul day.

The whole town came to the funeral the next morning, moved by the sudden and violent death, which had visited Kwasi. The police also attended taking their place at the rear of the church. Kwasi Amissah was laid to rest in the churchyard at noon. Hans, true to his word, paid the family's funeral expenses and gave money to have a headstone erected at the top of his grave. The inscription read: "Kwasi Amissah born 5th August 1923 – died, the result of a freak accident on 12th June 1940. Son of Saul Kwadjo Amissah and Yaa Mary Amissah, beloved brother of Salome, Wesley, Kwabena and Samuel. Resting with God. Alive in His Kingdom."

The following morning Fleur woke with what she thought was a cold. She remained in bed resting and did not appear for breakfast. By the time Mercy made inquiries, she was sweating in a hot damp state feeling weak. 'Let me call Dr Hoch. I think he will need to see you. Meantime I will bring you some water and I will wash your face.' Fleur hardly had the energy to thank her.

Dr Hoch arrived and saw the state she was in. 'I suspect a bout of malaria Frau Richter but just to make sure, I am going to take a blood sample for testing. This way I'll be confident in your treatment. Meantime, I am going to give you three amodiaquine tablets. Take these now and try to rest. I'll be back this afternoon after I have been to the clinic and tested this blood sample.'

Fleur felt her head had enlarged. Her body was so weak she had difficulty raising her head. Mercy arrived with extra pillows, a jug of water and a hand bell. 'Now give this a ring anytime and I'll come up. I see you have taken the pills so I think you should try to rest.'

'Try to rest, just what Dr Hoch said!'

Mercy laughed. 'I know I am not the doctor, but your body needs a good rest now, after these pills. Dr Hoch tells all the children when they get malaria, to drink and rest and let nature cure them after he has given them their medicine. You must too.'

Fleur tried to sleep. But the parasites had burst through her red cells. The repeated loss of haemoglobin was leading to anaemia and her spleen compensated to deal with the resultant debris from the ruptured red cells. The amodiaquine began the battle with the millions of parasites, but it was a battle, with only three possible outcomes: death of the patient, elimination of the parasites or the attainment of a variable balance between the body's defences and the parasites, whereby the latter persist in smaller numbers at the expense of ill health of the body.

Fleur slowly woke to find Dr Hoch sitting on the edge of her bed. It was late afternoon. He asked to take her temperature. 'Fleur, I can confirm the species of parasites you have are Plasmodium falciparum. They produce malignant tertian malaria. Now let me see...102 degrees. Still too high but we have identified the culprit. Two days complete rest and I'll bring you more medication tomorrow morning. You will probably not feel like eating but I'll ask matron to make a clear pepper soup tomorrow. It will be very hot, full of sharp pepper. This will help you sweat even more but it also helps you to clear the impurities in your body. Then you must drink water, lots of water. I'll see you tomorrow.'

Tomorrow came and went with Fleur not remembering much. By the following day she felt a resurgence of energy in her arms and legs. She had taken the hot pepper soup and it had performed its magic by making her sweat as she had never sweated before. She was at last regaining her strength. She looked in the mirror. She desperately needed a shower and a hair wash. She rang the bell and asked Mercy for some hot water. She announced she was going to get up and wash. Mercy arrived with a bucket of hot water and adjusted the cold to prepare the bucket shower. 'Shower ready Fleur. Come over to the kitchen after if you can, and have a cup of cocoa.'

'Yes I think I will manage that.'

Fleur stood beneath the bucket and released the cord. Warm water shot from the holes on the base of the bucket giving her a warm tingling sensation and with a native loofah, she lathered herself and felt good. She soaped her hair and stood erect to let the water run through her head and down the length of her ample body, to her feet where she felt the tickle of water on each toe. It was a marvellous warm, sensuous feeling. An invigorating freshness she had not enjoyed for almost four days washed over her. She stayed in the shower long after the soap had left her skin and scurried down the drain. She waited till the very last drop fell before lowering the bucket on the pulley and unhooking it. She returned to her room and stood naked in front of the mirror. She realised she had lost weight as a result of the illness. She turned to the side, yes definite loss of weight and the dimples on her cheeks responded to the smile that the apparition gave her. Not bad for her years she thought.

She dressed and left her room knowing her temperature was once again normal. At the dining room Mercy had prepared some Tom Brown corn porridge, toast and cocoa. While she was enjoying her meal, Comfort arrived and asked how she was. She was pleased to see she had made a good recovery. 'Thank Dr Hoch. He really is so very understanding. He is an excellent doctor.'

'Yes we are so very glad to have him here with us.'

Comfort was asked to bring Fleur up to date with what had been happening. 'Not much really. Kwasi was at rest in the churchyard and prayers were said for him at church at a memorial service. Oh and Hans Winkler has travelled.'

'Really, where has he gone?'

'Well he told me with the war on he could not go to Europe, but needed a break and he was due some leave so he decided he wanted to visit Mopti in French West Africa where he might get some agricultural supplies.'

'Mopti! How will he get there?'

'He told me he would travel north to Paga and cross over into Upper Volta. There he would take the road through Ouagadougou and then Ouahigouya to the river Niger at Mopti.'

'When did he say he would return?'

'He thought he might be away for six weeks.'

Fleur's thoughts jumped ahead. He was going to French West Africa – the part which Vichy France governs for the Germans.

Fleur finished her breakfast and returned to her room. There she took out her writing paper and recorded the recent events for the attention of Sir Ronald. There was much to record. She had a positive report to give about her Twi course that underpinned her creditability in the mission compound. That was holding firm. She had still to establish if indeed another German national was within the compound but there was no evidence of how any communication with any enemy forces was being undertaken, if at all. She reported the killing of Kwasi and the apparent sudden leave which Hans had taken to Mopti of all places.

Fleur completed the letter, folded it in a brown envelope but was careful not to address it until she posted it later that afternoon. Only then did her thought turn to the status of the French colonies.

Churchill was determined to prevent important units of the French Fleet at Otran from falling into German hands. The British admiral had been instructed to present the French with an ultimatum to come over to Britain's side, sail to a neutral port or scuttle their ships. When the French at Otran refused, the British sank the battleship Bretagne and the battle-cruiser Dunkerque. The battle-cruiser Strasbourg escaped to Toulon. This action against the French strengthened the British resolve to defeat Hitler at a time of dreaded and imminent invasion. Yet the summer of 1940 saw no glimmer of tangible success for the British stance.

It seemed that soon Britain would be assaulted from all angles. Fleur followed that thought. The Italians would drive into Somaliland, Kenya and the Sudan as well as Egypt. The Japanese would enter the war somehow and attack in the Far East. Germany, while still threatening Britain at home, might send armies to Spain, Portugal, Morocco and ...Dakar! Yes, Dakar, it lay at the terminal of the Mopti - Bamako - Dakar railway line. Perhaps Hans was not stopping at Mopti after all, but going on to Bamako and then taking the train from there into the heart of Vichy French West Africa at Dakar! From there he might even get passage to Vichy France itself or even to Germany.

Fleur opened the brown envelope and added a postscript to include her thoughts about Dakar. She had little evidence of her gut feeling, so she entitled the postscript simply, 'Thinking Aloud.' Without any further delay, she set off to the post office in Abetifi to post her letter. Sir Ronald would receive the letter within two days. One final note on the letter requested Sir Ronald to give her a few days' leave to visit Kumasi. She hoped she was not being too precocious in asking for leave. Had she done enough to earn it she wondered? Yet she was aware of being under a considerable strain living a double life. She noticed that when she cycled between Abetifi and Nkwatia or when she cycled for pleasure in the countryside away from the European enclave, she was relaxed, she felt at ease. Surely Sir Ronald would agree to some leave in these circumstances. Kumasi would be such a welcome break.

CHAPTER FOURTEEN

Not only had Sir Ronald given her a week's leave in Kumasi. He warmly congratulated her on her report and her 'gut feelings' which had 'hit the mark', whatever that had meant. Its greater impact was in gaining Sir Ronald's approval for a job done with no training. He obviously trusted her. She had deserved her few days off. This was going to be a personal homage to a city where her father had served at the turn of the century. The Ashanti kingdom was now a lively commercial and integrated part of the Gold Coast. The war of 1900 ensured that.

But Sir Ronald had ended his letter with an invitation! Fleur was invited next Friday evening, to join him at a reception at the home of Mr and Mrs Hall of the Ashanti Timber Company at Mampong Road, near the Wesley College in Kumasi. Had Sir Ronald remembered Madge had sailed out with her? His invitation was so formal. There was no hint of a reunion, or whether the Halls knew what she was doing at Abetifi. Nevertheless it would be wonderful to catch up on Madge's gossip and friendship. What a pleasant coincidence this had turned out to be. She knew she would enjoy this break. She put the doubts about her security cover out of her mind as she concentrated on packing. After a light and early lunch she set out to Kumasi.

Now that Fleur knew the Kwahu ridge descent was one-way, she was able to enjoy the descent through Mpraeso. The lorry swept round each sharply angled curve, taking the lorry's wheels to the very cusp of the road. The sight beneath her was of soft greens of the dense forest. A deceptively soft jungle for no one had survived a fall from such a height apparently. The lorry drivers were the bravest of the brave. None was under the age of thirty-five. This was not a learner's hill. Soon the descent was complete. The warm sticky heat of the plains engulfed them and the lorry pulled into the Nkawkaw lorry-park. Chickens darted from beneath the wheels of moving lorries and mothers grabbed the arms of straying youngsters. Tables of okra, tomatoes, plantain, bananas, sugar, salt, peppers and palm oil formed a border around the lorry-park. Beyond the food market were more wooden stalls, some with fine Java print cloths on display, others with material decorated with traditional adinkra symbols and others displaying colourful Ashanti kente cloths. Yards of plain colours, every day use cloths, funeral cloths and more happy, special occasion cloths were to be seen. Traders and customers mingled. Different languages were heard. Fleur heard Ga and Ewe, Dagomba and Hausa even without understanding them. Tall elegant Fulani traders were recognisable as they stopped on their long journeys from the north to the coast and from the coast back home. Their flowing robes and pillbox hats emphasised the cosmopolitan nature of the town's trading.

Fleur found a lorry heading for Kumasi and boarded it. She was invited to share the driver's passenger seat, but thanking him, she insisted on sitting in the back with the other passengers, to enjoy the fresh air which the movement would provide and, of course, the camaraderie of the travellers. The lorry filled up with passengers, goods and livestock. Live chickens with strips of cloth tying their feet together were brought on board while other more bulky items were secured by rope, on the lorry's slightly convex roof. On the side of the lorry read the inscription: *A Stranger is Like A Child.* Fleur recognised the Twi proverb. How true! The stranger is treated with the belief that they will be lost, in need of direction and sustenance. It was at the very heart of African belief. How that contrasted with the European experience where suspicion predominated.

The lorry set off slowly through the park, negotiating the potholes still filled with rain. The lorry lurched one way then the other before it climbed back on to the main Accra – Kumasi road and began to pick up speed. The draught added freshness to the travelling faces and Fleur took a deep breath of this invisible delight.

The lorry proceeded to Konongo where passengers, goods and livestock descended and new passengers joined. On noticing Fleur unexpectedly, gasps of '*Oh Oburini!*' were heard. She smiled. They progressed through Juaso, Boankra, Besease and finally Ejisu. Then amid its hills stood the Ashanti capital, Kumasi.

The vehicle climbed Bimpeh hill and turned right at Asafo market square. It terminated its journey by the central market at the Kejetia lorry-park. Fleur had reached Kumasi.

She found accommodation at the Government rest-house. It was central, gave her breakfast and an evening meal each day and even provided a laundry service. Fleur paid her week's accommodation in advance and settled into her room. She obtained a Kumasi street map and planned her itinerary.

According to legend, when King Osei Tutu, the unifier and liberator of the Ashantis wished to select the site for his capital, his high priest planted two branches at different places. One of them withered and died. The other grew strongly and sprouted flowers. The interpretation of this portent was obvious. The one that flowers, *Kum – asi,* was chosen and the city was named.

Fleur made her way past the pink brick Methodist Church, along the walls of the town's prison, past the facing Commercial Bank and the Court House. There she saw for the first time, the distinctive shape of the fort. It was a solidly built structure, with turrets at the end of each side giving a commanding view of the neighbourhood. Turrets were not manned. Fleur focussed on the turret and imagined the Scots Guards in post. She focussed more closely and saw in her imagination an officer, her father, surveying the land around the fort. She looked at the solid wooden double doors. Only one was open. She remembered how her father had ordered for them both to be opened to engage the trust and friendship of the African people. She entered the fort and made her way to the trophy room whose displays once belonged to a British Officer. She spent much time viewing the fort's photograph albums. They covered a span of several years, encompassing the war of 1900 against the Ashantis. She carefully leafed through the album, recognising her father's regiment and in no fewer than sixteen photos she had seen her father. She knew these were happy times for him but the poignancy of seeing him again so soon after learning of his death brought a tightening to Fleur's throat. She knew she was close to tears.

A painting caught her attention. It depicted the fort being attacked by the Ashanti, who had emerged from the Asantehene's palace and were proceeding across a deep ravine. But the British had burned the palace down and the ravine was now filled in. It no longer existed. This made Fleur question just how much had changed over the forty years since her father trod these very same steps.

Fleur returned to the fort on the third day of her leave and spent more time with the album, trying to capture her father in various poses and activities, for her to recall to her mother one day. She walked around the fort's perimeter. She pretended she was a Scots Guard officer on patrol, but many parts of the fort were off bounds. European soldiers at the fort were training West African Forces. This brought home the reality of the wider war in progress.

Fleur's thoughts then turned to remembering how Madge and Joan had sailed with her from the Broomilaw. A three-month visit she seemed to recall. Then she wondered how the war would have altered their plans. Then the problem of Sir Ronald! Fleur wondered how she could retain her cover at the reception. The Halls knew she was to be appointed as Sir Ronald's Hostess, but if any of the Basel Mission heard of this, they would soon realise she was not the anthropologist she declared she was. She knew she would have to be very careful with her socialising and ensure that not too much alcohol was consumed. Had Sir Ronald taken her anxiety into consideration, she wondered?

That Friday she took an extended afternoon nap and woke in time to laze in a warm bath, full of anticipation of the evening's gathering. She had chosen to wear a traditional long skirt and jacket, topped off with an African headscarf. This attire was all in a yellow and blue Java print, with a matching shoulder wrap. It had been ironed perfectly and lay on her bed until darkness fell at 6.20pm. At five minutes to seven she arranged for a taxi to take her to the Halls' residence. The car crossed town to the Mampong Road and two hundred yards before the turning into Wesley College, on the left side of the road, was the Halls' home. It was lit up on all sides and live music was seeping into the surrounding district causing some young children to dance spontaneously outside the garden perimeter.

Fleur paid for her taxi, entered the driveway and climbed the steps to the house. Mr Hall met her at the entrance. He didn't know who she was. Just as she was about to introduce herself, a familiar voice greeted her.

'Mrs Richter, how nice to see you.' Fleur thought quickly. This was a chance to get Sir Ronald's approval of her identity.

'Sir Ronald. Delighted to see you again. You must call into my classes sometime at Nkwatia.'

Sir Ronald agreed with the cover. 'Ah yes, I'd forgotten you were there studying Twi. You will be anxious to get your anthropological work underway soon.'

'Yes, I look forward to that in the near future.'

Over his shoulder, she saw Madge hold her breath and look puzzled. Fleur asked to be excused as an old friend had just appeared. But what was Madge so surprised about? Was it the reference to anthropology? Or because she was greeted like a long lost friend, by her employer Sir Ronald, or the native dress she was wearing? She was not sure.

'Certainly, perhaps we can have a moment together later. Meanwhile do help yourself to a drink.' Sir Ronald turned to greet the next arrival.

Fleur approached Madge warmly. 'Didn't you know I was coming then?' she whispered in her ear as they exchanged an embracing greeting.

'Why, yes, David sent the invitation list to Sir Ronald but I added your name! That's how we knew you would be coming. That part was arranged but when he greeted you it was as if you had never seen each other and he said you were studying Twi and hoped you would be starting your anthropology work soon. It does not make sense. Does it? Fleur, what have you been up to?'

'Madge, you are right. Can we talk somewhere alone?'

Madge ensured they each had a glass of wine and took Fleur through the house into the garden where the band played in the grounds and there was generally more privacy.

'Oh Madge, I am so pleased that your husband and Sir Ronald are good friends. But what I must tell you, must never be repeated or discussed in any form. Do you realise?'

'Yes, all right.'

'Are you sure? You must tell no one. There is a war on.'

'Trust me Fleur, just tell me what you can. I won't tell anyone.'

'Well, when I told you on the Royal Palm I was to be the Hostess to the Governor of the Gold Coast in Accra, that was true. Except when I got there, Sir Ronald told me the history of the Basel and Bremen mission in the Gold Coast and what happened during the First World War. What he wanted to know, was what German sympathies were around now that the Second World War has begun and so he sent me to the bush, as it were, to find out.'

'Near Kumasi? Is that why you are here?'

'No, not really. I had earned some leave so I decided to come to Kumasi where my father had served in the army at the Kumasi fort at the beginning of this century. I am staying at the Government rest-house. I'll leave again on Monday. I am working from Abetifi and I am learning Twi at Nkwatia. That's where all the German speaking community lives.'

'I see, it's a sort of cover.'

'Well, yes. I suppose it is. Anyway whatever it is the Basel Mission must not think I am on the Governor's staff and that goes for everyone this evening. If they ask, tell them I am learning Twi. I'm an anthropologist. That's all.'

'It's a deal. Now let's meet some of my friends. Oh Joan! Joan, see who's here.'

Joan, who had been helping to serve trays of drinks, bounded over to meet Fleur.

'Fleur how nice to see you again. Did you come up with Sir Ronald?'

'Ah... no, Joan, I came myself. But tell me about you. What are you doing now that the war has begun?'

'I've been allowed to enrol at the Wesley College, across the road. It's great. I enjoy it very much. I have many friends there. And I am studying hard. Are you still playing your oboe?'

'Not as much as I used to. I would be happy to join the band, but I don't have my oboe with me. They are good aren't they?'

'Yes, it's the Kumasi Police Band. They are very popular.'

'Actually, I have been very busy learning Twi.'

'Oh that's useful. I know a few sayings, but I wish I could speak Twi fluently,' said Joan.

'Perhaps you will have an opportunity, especially if the war goes on any longer.'

'Do you think it will go on for a long time then, Fleur?'

'I really do not know. It's not going very well for us yet but if America join us and if Russia fights Hitler on his other flank, it may turn the tide of war. Anyway I don't think we'll have fighting in the Gold Coast so it is better to be safe here perhaps.'

Just at that moment the Chief Superintendent of Police approached. 'Good evening, Miss Hall. Perhaps you will introduce me to your companion?'

'Certainly. Chief Superintendent, this is Fleur Richter. Fleur, Chief Superintendent Kwame Bruce.'

They shook hands. 'I hope you like the Police band. There is much competition to get into it and they have a very wide musical range. One of my difficulties is turning down requests from places too far afield. Only yesterday the Tamale Chief Superintendent asked me if I could send the Police band to a durbar in his town up north. I would love to, of course, but it means constant travel and practice. That can deplete my force numbers. You see, all the band members are serving Police Officers too.'

'I see your predicament. They play particularly well. Do you play any music?'

'Well, Mrs Richter, it depends what you call music! The police also have a pipe band. I play the Scottish bagpipes. They are not compatible with this evening's dance music!'

Fleur looked at the Chief Superintendent. She guessed he was a man of perhaps fifteen years her junior. 'I do apologise Chief Superintendent, I did not catch your surname.'

'Not many people do first time actually, Mrs Richter. It's Bruce. A Scottish name in fact. As you can see, my skin is much lighter than the Ashantis. I am half Ashanti, half Scottish.'

'Really!' Fleur was astonished at what she was hearing.

'Oh yes, there are quite a few mulattos, people of mixed African and European race in our country now. My father was in the Scots Guards. He was the fort commandant here. He met my mother who was a seamstress in Kumasi.'

'She is still alive?' Fleur found herself asking.

'No, she died in 1931.'

Fleur studied the man's face. She detected two dimples hidden in his light brown cheeks. She realised she was standing beside her half brother. Why a half brother, she thought? Her brother ...she had a brother! A numbness of delight came over her but the Chief Superintendent was totally oblivious to what Fleur Richter was experiencing.

At that poignant moment Madge suddenly appeared. 'You two look so serious. I hope I am not intruding on an arrest!' she joked. Kwame Bruce enjoyed the joke. Fleur could hardly raise a smile. She was numbed to the core. The realisation of their relationship was profound with an overpowering intensity of feeling pervading each and every sinew of her body.

'Come into the body of the kirk. The Governor is about to address the gathering,' urged Madge.

The moment of truth was lost. The Chief Superintendent excused himself and the gathering made a large semicircle into which Mr Hall strode.

'Governor General, Chief Superintendent Bruce, Ladies and Gentlemen, I need not remind you that we are in troubled times. A time for us to know for certain who our friends are and to give each other mutual support. It is my privilege to welcome the Governor General to Kumasi and I invite him to address you.... Sir Ronald.'

Applause broke out as Sir Ronald stepped forward. Fleur vaguely remembered his address to the assembled good and worthy of Kumasi. She was vaguely aware that he did not bring any specific news good or otherwise. Had he done so, she was sure she would have picked up the information. Instead, she stared at the Chief Superintendent. What was her duty in these circumstances? He was obviously quite unaware of his relationship to Fleur. Should it stay that way? What would his wife and family think? How many new relatives were about to be uncovered? Was he an only child of this relationship? The incredulity was not confined to Chief Superintendent Kwame Bruce. Her father, Colonel James Bruce, had lived a lie since the turn of the century. Yet what circumstances had led to his unfaithfulness? Could the Ashanti War be the cause of this union? Was the policy, his policy, of fraternising, responsible for the consequences?

Sir Ronald's speech came to an end with the playing of the National Anthem. The Chief Superintendent then shouted 'Three cheers for Sir Ronald and the war against the Nazis. Hiphip ......Hiphip.....Hiphip.......' The band then played an appropriate medley of rousing military marches.

Sir Ronald approached Fleur. 'It is good to see you again Fleur. I must say you are having an interesting time at Abetifi. Your character assessments are particularly good. I'm pleased you are doing so well at Twi too. That is always appreciated.' They moved towards a less crowded area at the foot of the stairs.

'Now can you tell me any more about this Hans fellow?'

'He is certainly a Hitler sympathiser, even although he is Swiss. He accidentally killed a young farm worker. Well, there was no collaboration is the point I am making. His version of the fateful event was accepted by the police. I then fell down with a nasty bout of malaria ....'

'Yes, I was very sorry to hear that. How are you now? Are you fully recovered?'

'Much better thanks...yes, yes.... but when I got out and about again, I discovered Hans had gone to Mopti. He said he could not go to Europe, so he decided to see what agricultural items he might find in Mopti.'

'I don't think it's agricultural. We had him followed discreetly. He did not stay long in Mopti before going to Bamako. He got the train to Dakar as we suspected.'

'You knew he was going to Dakar?'

'Not at first. But we put two and two together. The railway is at Bamako and you told us he was gone for about six weeks. Six weeks in Mopti would drive the best of us insane! So we put a man on him and sure enough he got the train straight away for Dakar.'

'But what's the interest in Dakar?'

'Well, Churchill is not in de Gaulle's good books after the British sunk the French navy. So it seemed de Gaulle would have nothing to offer the Allies. However in Chad, the black Governor, Felix Eboue, originally from French Guyana in South America, made a bold and swift decision to support the Free French. The Governors of other French Equatorial territories fell in behind him. So de Gaulle declared that all French Equatorial Africa is on the Allied side now. But the Vichy government had French West Africa. I can not give you any more details about what's happening but it may be that de Gaulle will be able to bring the Vichy forces in French West Africa over to the Allies. It all depends on a sudden, surprise attack on Dakar, where the Vichy fleet is based. So you see we need every bit of information we can. That's where you are being very helpful.'

Fleur smiled. She was reassured by what Sir Ronald was telling her. Madge was overseeing the departure of guests. She came over to Fleur. 'I have arranged for the Headmaster of Wesley School to drop you off at the rest-house Fleur. I'll bring him over in a minute. But you say you are leaving Kumasi on Monday? Perhaps you will join us for Sunday lunch, at 1pm after church?'

'Yes, Madge, that will be delightful.'

Fleur remembered little of that journey home. Still the thoughts returned to her. How would she be able to break the news to her mother? What relationship could she have with this brother? Since her husband's death, she had no close male confidant. It was certainly not his fault to be brought into the world and he had done well in his promotions, reaching his present rank. She resolved to contact him the next day and ask him to call at the rest-house. Having made that decision, she lay down though sleep was not readily accessible.

After breakfast on Saturday morning, she telephoned Police Headquarters. She asked to speak to Chief Superintendent Bruce. The call was put through to his office.

'Chief Superintendent Bruce speaking.'

'Good morning. This is Mrs. Fleur Richter. I had the pleasure of meeting you at last night's reception for the Governor.'

'Good morning. Yes I remember you well. How can I help you?'

'Well, firstly I should say that this is not a police matter. A delicate matter describes it best. One, which I have slept on and I am coming to appreciate very much. I would rather speak to you in person about it. Are you able to come to the rest-house some time today?

'You have me intrigued! As it's Saturday, I am only on duty to check the overnight diary. Let me see...I could be with you in half an hour.'

'Then that would be about 11o'clock. I look forward to meeting you then. Good-bye.'

Fleur replaced the receiver but held on to it for a moment. She was about to confront this police officer and inform him that she was his sister. Was she doing the right thing? It would have been easier to ignore the whole situation after all. What would she be unravelling for the Chief Superintendent? What repercussions would follow back home in Scotland? Whatever was about to unfold, she could now no longer reverse her fate. She returned to her room, knelt on her knees and prayed that this encounter would be honourable.

She took two wicker chairs from her bedroom to the balcony outside. She could not entertain him in her bedroom and the compound's public room was not suitable for such a private discussion. She returned with a waist high table on which she had placed two teacups, borrowed from the communal kitchen. The table was covered with a gingham blue and white patterned cloth. She placed five custard cream biscuits which she had purchased from a peripatetic trader, on a matching plate. The sugar bowl did not match the crockery but it was at least on speaking terms and consequently did not look too much out of place. She then covered the tray with a net cloth that was weighed down at its edge by a long border of blue glass beads. The rest-house manager had provided a vase of cut flowers on being told of this impromptu meeting by Fleur.

She went to her handbag and removed pictures of her parents and sister. She placed them in the drawer of the table on the veranda. She was not sure why initially but then thought that was a good idea. If the meeting went well, she could open the drawer with ease. If he wished no contact or details, then they would remain there until his departure. This might save her fumbling in her handbag. She wandered round her room and fussed over the bedspread making sure its length from the floor was equidistant on all three sides. She sat on the corner of the bed and gazed through the window towards the entrance of the building. She breathed deeply, holding her breath for twenty seconds at a time, to steady her nerves. The adrenaline came in waves and she felt tightness in her stomach. She practised introductory remarks but failed to remember them. She rose to walk round her room once more when she became aware that a car was entering the compound. It went to the office and a hand pointed to the room Fleur was occupying. The car swung round and slowly approached.

Yes, she thought, she could not have let this meeting lapse. It would have haunted her for the rest of her life.

Fleur descended the few steps bringing her to the dusty compound. The Chief Superintendent rode in the back of the car and waited until his driver parked and then opened the door for him before disembarking. He walked forward smiling and just when Fleur felt it appropriate to offer her hand in a handshake he came to a sudden halt, saluted her, then took off his hat and shook her hand. Pleasantries were exchanged in Twi and Fleur was complimented on her language understanding. Fleur complimented the officer on his impeccable English.

Fleur showed him the way to her balcony and offered him tea or coffee.

'Morning coffee and afternoon tea for me. Very traditional I know but it helps to remind me which part of the day it is!' he laughed. 'Are you comfortable here?' he enquired.

'Oh yes, it has been very pleasant and relaxing. However on Monday I must return to the Kwahu ridge, to Abetifi.'

'Abetifi, ideal for you Europeans. It is high up in the mountains. The missionaries knew where the most pleasant climate was to be found.'

‘You know the area well?’

‘Yes. I have been there on many occasions. Obo is where the wealthy people live, Nkwatia has the White Fathers mission, Abetifi has the Basel mission house, and Mrs Richter, I imagine that is where you will be staying. Am I right?’

Fleur gave a nervous smile and poured the Chief Superintendent’s coffee.

‘Right yes. Well detected! My beautiful Abetifi. But all is not quite what it seems. You see I must explain that I am a widow of a German doctor. That is why you presumed I was perhaps Swiss or German. The fact that I am not, is why I wanted to meet you privately.’

They were sitting at right angles to each other, each with their coffees. ‘A biscuit?’

‘Thank you.’ Chief Superintendent Bruce crunched into his custard cream.

‘No, I am not German,’ Fleur continued ‘I am Scottish. My father came to Kumasi as part of the British Army when the Ashanti war took place forty years ago.’ Fleur felt a tear well up in her eye. She became much more informal.

‘Kwame, ……my father was ……..Colonel James Bruce. I am Fleur Bruce, …your sister!’

Kwame froze momentarily, taking in the magnitude of what Fleur had just said. It took him by complete surprise. His stunned response did not reflect his formal police training. He had had no idea why he had been invited over this morning to this German woman’s temporary accommodation. Now it was beginning to make sense.

He stood up, he looked Fleur in the eye. ‘Yes. It must be true. ….how…how wonderful.’ He noticed a tear fall down Fleur’s face into her dimpled cheek. He held both of her hands. ‘Fleur, let me hug you.’

Fleur did not need to reply. She held him tight, crushing herself against his tunic buttons, a brother at last. They embraced for three more minutes to abate Fleur’s sobs, allowing them both to come to terms with their inner feelings. They were oblivious to Kwame's driver and the office staff who had noticed sudden physical developments on the veranda.

Two tear-filled faces finally parted to resume their seats. They saw each other’s faces, smiled and then laughed out loud.

'I am so relieved. I had no idea how you might react. I thought you might be very angry.'

'Why angry?' asked Kwame. 'These were dangerous times. Times when trust had to be built up. Your…I mean ….our father was a very popular man in Kumasi, I was told. He did a lot to harmonise the Ashantis with the colonial administration.'

'A little too much harmonising?' ventured Fleur.

'No, not at all. I am proud to have his blood in me. He was a good man. He left money in trust to see I had a good education too. I thought about joining the colonial army but in the end, decided to police the Ashanti capital just as my father had, in his own way. Tell me, is he still alive?'

'Kwame, no. Sadly, he died earlier this year. My mother wrote to tell me.'

'I suppose, she does not know about me?'

'No. I am sure she does not, nor my sister.'

'Ah that means I have two sisters!' Kwame declared.

'Yes, my sister's name is Ada. Do you have any brothers or sisters?'

'My mother died as I think I told you last night. She had no more children. She always felt she was married to your father. …..But you must have known last night we were brother and sister, when I told you about my father.'

'Yes. It came as quite a shock for me too, but it was not the place to disclose our relationship in view of so many people present. I hope you agree. That's why I had to telephone you this morning. May I ask what family you have?'

'I am married to Abena Bruce and we have two sons and a daughter. Alice is just ten years old and the boys are twins aged fifteen years.'

'Identical twins?'

'Yes, to everyone except us!'

'One moment, Kwame.'

Fleur opened the desk drawer and brought out three photographs. 'This is my mother. This is a picture of my father, mother and sister. This is my father…. our father. If you wish, I would be very pleased to give it to you.'

'Thank you very much indeed. I will treasure this photograph. Fleur you have made me a very happy man. You must come and visit my family but let me first give them this good news. Can you come for Sunday lunch tomorrow?'

'Tomorrow? Oh dear. I have been invited to lunch with the Hall family and on Monday I must return to Abetifi. Perhaps I could visit in the afternoon. Around 4pm?'

'Certainly, that will be fine. 4pm. I will come to the Halls' residence to collect you. By then, I presume you will have told them about our news?'

'Oh, I am certain to have by then.'

Kwame waved his driver over. 'Then I must ask now to depart. I can not describe how happy this news has made me. I hope that it will be that way for your family in Scotland when they learn.'

'I am sure when I tell them about you, they will forgive my father and wish you well.'

Kwame stepped forward hugged his sister then kissed her forehead. 'Till tomorrow.'

CHAPTER FIFTEEN

Sunday lunch at the Halls was a very grand occasion. It started with pre-dinner drinks on the lawn. The scent of the frangipani in full bloom attracted the most beautiful butterflies and the red flames of the flamboyant tree, set against the milk bush hedge, was the quintessential essence of a European colonial residence of splendour. The garden city of Kumasi was a bounteous provider. The sky was light blue with no hint of a cloud. The sun was at its zenith and shade was necessarily sought. Lunch was served in the dining room, dominated by an electric ceiling fan. The wicker propellers wafted cool air over the table and its seated occupants. Mr Hall said the Selkirk Grace, delivered firmly in his Glasgow accent.

'Some hae meat, and canna eat.
And some wad eat that want it;
But we hae meat, and we can eat,
And sae the Lord be thankit. Amen.'

The meal began with boats of avocado served on saucers. Inside each concave of light green flesh, finely diced onion sprinkled with vinegar rested. A rim of salt surrounded the rind. The bland avocado came to life.

'Kumasi is so rich in fruit and vegetation. These must be local avocados,' assumed Fleur.

'Look towards the side of the garden. See that tree over by the shed? That's where they came from. Home grown, I assure you. You came in the right season,' said Mr Hall. A house servant came to remove the plates and prepare the next course.

'I am not used to such service. Let me help serve the next course.'

'Nonsense Fleur, you are our guest and, today, I am your Hostess!' joked Madge.

On to each plate Madge served a circle of hot fluffy white rice. In the centre, Joan ladled a portion of groundnut soup in which diced chicken breasts were submerged. 'Help yourself to the accoutrements on the table please.' Joan was referring to the sliced oranges, shredded coconut, hot peppers, sultanas, diced banana and pineapple.

The opportunity came early in the table conversation when Madge had casually wondered what Fleur had found to do in Kumasi yesterday.

'I met Chief Superintendent Kwame Bruce. You know, the officer I met here on Friday evening.'

'Oh yes, we know him well. He is very pro British. Not all Ashantis are. Some harp back to their dealings with the Dutch and have ambitions to go to Amsterdam rather than London. But Kwame does a good job in Kumasi and gets on very well with the colonial powers.'

'I'm glad you approve of him. As it turns out..... he's...well...here's a surprise...you will not believe it at first....but .... well.....he is my brother!'

'What! You don't mean your birth brother do you?' asked David Hall.

'Yes, exactly that. My father, Colonel James Bruce, was an officer in Kumasi during the Ashanti War at the start of this century and lived for many months in the fort in Kumasi. Now I discover he fathered the Chief Superintendent.'

'Well I never. What a scandal,' remarked David.

'David!' reprimanded Madge.

'The scandal is not Kwame's and I am not embarrassed. It did take me a little getting used to though.'

'But whatever will your mother say, when you tell her?' asked David.

'I'll be prepared by then. She may be disappointed in her husband for not being faithful, but he is dead now and we can not undo the past. Oh and, by the way, I have to tell you. He will be coming here at 4pm to take me to his home to meet his family. I trust that is agreeable to you? It was the only time available as I leave Kumasi tomorrow.'

'Of course it is Fleur,' said Madge. 'I think it is wonderful to find you have a brother in Africa. I mean, it is isn't it? After all we never question the mulattos when we see them in Accra or here. We never ask who their parents were. It's just that we know the Chief Superintendent of Police and it's all very much a surprise. Well isn't it?' flustered Madge. 'A wonderful surprise. Fleur, I really am pleased for you both.'

'I think it's terrific,' said Joan who had listened to the unfolding conversation. 'You know Dr Aggrey at Achimota

College once said that you could play a sort of a tune on all the black notes of a piano and you can play a tune on all the white notes. But if you wish a harmonious tune, you need to know all the keys and be able to play both black and white notes together. Everyone agrees. Now here we have the living example and they are friends of my parents. I think it's great news.'

'Then great news it is.' David had had the final word. His body language however conveyed his own reserved view on the matter but he knew to keep it to himself and to respect his present company.

The meal progressed satisfactorily without further reference to inter-racial breeding. All agreed that although the war was not going well for the Allies, at least Hitler had not invaded Britain. Some time was required to get our plans together. It was only hoped that time was still available.

Madge served pawpaw in lime juice to conclude the meal. She pointed out of the side window. 'The pawpaw is from that tree over there.' They spooned the orange flesh from the fruit and the lime juice brought Fleur's dimples into prominence once more.

'Have we all had sufficient to eat?' enquired David. When he was satisfied that all had finished, he concluded the meal with a second grace.

'Lord, we thank, and Thee alone,
For temporal gifts we little merit!
At present we will ask no more –
Let Madge bring in the spirit.'

'Not that we have a great choice here and with the war underway we may not be able to restock but this is a special occasion. Crème de Menthe or Drambuie perhaps?' offered Madge.

'Drambuie please,' Fleur requested, in keeping with the Scottish flavour of the gathering.

The drinks were served and a round of toasts spontaneously erupted. 'To the Royal Palm for bringing us together,' began Madge.

'To Bonnie Scotland,' perked up Joan.

Fleur took her turn. 'To my hosts for a delightful meal and good company.'

'To you all and our safe return home to Scotland after a successful conclusion to this awful war.' David's sombre note seemed to conclude the formalities but Madge had the last word. 'To Fleur and finding her brother, our friend, Kwame Bruce.'

At precisely 4pm Kwame arrived. Whether it was his Police training or his British punctuality, no one could decide, but indeed it was as the grandfather clock in the hall struck 4 o'clock that the Chief Superintendent's car arrived. Kwame was dressed in his traditional Kente cloth of gold, red, blue, green and black. He wore black traditional sandals. A gold ring adorned his finger and enhanced the gold thread of his cloth.

'Good afternoon.' He approached hesitantly unsure how the Halls might regard the information that he was sure Fleur had shared by now.

'Good afternoon, Kwame. Come to collect your sister?' cheerily greeted Madge.

Kwame was able to relax.

'I think this is quite wonderful news. In fact I think I can even see a resemblance. It's in your faces. To be more precise, it is in your dimples. That must be a Bruce trait!' Fleur smiled as if to show her dimples on demand. Kwame reciprocated unconsciously revealing his.

They took their leave vowing to meet the Halls again at either Abetifi or Kumasi. Kwame opened the car door for Fleur.

'No driver this afternoon. I am not on duty.'

As they left the Halls' driveway, Fleur anxiously turned to Kwame. 'Tell me how your family have taken the news.'

'They are delighted of course. Abena had wondered and I had too, before now, how many siblings in Scotland we had. We never thought we would find out. But now, quite by chance you and I met at the Governor's reception and you did the detective work!'

The car turned into Ofinso Road and returned to the heart of Kumasi. From there it proceeded past the Manhia Palace onto the Zongo Road, in the Dichemso district. Kwame's home was a long bungalow, set in a walled perimeter. Pawpaw and palm trees grew along one side. Hens and two goats scurried on the car's arrival. The identical twins came to greet their father. Abena stepped out of the house and came out to greet her sister-in-law. Alice stood apart shyly, from a respectable distance, examining her new aunt.

They talked for hours. Kwame drew two family trees. One of

his family tree to give to Fleur and one drawn, with Fleur's assistance, of the Bruce family in Forres. Fleur declined a meal as she had eaten so much at the Halls but, later in the evening, Alice stood beneath a pawpaw tree while her brothers climbed to the top to pick a ripe fruit. It was served in chunks moments later, draped in lime juice. She did not admit that she had eaten this refreshing plate just a few hours ago but, nevertheless, it was a plate she always enjoyed and an ideal light meal to follow her feast.

Fleur was returned to her quarters at 11pm. It had been an eventful week in Kumasi, one that she would treasure all her days. She knew Kwame shared this mutual feeling. For the first time in her life, she had a brother. It was a good feeling.

By midday the following day, Fleur had returned to Nkawkaw. She awaited transport to take her up the Kwahu ridge to Abetifi. In the market place she caught sight of a Daily Graphic newspaper headline. "Britain Bombed by German Luftwaffe." She purchased a copy.

She read that on 13th August 1940 Göering ordered his Luftwaffe to start an air offensive against Britain. Previous coastal bombing had been experienced. Now they had begun to extend towards the capital. The talk of a corridor between Folkstone and Bognor was seen to be the pathway for the great invasion before long. This was the most depressing of war news Fleur had received to date. She folded the paper, placed it in her bag and boarded the lorry heading for Abetifi.

After greeting her fellow passengers, she sat thinking of the repercussions of Germany invading Britain. The thought was unresolved in her mind. What would Otto do if he invaded Britain? He spoke English well, if with a slightly Scottish accent. Surely Hitler's generals would make use of this ability? There was no one to answer her questions. As usual, all were concentrating on the driver's ability to negotiate the Kwahu ridge.

On reaching the Ramseyer Centre, Fleur was greeted as if a long lost cousin. '*Akwaaaaba*', she heard from across the compound. It was Mercy. 'How are you? How is Kumasi? How are the people of Ashanti?'

Fleur gave the traditional responses. 'I am fine, by the grace of God, the Kumasi people are fine, they greet you.'

Fleur went to her room, unpacked and sat on her bed. Am I fine, she wondered? This had not been a normal break. This had been a seminal experience. Yet it was only one of the many concerns racking her mind. A son in the German Army, a brother who was an Ashanti Police Officer and her own precarious position as a British Foreign Office Hostess living in a Christian community. A surreal set of circumstances which life had thrust on her. At times like this Fleur sought the comfort of her black box. She opened it. Carefully, she lovingly assembled each piece of the oboe. This was her friend. It responded to her touch. It spoke through its musical notes. Some strained, some pure, some with gravitas, some with mirth. It was a living friend. It was her closest friend. She never played it when pressurised or anxious. She knew it would respond in a like manner. But when she sought reassurance and needed to revive a flagging soul, it was the elixir.

She thumbed through her music, undecided. She alighted on a tune she first sang in her primary school more than forty years ago. She made an impromptu music stand by opening the second top drawer of her chest of drawers a few inches and rested the music securely in the created gap. She dampened the reed in a thimbleful of water for a minute then secured it in the instrument, aligning it so that she peered down the finger holes. She pursed her lips, engaged the reed and began to play.

As she concentrated to ensure each note was played perfectly, she was oblivious to the visitor who now stood by her door. He made his presence known by a rich baritone voice and sang to the music. Fleur did not stop playing. Instead she nodded her approval and encouragement when she heard him sing tunefully along to *The Ash Grove:*

'Twas there, while the blackbird was cheerfully singing,
I first met that dear one, the joy of my heart!
Around us for gladness the bluebells were ringing
Ah! Then little thought I how soon we should part.'

Fleur repeated the last line, drew the tune to a perfect conclusion and welcomed Osofo Emmanuel Okine to her room.

'You play very sweetly, Fleur.'

'Thank you very much. I have not played for some time.'

'Would I be right to think you have lost your heart to someone in Kumasi?' he smiled.

Fleur paused, turned to him with the oboe held firmly and said,

'How ever could you know?' She looked perplexed. 'I told no one!'

Osofo Okine was shocked to think he had intruded in her personal affairs. 'Fleur, I apologise. I was only repeating what I have just sung with you. He hummed the preceding line then sang, "I first met that dear one, the joy of my heart, Then little thought I how soon we should part." It was only a little joke!'

'I am sorry, very sorry indeed. My emotions got the better of me, Osofo. How ridiculous of me. Please sit down and let me tell you about my brother.'

'You met your brother in Kumasi?' the bursar enquired.

'Well yes. I discovered him in Kumasi.' Fleur explained how it had come about and how confused she was at first. Osofo Okine took the news as a blessing. 'We must celebrate this evening. I will make an announcement at the evening meal. We need some good news.'

'Oh that puts me in a difficult position.'

Fleur realised she needed to share her news but she decided it was also in her interests to share her confidential mission with her trusted bursar.

'Let me share a confidence with you. You see because there is a war on, I have a responsibility to report any unfriendly attitudes against the Allies and here in Abetifi, we have a potential weakness. That is why I prefer to be seen as a heavily influenced German anthropologist and not the daughter of a British Army officer. Am I making any sense?'

'You are indeed. We appreciate your presence and I respect what you have told me. I shall not let any of your words slip from my lips. You have my word. I will make no mention of your brother. I fully understand. However, Fleur, I am delighted that you have found your brother. Let that be our secret for the duration of the war.'

'Thank you very much, Osofo. I knew I could confide in you. This has taken a weight from my shoulders. But I remind you that it is only you who know about this.'

At meal time all on the compound gathered as usual. Fleur had already met them since her return and responded to their greetings.

'Lord most wondrous and bountiful,' the pastor began the grace, 'we thank you for bringing us to sit together to enjoy the fruits of the land at the end of this day. We thank you Lord for bringing families together secure in their love for each other.' Osofo opened his eyes and met Fleur's. He winked without anyone being aware of the significance of his grace. We thank you for all God's mercy shown to each of them. Now we ask that our table is blessed and the food we eat strengthens us to uphold your kingdom here on earth. Amen.'

As Fleur left the dining hall and set off to her room, the lay preacher, Daniel Tettey, asked to accompany her. Fleur gratefully accepted his friendly offer.

'Madame Fleur, I wonder if you can help. I have a problem. Not a personal problem, a very difficult situation in fact.'

'Well I'll try if I can Daniel. Is it a family matter?'

'No, not exactly. It is the farm boys who work for Hans.'

'Really, what is the trouble?'

'Firstly, one of the boys said he was not going to work again with Hans. When his parents made some enquiries, they found that two of the other boys agreed. Now none of them are going back to work with him again.'

'Well, that is in order. If they find work when he is away in Mopti, then they should apply for it and, if they are successful, then Hans can employ new farm workers when he returns. I don't think Hans can complain about that.'

'Oh Fleur, no. It's not like that. They will not work for him again and they will advise others not to work for him either.'

'Why ever not?'

'Well, and I have no evidence of this myself, you realise, but it seems if Hans is unhappy with the workers, he sets an example.'

'You mean he is too strict?'

'More than that. The boys say he plays a game. He tells them the story of William Tell. Then he says there are no apples in the Gold Coast so he takes a tin can and places it on the head of the worker who has offended him, for whatever reason. Now we all know he is a good shot with his pistol, but the margin of error is very slight. The boys tell me he always hits the can but it is frightening. The can always falls from the head of the boy but they fear that on the day in question, which was very wet and windy, he may have been giving this treatment to unfortunate Kwasi Amissah.'

'Daniel, are you sure of this? Are you sure the boys are telling the truth?'

'Yes, honestly. I believe them.'

'But this is a serious allegation.'

'Yes. The boys think Kwasi tore the sheet by accident in the storm when he was trying to secure it. If they had done this, they would surely have been given the William Tell treatment too, even if it was an accident. So in the wind and rain Kwasi was probably asked to stand up and place a tin on his head. How else would the bullet have hit Kwasi between the eyes?'

Fleur's prejudiced view of Hans was proving to be a concern. 'What do you think I should do?'

'Well I think we should at least tell the police.'

'You are right, these are serious allegations. We must act before he returns.'

Fleur wrote to Sir Ronald that night and sought his advice. She also revealed Daniel's allegations to both Reverend Emmanuel Okine as the bursar in charge of the Ramseyer Centre and Reverend Jurg Fendler as the senior Basel missionary. They made a report and took it to the Abetifi Police Inspector the following day.

Meanwhile the Germans were offering Pétain peace on the conditions that:

(1) Alsace-Lorraine was restored to Germany;

(2) Alpes Maritimes department was given to Italy;

(3) Germany was allowed to remain in possession of the Channel ports and a corridor down to Spain for the duration of the hostilities;

(4) half Tunis and Algeria was ceded to Italy;

(5) Morocco was given to Spain;

(6) the French colonies in Africa were administered by a joint German-Italian and French Commission;

(7) All French bases and aerodromes in Africa and the Mediterranean were placed at the disposal of Germany and Italy;

(8) France was to 'safeguard' the flank of Italy's attack on Egypt, Syria and Algeria; and

(9) The French Fleet in the Mediterranean was placed at their disposal. If the French did accept these terms, then their prisoners would be released and they would be given food. Pétain assented to Hitler's offer adding that 'the Axis Powers and France have an identical interest in seeing the defeat of England accomplished as

soon as possible.'

In defiance, in late August, a small Free French expedition rallied the French Central African territories of Chad, the French Congo and the Cameroons to de Gaulle's cause. It was a desperate attempt to save Free French faces. But 'Operation Menace' devised by Churchill and de Gaulle, targeting the strategically significant port of Dakar in Senegal, had been sabotaged.

In Dakar, Hans Winkler had a workforce of more than a hundred Senegalese men. Some were carpenters, others were painters. Some had more expertise in electronics and chemistry but all had sworn their allegiance to Vichy France and all wished no destruction to come to their beloved city. They were engaged in a massive deception. They set up a fake harbour in a bay slightly to the north of Dakar with dummy buildings, lighthouses and even anti-aircraft batteries that flashed. Fake tanks were positioned further up the coastline and to support the fake scenario, a false railway line was constructed and loudspeakers created a hub of activity, which was otherwise non-existent. Hans Winkler supervised the creation of this stage, on the instruction and in the payment of the Vichy French government. They needed to stop de Gaulle claiming that part of Africa to the Allies.

Dakar was of immense strategic importance. Situated on the westernmost point of West Africa, it was clearly the eastern end of the shortest trans-Atlantic route. It had an established airfield and one of the most developed ports in Africa, not to mention a large naval base. This was of course strongly fortified and of great importance, in holding the West Atlantic sea-routes. Conversely, in Hitler's hands, it would be the ideal base from which to attack the significant sea communications between Britain and South Africa's Cape. Dakar was also a rallying point for the sparsely settled and populated West African French colonies. Churchill and General de Gaulle sanctioned the occupation of Dakar known as Operation Menace.

The optimistic belief that the population of Dakar would welcome de Gaulle proved ill founded and real shore batteries from the southern bank opened fire on the Allied fleet hitting HMS Cumberland and Foresight. On 24th September 1940 HMAS Australia was engaged in a general fleet bombardment of French ships and forts and was twice subjected to high level bombing attacks by Vichy French planes. Many of Australia's salvos landed on Winkler's toy town. On 25th September HMAS ships the Australia and Devonshire moved in towards Dakar to attack French cruisers. During the engagement that followed, Australia received two hits aft and her 'Walrus' spotting aircraft was shot down. Fifteen minutes later after engaging the French ships, the British cruisers withdrew. What was certain was that Dakar had been prepared for 'Operation Menace.'Hans Winkler's activities had contributed greatly to an Axis victory and de Gaulle's Allied defeat.

Fleur resumed her classes in Nkwatia each day making the customary post office box visit on her way home. For days there was no communication. She concentrated on the past tense by telling Kofi Frempong about her life in Germany and in the more recent past, her adventures the previous week in Kumasi, though not divulging her relationship with Kwame. These Twi classes were providing her with an opportunity to review her eventful life. One afternoon as she was riding back to Abetifi, she stopped to eat a banana at her favourite haunt.

She peeled each side of the fruit to reveal the soft cream texture. How like her own life she thought. Stripped of the protection of family, roots, belief! She thought of the people she was staying with. They had purpose in life, belief in what they did and faith in their lives. Was she different? She had not the Christian calling which they had but that made her no less acceptable in their midst. Would she be a better person if she had their faith? How was it acquired? She took a bite. The coolness and the sweetness of the banana filled her mouth. Religion had not featured much in her life. There was no doubt it would be in the front of the minds of those in war-time danger, in battle distress, but in her daily life, she had her doubts. She looked up and saw the beauty of the sweet-smelling jungle all around her. Was this created with or without a God?

With these thoughts occupying her mind, she noticed Osofo Okine approach.

'Good afternoon, Fleur. You are returning from class?'

'Good afternoon, Osofo,' giving Osofo Okine his native title as a man of the cloth.

'Yes a moment's rest to think about life.'

'Just what I am doing.'

'Really? Then tell me your thoughts if you can, Ososfo.'

' Well, what I see as my commitment, is the will-to-love over rational thought based on raw will-to-live. As a thinking being, I must regard all life, other than my own, with equal reverence, because I know it longs for fullness and depth of development as I do myself. All of us are endowed with a potential fullness of being which we are intended to actualize. So we have the farmer, the teacher, the mother, the pastor, the trader and so on. Each of them is playing their part in the scheme of things. This potentiality is 'given' to us in mysterious ways we can not fully understand. But as I see it, this 'essential nature of the will-to-live' can not be complete without a decision on our part, to be faithful to our destiny. So, I see why God so loved the world that He gave His son to us.'

'So the will-to-love drives your life?' Fleur clarified.

'Yes'. ...Osofo laughed loudly. 'Simple, really isn't it? But it is the thing missing from so many lives. That's why we have war again. People do not trust each other. They do not love. St Matthew chapter 5 verse 44: Love your enemies. Now there's a challenge!'

'Beautiful words, Osofo. But tell me. You are a Kwahu man. This white man's religion is only a hundred years old in your culture. How can you so quickly reject the old and take on the new?'

'My dear, Fleur. I do not reject the old. We knew God before the white man came. Traditional religions neither send missionaries nor make proselytes. Instead their strength lies in being fully integrated in all aspects of our human life. So you see, they will never be washed away. Africans do not know God as a man. They see him as Father, Mother, as a Friend and God of the forest, the woods, the bushes and groves, sacred trees, the rivers, the earth and earthquakes and the continuation of God after death. What we have now in addition, is the love of God, through his son, our Lord, Jesus Christ.'

'I admire your faith, Osofo. It seems to me some of us have it and some do not. Some are more able than others to acquire it and some just don't want to know about it. They see religion as divisive, war mongering. Can you blame them?'

'God loves us, he does not control us, Fleur. I have to earn God's respect. You know, that it is easier for a camel to go through the eye of a needle, than for a rich man to enter the kingdom of God? I tell you, it is not easy being a pastor, but remember one thing, Fleur, have we not one father? Has not one God created us?'

Fleur smiled and nodded. She had heard much to consider. She arose and threw the banana skin into the bush behind her. 'Well I suppose I had better carry on along the road to Damascus or is it just Abetifi?'

'I'll start heading back too. Just remember, Fleur, many waters cannot quench love, neither can the floods drown it.'

CHAPTER SIXTEEN

Kofi Frempong arrived at class with a large stamp album the next day. At lunchtime he showed it to Fleur. He had been collecting foreign stamps for a number of years.

'I've not got stamps for every country yet, but perhaps if I keep this album till I am very old, I may have stamps on every page. Do you want to look at it?'

Fleur opened the Ace Crusader stamp album carefully. On the first page was a map of both Africa and Europe. 'Show me your home town please.'

She hesitated for a moment seeing both Scotland and Germany in close proximity. She focused on Hamburg and Forres for a fleeting moment, before pointing to the straight coastline running from Fraserburgh to Inverness. She found it strange to identify her Scottish home not having lived there since 1912.

Kofi asked her to point out which countries were at war with each other. It was a sobering picture she portrayed. 'Britain is surrounded by enemies. Do you think you will beat Germany?'

'Probably not on our own. We were caught unready at first, but if Russia and America join us, then Germany will retreat eventually. Let's hope so anyway.'

The next page was a double page of the world. Dakar was so prominent on the route from Europe to South Africa and sailing due west from the port, would take a ship into the Caribbean islands. Surrounding Nigeria and the Gold Coast was the large area of French West Africa. It was not significant in terms of population, nor rich in vegetation or products, but significantly it was Vichy territory. Only French Equatorial Africa remained loyal to de Gaulle and the Allies. She turned the pages. There were no stamps for Abyssinia, Afghanistan, Aden, Albania or Andorra, but Antigua had a two penny stamp of Nelson's Dockyard.

Argentina had two 5 centavos stamps, with General Jose De San Martin's pose on both. There were several Australian stamps that Kofi had purchased in the market at Obo last year. That had been the source of his Bermuda stamp too. A few Belgian stamps and even one Brazilian stamp followed. Fleur showed her interest in each page and commented on the colour, the cost and the detail and condition of each stamp. Canada had a grand selection of recent stamps. But there were empty pages headed China, Cuba,

Crete, and Cyprus. Denmark had two 15 krone red stamps, showing a Viking ship at full sail. Inevitably Fleur explained about the times when the Vikings dominated the North Sea and the waters around Britain. She explained Viking settlements had been discovered in Scotland and that in Shetland, many Viking traditions were still celebrated.

Egypt and Finland were empty pages but France had a full page of stamps. 'Obo stamp market?'

'No,' replied Kofi. 'Passing Moslem traders often have French stamps and for a few coins, I get so many. They are very good to me.'

Gambia had one stamp, Gibraltar had none, but the Gold Coast, whose first issue was in 1875, had a very full page and an envelope containing even more. She peered into the brown envelope and inserted her index finger to gently separate and view the additional stamps.

After a moment she realised that she had missed a page. The previous page was full too but Fleur noticed it was no longer the Gold Coast, it was Germany! She looked more closely at these stamps. Some were old, but some were very recent and some bore the swastika and portrait of Hitler. This page was full except for three white squares.

'Obo market?' she asked.

'No, I get them from Gisela.'

Fleur though for a moment. The Swiss border was very near Germany but the Swiss had their own stamps. Why so many stamps from Germany, she wondered? 'Does Gisela bring them often?'

'Not as many since the war began. She used to give me her Swiss ones and the German ones too. You know, letters from her family but I don't think it is so easy for her to get letters now.'

'Do you think she has relatives in Germany?'

'Yes, I know she does.'

Fleur digested this information. Gisela was the fair complexioned wife of Reverend Andreas Schmidt from Brugg in Switzerland. She remembered Gisela being introduced to her and that she came from a town thirty miles away. That surely implied she was Swiss. She knew she had noted everyone's names and where they came from and kept them in her diary. She took the diary from her bag.

'Do you keep all your secrets in your diary like me, Fleur?' asked Kofi.

'Not secrets, it's my way of remembering who is who. When you get to my age, memory begins to fade. Mark my words. Now S let me see...Schmidt ...Gisela from Schopfheim. Now what I need is a good atlas.'

'I know,' said Kofi. 'Let's go over to the school and ask for an atlas with a good European map. They will have one in the geography department.'

'A good idea. I suppose they will not mind.'

They crossed the school compound and entered the main entrance of St Peter's Secondary School. Fleur asked the school secretary if she could borrow an atlas and a school pupil was summonsed. He was told to bring an atlas to the school office promptly.

The large atlas arrived and was laid on the office table by the window. Fleur turned to Switzerland. Brugg lay east-south-east of Basel. With Brugg as the centre she described a 30 mile arc round the town. Schopfheim was not marked. Then suddenly Kofi declared. 'Look there it is! Thirty miles north west of Brugg, in Germany, in the Black Forest!'

Sure enough, on the river Weise in the Schwarzwald, lay Schopfheim. So Gisela was after all the second German in the mission station. She knew she would have to report this to Sir Ronald, but there was something serene, something wholesome about Gisela, that made Fleur doubt she could be of any harm in the war. She helped her husband prepare prayer groups for the outlying farming congregations in Kwahu. They were popular meetings and the Africans spoke well of the Schmidts. Fleur had spoken frequently to Gisela and she was fond of her. They spoke in German but that had not raised any doubts about her apparent Swiss nationality. But why had she not been told Gisela was from Germany? Neither Sir Ronald nor anyone on the compound had mentioned the fact. It had never been mentioned even when the war was being discussed. Why the implication that she was Swiss? Was this to allay suspicion or was it deliberate to engage more freely in enemy preparations? Fleur decided to do nothing until she had heard from Sir Ronald.

The next few days let a melange of thoughts occupy her mind. Osofo Okine's words had left their impressions on Fleur. It was so simple in a way. The will-to-love was a powerful concept. But to place this before the will-to-live, seemed an uncalled for challenge in itself. There was Fleur, independent, with a purpose in life, a will to see it through, to all intents a will-to-live in action. But a will-to-love, how could she love when she was reporting Gisela? Could this mean deportation? Separation if her husband stayed? What sort of love was that?

Her Twi was progressing at such a pace she wondered what use she could make of it once the war was over. If her course came to a conclusion she would have no reason to remain in Abetifi. Had Sir Ronald thought this through? She then heard from him by letter. Sir Ronald was pleased with her ability to find out Gisela was German. Operation Oboe was producing a clear note, he reported. He was particularly anxious that Hans Winkler was arrested on his return, on suspicion of murder, but the main thrust of her work was to continue to observe any anti-British activity. He was not taking any steps over Gisela but had reported her to the police as a German national, not declared by the Basel Mission. As she was the wife of a Basel missionary, she would have been regarded as a nominal Swiss citizen but in war time, this convenience could not be overlooked. Meanwhile the colonial government asked the Basel Mission to ensure no other German employee was in the country. Furthermore any anti Allied action by any Basel mission staff member, whether Swiss or otherwise, must be reported instantly. All movements of Basel missionaries around the country must be logged and made available to the colonial office on request.

The following afternoon, after Fleur had enjoyed an hour's siesta, Gisela came to her room. She gave the traditional announcement of her arrival. '*Agooo*'.

Fleur responded '*Ameeee.*'

'I was wondering if we could talk for a while, Fleur.'

'Let's take these two chairs onto the balcony outside. It is so peaceful and shaded at this part of the day round here.'

They settled into their cushioned chairs, aware of an important if not official and possibly argumentative atmosphere stirring. 'Fleur, it is so hard to think of war in this beautiful part of the world at times. At least we are sheltered from the horror, the deaths, the anger, the suffering of so many. Kofi came to see me yesterday and asked if I had any more stamps to give him. I told him that the war had made this difficult. He said he understood about the German stamps, but thought Swiss stamps might arrive. We discussed his stamp collecting a little longer and I discovered you were interested in why I had German stamps. I thought I'd come to tell you.'

Fleur felt a little embarrassed and a little disappointed that Kofi had let slip to Gisela her apparent interest in his stamp collection.

'You may find this difficult to accept, but I am actually German by birth. Of course, Swiss by marriage but I can not deny German by birth and of course I have family in Germany.'

'That really is quite strange, Gisela. The position that you find yourself in now, was the position I found myself during the last World War. British, married to a German in Germany in the First World War. The tables are turned.'

'Yes indeed. But there is a difference in these two wars. Great Empires were at stake in the first war. Civilisation is at stake in this one. Fleur, Hitler is evil. The Churches are silenced. I for one am privileged to be out of Germany. I am pleased to be married to a Swiss national. But you are right, I do have family in Germany. As you do, too, I believe Fleur. My mother and sister live in Wentorf just outside Hamburg.'

'Wentorf!' repeated Fleur. 'Oh yes, I know Wentorf too.'

'Yes. Near where you lived for so many years. I also have a brother. He is in the army.'

'And I have a son, Otto, in the army too,' Fleur said sadly.

'I think we can be of help to each other, Fleur. I could try and make contact with your son. While ....you could.....well.....ensure that I stay here in the Gold Coast. Does that make sense to you?'

'Gisela, I have no concerns about you, but what you are saying, if I have understood you correctly, is you can get information to me from Germany perhaps and if you do, I must keep that secret?'

'Exactly. If I get you news from your son, you promise that you do not give me away?'

Fleur realised she was being compromised but the need to hear from Otto and how this communication was achieved, was compelling and made her decision for her. 'Agreed'.

'Then let's shake hands on this,' said Gisela and they did.

Fleur gave Gisela, Karl and Renate's address in Hamburg. Although she was not going to inform Sir Ronald about this arrangement, she knew she was living two lives all of a sudden.

Yet she felt quietly confident, that Gisela was not a risk. It was nevertheless desirable to keep a note of Gisela's movements.

'Let's attend the durbar tomorrow in town. I saw the ground being prepared with seating and shelter this morning. Long palms were being woven together. It will be enjoyable. Shall we go to it together?' asked Fleur.

'Why not. We could do with some music and dancing. 2pm tomorrow? Another deal!'

With that agreement concluded, Gisela took her leave. Fleur stood forward leaning over the balcony rail. Life was throwing challenges at her. She thought of an appropriate Twi proverb: *It is not mountains, but the small stumps on the way of life that cause our downfall.*

Around 12 noon the next day, drumming could be heard from the town. After a light lunch, Fleur dressed in a traditional dress and called on Gisela. She was similarly clad in a tight two piece long skirt and blouse with a broad headband, made of the same azure material, completing the outfit. Fleur had no headband but instead additional cloth that she could use either as a shawl or a waistband. She wore it as a waistband and secured her purse in its folds as the local women did. They walked down from the compound to the town together, along the main street which was packed with townsfolk wearing traditional clothes and happy children making their way to the durbar.

They entered the ground and were shown to seats under the palm woven open canopy. The chief sat on his podium with a fly-whisk doubling as a hand fan. The sky was cloudless. Traders supplied the audience with trays of oranges, already quartered and nicked for easy peeling and consumption. Trays of roasted groundnuts and bananas were on hand and a large urn was mounted on a table, supplying cool water.

The durbar began with a procession of represented associations, circulating the ground and bowing before the chief. There were groupings of six or ten people representing singing bands, tailors' associations, seamstresses, palm oil producers, car mechanics, and other service providers. Then came representatives of different tribes paying respect to their host chief. From the east the Ewe representatives, the Fantis from the coast and Ashantis from Kumasi and Brong Ahafo further north. From the Northern territories there were representatives from Navrongo, Paga and

Bolgatanga and, in their flowing white and blue gowns, the Fulanis from beyond the northern territories, north of the Gold Coast. Every grouping in Abetifi and its surrounding areas was represented, resplendent in their finest attire.

When all were seated, a traditional priest in his white robes and hat stepped forward and bared his chest. He summonsed up the spirits and dribbled a bottle of schnapps in libation as he invoked the spirits to bless this occasion and honour the chief.

The chief was a well-educated African and chose not to speak through his interpreter. He also had a marvellously rich deep bass voice that hardly needed the artificial amplification that was supplied.

'Abetifi People! I welcome you to this annual durbar. It affords me no little pleasure, in having this opportunity to welcome you here on this grand July day.

The country, as my people are aware, is passing through a most difficult period in her history. Before I come to that, I should like to take this opportunity to express the appreciation of all chiefs to the Colonial Administration. For they uphold the Chieftaincy Act, thus ensuring the chiefs of the Gold Coast work with their people, to do their very best to support Britain in its hour of need. Soldiers in our midst are already in an advanced training programme preparing to serve overseas with the Allied Forces. The Kwahu district is proud to have so many fine men undertaking this intensive training. Furthermore the 1925 Native Administration Ordinance has given us the organs to modernise our country by training us in the skills required to build and serve our communities. Even since last year's durbar, Abetifi has seen the completion of the main drainage system in our streets and we have been provided with two more generators for additional electricity. Our water supply has been expanded and a new post office has been approved. Building on the present post office site, will commence in the New Year. Governor Sir Ronald Murray, we salute you for all you do for us in Kwahu.

However, and I make no apologies for saying this, it goes without saying that it is in our best interests to ensure an Allied victory, so that we can proceed as a responsible democracy to have greater say in our political life. In stating this we remember how the women in Britain worked during the First World War and gained their voting rights. Why not then, if we work hard, produce the gold and timber the Allies need and provide brave fighting men, can we not too gain in the resultant victory and peace?'

This call was met with wild excitement and the police on duty rose to quell the noise. Fleur looked around as batons were wielded but wondered if this sudden show of martial order was not just for the benefit of herself and Gisela who were the only Europeans in attendance.

'Chiefs have already, in diverse ways, indicated what they can do. Now with the present advancement in education, when many chiefs can now stand shoulder to shoulder with the best-trained minds in our nation, there is no limit to the contribution they can make towards the national welfare, if given the chance.

Change there must be in the lives of people and nations alike, but change must follow the progress of civilisation. To do this, we are of the opinion that no community can afford to jettison all the age-old and time-tested values that have sustained that community in the past. We, therefore, believe that those values enshrined in Chieftaincy, which have in past centuries made it possible for our people to develop, must be respected.

In return we respect and work together with the Basel Mission in our community and the British Colonial Government. Together we will make our people prosperous, in mind, in spirit and in wealth. It is that success which we acknowledge today in our proceedings. So I once again welcome you. Thank you for attending in such great numbers this afternoon and I now declare the 1940 Abetifi Durbar underway.'

On that announcement suddenly a number of boys ran forward and launched themselves into a series of tumbles, accompanied by rhythmic drumming. They created a pyramid with the smallest boy running towards it, climbing on many bent knees and shoulders, taking him to the top, where amid great applause, he stood erect with his hands raised. His descent was equally stupendous. The pyramid collapsed like a pack of cards, yet each descending gymnast took responsibility for the small boy who was passed from one arm to another so that he landed as deftly as a butterfly on a leaf. Then a brass band of sorts appeared bringing a set of eight dancers to the fore. The music was traditional with a euphonium providing the melody. Groupings of drummers joined in and the noise enveloped the arena. One set of dancers gave way to another and then another. Despite the number of groups dancing, each told its own story. The delicate flapping of the arms denoted birds flying, while clasped hands in a stirring motion portrayed cooking activities. To each dance, the chief's linguist narrated a story. He used the loudspeaker cone to its full advantage.

The gathering was not always seated during the events of the durbar as people passed by on their way to greet others, seek refreshments or head for the latrines. Gisela and Fleur found themselves greeted by local friends. Wives would always shake their hands, while men acknowledged them by nodding and vocally greeting them. Fleur always replied in the local Twi language using her growing proverbial Twi to good effect. *'Much of our troubles today stem from our deviation from traditional ways of life.'*

This was met with enthusiastic agreement. Then when her efforts at using such profound Twi were acknowledged she remarked '*bad dancing will not harm the ground.'* This time her efforts were applauded causing a stir around the durbar.

Fleur noticed a handsome tall man in a long blue gown approach. 'Madame Gisela, Good day.' He turned to Fleur. 'Good day, Madame.'

Fleur smiled, 'Good day.' This was not a local Kwahu man. He was a northerner, but Fleur had no idea where he was from.

Gisela obviously knew this man and spoke to him with fondness. 'You are wearing your finest robes today, Babatu.'

'Oh no, Madame, I have even finer robes with more silver stitching around the neck and cuffs. I keep them for very special occasions.'

'I have not seen you for a few weeks. Have you been travelling?'

'Oh yes, I have travelled. I have been home twice since I saw you but I will be returning in two days. So if you have any letters please have them ready.'

Gisela knew that Fleur was taking note of what was being said and made little attempt to disguise her business dealings with Babatu.

'Fleur, if you have any letters to send home to your son, please have them ready by tomorrow evening.'

Babatu saw a trade opportunity. 'Madame Gisela, your friend wishes to use my service too?'

‘Yes Babatu but remember this is our secret. We should not be discussing this here. Not so?’

‘Oh very sorry, Madame, please forgive me, I beg you.’ Babatu made a slight bowing motion avoiding further commotion.

‘Then I see you on Monday afternoon Madame Gisela?’

‘Yes, I’ll be there around 2pm.’

‘Then I ask permission to depart. Enjoy the durbar ladies.’ Babatu bowed once more and in a sweeping movement of his robes, he was lost in the crowd.

‘So he’s your contact, Gisela?’

‘Yes. Always Babatu. I’ve known him for a number of years. He has been trading in Kwahu for more than ten years.’

‘But how does he get letters to Germany?’

‘He is a northerner from Bawku but he regularly trades with the nomadic people of the Sahara, the Peuls. He crosses the northern border of the Gold Coast and goes to Mopti, via Ouahigouyou. That is where the Vichy French collect mail to take firstly to Bamako. From there it flies to Paris and beyond. All German post is sent that way. Babatu has a post box in Mopti. I will give you the number when we get back. Always use it on your correspondence both inside and outside the envelope. Never mark it Gold Coast.’

This was really compromising Fleur. She was about to engage in communicating with Germany. This could mean serious trouble if this was discovered. How would this fit with Operation Oboe? Was it treason? She looked at Gisela. What information was she sending to Germany? She asked her.

‘Oh, I have nothing to report other than our health, what we are doing and how the war is affecting us but it is the communication from home that is special. I will show you my letters. You will see it is only family correspondence.’

‘How long will it take to get to Germany and how long is it before you get a reply?’

‘It really depends on so many factors. Firstly, Babatu has apologised once or twice as he has taken my letters on the day I thought he was going north but decided to go to Accra first! So he is not always reliable in that way.’

‘What! What if he lost the letters in Accra? That would be serious for us.’

‘Yes, of course, but I assure you he is thorough. In fact I have a way to ensure it is in his best interests the letters are delivered.'

'How?'

'Quite simple really. I pay him for replies received, not for sending the letters.'

That evening, Fleur started to write with a passion and purpose that she had not experienced often before. She began with a letter to Otto c/o Karl and Renate. She intended to write to Renate as well but the generator cut off as usual at 9pm. By then, Otto had been fully appraised of his mother's life since sailing from the Broomilaw. The murder on board, the friends she had met, the language course she was enjoying, and after some thought, the revelation of her brother, Kwame, in Kumasi. Nevertheless her letter made no mention of the specific duties she had been given, under her position as Hostess to the Governor. To reveal any more would have breached the trust of her employer. It would have meant information to an enemy too. That was the incongruous aspect of her letter to her son. Anyway, as long as she had enough substance to make a letter of some interest, her purpose was to encourage replies on this first attempt at correspondence. The letter to Otto, like a carefully selected fly being cast on the turbulent waters of war-ravaged Europe, was sent more in hope than expectation of arrival. Yet it was such an important possibility. She lay it by her bedside unsealed. She released the mosquito net curtain around her four poster bed, tucked in the corners, leaving a gap for her to enter, then opened the window for fresh air to aid her sleep. She climbed back into bed and placed her head on the pillow. Sleep would not come to her easily. Realisation that she could make contact with her family in Germany gave her an excitable energy inappropriate for this time of night. It was nevertheless an energy she thought had been lost long ago, to decades gone by. Feelings of hope mingled with feelings of fear clouded her thoughts and tightened her throat. The excitement cramped her stomach. She knew she would wake at first light and complete her letter writing. Sleep, she hoped, would provide an orderly chain of thoughts for her letter in the morning. Then concentration would enable her to check the contents of the letter for security, meaningful communication and love, for above all it was love, which Fleur wished to impart to her son and his carers.

Fleur wakened the next day with the sun casting a column of

bright light across her bedroom. It lit her table and the door. She sat up briskly. Otto's letter was gone. She pulled up the mosquito netting and crossed to the table. The letter was not where she left it opened last night. A panic set in. She stood in the centre of the room and turned 360 degrees. No letter! She crossed to the door and turned the handle. It was still locked. Adrenaline rushed through her body. Was she alone?

By now she was fully awake and mystified as to what could have happened. She rolled up the mosquito net on each side and stripped her bed. Still no letter could be found. Then she bent down to look under the bed. She startled. A gecko met her eyes head on. Its dull colour was almost camouflaged by the dark brown floor panels in shade. In contrast to this was Otto's letter a few inches away. The relief was almost audible. The stress released itself like a balloon to the sky. How silly she felt. The breeze had dislodged the letter from the table during the night and it had been blown under her bed. It showed Fleur nevertheless that what she was doing had serious consequences if it went wrong. Yet the prize was too tempting: contact with her son and relatives in Germany during the war.

She opened her door, let day come in and the skittering gecko went out. After breakfast of porridge, tea and pawpaw she returned to complete her second letter. Her sister-in-law's letter covered much of what she had written to her son. It lacked no less warmth as they had enjoyed years of sisterly friendship. Had she really made the right decision to leave Germany? Should she not have stayed to see the war through with her son, with Karl and Renate's support? Both letters concluded with the wish for a conclusion of the war quickly, but Fleur knew that the Allies were not making sufficient inroads into the machinery of the Axis powers.

On 14th October 1940, German bombers were sent low over London, in groups of threes. The East Enders wondered if the country's defences had run out of shells. One bomb dropped in St. James's Park. Another left Leicester Square in ruins.

On 5th November, Churchill made a statement to Parliament. He was grim. He brought home to the House, as never before, the gravity of the shipping losses and the danger of the Allied position in the Eastern Mediterranean. It had a good effect. By putting the grim side foremost, he impressed the House with his ability to face the worst.

The worst was what Fleur knew of the Allied cause, for no positive news on any front had filtered through. De Gaulle's defeat at Dakar was as close as the war had come in West Africa. Meanwhile her skies were bright blue, cloudless and hot. She wondered if the Allies were to lose the war, whether the Gold Coast would simply revert to a German master once again. A master who, unlike the Portuguese, the Dutch, and the British, had not governed these parts, but whose only influence had been the Basel and Bremen missions. There was no sign of ambivalence in the colony. The Gold Coast was putting its resources both material and manpower at the disposal of the British cause.

Gisela approached Fleur's room. 'Good morning. How are you today?'

'Well, after a good night's sleep. And you?'

'I can't say I slept as well as I might. I suppose it was thinking through what I had told you. After all, you are British, well I mean Scottish. Yet you are as keen to use my contact with Germany as I am. Life seems so much easier for my husband who is Swiss and your brother who is a Gold Coast native. Isn't it strange? Anyway I have brought you the return address in Mopti. Are your letters ready?'

'Yes, here they are. ......So you have heard I have a brother in the Gold Coast?'

'Yes Fleur, I thought it was common knowledge. I think that is wonderful news. You must be wondering who told me?'

'It would be of interest.'

'It was a market trader in Abetifi, you know the one who sells paraffin by the crossroads. She had been in Kumasi last week and she heard about it there. She told me. She said he was the Chief Superintendent of Police. Is that not so?'

Fleur felt she had to let go most of her cover now and hope it was a case of damage limitation.

'Yes. It's true. I have a brother at last. I am really very proud of him, Gisela.' There was no need to reveal any more about the circumstances. There was a job in hand. Fleur gathered the two letters and took them from her dressing table. She added a brief postscript to each letter with the return address for them to post their replies.

'BP 169 Mopti, Mali, Afrique de l'Ouest. Shall I put this on the back of the outside of the letters too?'

'Yes, then if you have written them both, seal them.'

Gisela added hers to Fleur's letters. 'Keep them till this afternoon and we will give them to Babatu.'

'Will he come to collect them?'

'No, I do not let him visit the Ramseyer Centre. He knows I live here, but we meet him in the town where he stays with a fellow northerner.'

That afternoon Gisela took Fleur to Babatu's quarters in Abetifi. It was a modest home where his brother had lived for a number of years. Babatu had a room when he visited and that was where he was found.

'Come in, ladies. You are most welcome. How are you both?' He brought some tea for them and poured the fresh brew into saucerless cups.

'I will go north at 7pm this evening,' he announced.

'Is that when you usually set off?' asked Fleur.

'I will wash at 4pm and eat at 5pm. At dusk I will join my brothers in our salat prayers. Then I will be ready to travel.'

Fleur remembered his Moslem custom was responsible for his timing. They produced their letters. He took them carefully and placed them in a leather pouch that he hung up on a hook on his door.

'You won't forget them when you travel?' teased Fleur.

'If I do not have my leather bag, I do not travel. It contains my money!' he laughed.

'We will not take more of your time. Travel safely,' said Gisela. They took their leave and began to head back up the hill to the Centre.

'Gisela tell me, how did you come across Babatu again?'

'It began when Andreas thought he would try to engage the Moslem community in understanding them and letting them understand the Basel Mission more. So he went to meet them, to show how he respected them and their religion and to share what the Basel Mission was trying to do in Kwahu.'

'How interesting. How did they get on?'

Gisela explained how Andreas had no intention of bringing any Moslem into Christ's fold. Rather it was conducted on a personal basis. The apparent impregnability of fortress Islam had channelled his interest into two main directions. First, it had provoked a profound and scholarly examination of the Moslem religion, culture and history by Europeans of wide sympathy. Gisela remembered the piles of books on Moslem custom and religion that had filled the house a few years ago and the notes which her husband had taken at the time. She remembered asking where all this knowledge was taking him and he told her that he could not minister to the agricultural and rural community without knowing and understanding his Moslem brothers. His vocation at that time, was to interpret the two worlds of Christianity and Islam to one another and to create the atmosphere in which tolerance, understanding, goodwill and mutual concern could replace that of fear, mistrust and violence which had characterised the past.

It was Andreas' understanding that his mission was to reveal Islam from within, as a belief system worthy of concern by Christians and held by peoples who were our equal in the sight of God. They were in as much need of salvation as Christians. They demanded a more worthy destiny than to be played off against one another in the game of world power politics, a game in which the Middle East had been embroiled by the West in the past and was most likely to be once again.

The clerics at the compound agreed with Andreas. It was also their mission to Islam to convince the Moslem community in Kwahu that the claims of Christ and the power of his salvation have nothing to do with any thought of subjugation by the west, but are absolute, priceless and unique in themselves. It was hoped this would lead to persuading the Moslem brothers to examine the Christian claims from Christian sources – above all to read the Christian scriptures and to realise that they were not corrupt. And that was what led Babatu to the Ramseyer Centre where he met to discuss the two religions and study in the library.

'He was a most diligent student. He eagerly asked questions that Andreas thought worthy of divinity students back home. He also had a real and deep understanding of his own religion, which he faithfully followed and a real interest in the Christian beliefs he was discovering.'

'So he used to visit the Ramseyer Centre?'

'Oh yes, he was a very regular visitor, when he was in Abetifi. He no longer comes as the classes and inter-faith studies are no longer taking place. Suspicion might lead others to ask why we have an interest in his activities. So he agreed we should not meet at the Centre.'

Gisela continued with her account of the work Andreas had undertaken. 'Then his second task was to show how the missions had attempted to bring the Gospel to the Moslems through works of charity. Christian love could always be shown in the midst of a Moslem community, even when direct preaching was not possible. That was why so much of the Christian effort was concentrated in providing schools and hospitals. So the scholar, the doctor, the nurse and the school teacher were showing their Christian love by their deeds. Babatu was impressed that he and his brothers could always go to the clinic in Abetifi or the church hospital at Agogo. There they saw evidence of Christian faith, where Moslems and Christians were equal and they had access to the same health services. So Babatu and Andreas met regularly and got to know each other very well.'

'Did Andreas visit the mosques?'

'There was one in Nkawkaw that he visited. So that led to getting to know Babatu better and we learned of his travels and his trading activities. When the war began, we realised he was able to travel freely into French West Africa and he agreed to take our post. It was really as simple as that.'

'Does he realise he is communicating between you, the enemy and the Gold Coast?'

'I have no doubt about that, Fleur. But that is of little consequence to him. It is very much a white man's war for Babatu. He is happy to get some business out of the deal.'

'I see. Does anyone else use this service?'

'Just the three of us now.'

'Three?'

'Yes me, you and Hans.'

Fleur smiled but behind her acceptance was a worry. She had hoped to keep her friendship with Gisela, untainted. Hans muddied the waters.

CHAPTER SEVENTEEN

Four days later a police van drove into the compound shortly after 8.30am. Two officers spent the day taking statements from all the staff of the centre. They visited Hans' room and took away a bag that seemed to contain written documents. His field rifle protruded with no effort made to conceal its potential menace. Their work came to its conclusion at 4.20pm.

Fleur knew that they were being thorough in taking accounts of Hans Winkler's activities in Kwahu and wondered what the officers' superiors would make of their information. She did not have to wait too long.

The very next day at 5pm, Hans Winkler arrived at the compound. He was greeted in the normal manner and given time to settle in. He heard the dinner bell at 6.30pm and joined the table for the evening meal, unaware of any interest that had been shown in him recently. Hans was given a brief account of the happenings since he had been away. Fleur's malaria began the list of events, the black cobra in the compound, the recent durbar and the arrival of a duplicating machine from Accra seemed an adequate opener. Mention was not made of Fleur discovering her Kumasi brother. All of them were anxious to hear from Hans.

Osofo Okine then turned to him. 'You have been away some time Hans. How was your trip?'

'Yes I've been away a little longer than I intended. You know what it's like, you meet a few agriculturists and they promise supplies and some new equipment, but it never comes. So you announce you are about to depart and then you hear it is on its way. It's amazing how much time is lost that way.'

'Must have been very frustrating,' sympathised Fleur.

'Yes frustrating on one hand, but relaxing on the other. The markets were well supplied and I ate well. But it took me some time getting there. I left here and only got at far as Mampong the first night. The lorry I took from Kumasi had a puncture and the time it took to repair set me back. However, I got to Tamale the following day by 2pm so I decided to go on to Bolgatanga that day. It was night before I arrived but at least I felt I was well on my way. The air was dry and pleasantly cool at night but during the day, the temperatures soared. I bought a wide-rimmed northern hat. I grew very attached to it. You'll see me wearing it around here from now on.'

The bowl of yam was passed round again and the fish and kontomere stew followed. Water glasses were filled as the assembled group latched on to the account of Hans' travels.

'And did you visit the sacred crocodiles of Paga, Hans?' asked Comfort.

'Yes and what a surprise! I had heard about them but not realised what I would encounter. So I made a point of going to Paga. I went to the area of the four lakes where there was a sign to the Sacred Crocodile. I made my way along to a farmer's house where I met a man of considerable age. He told me that an ancestor crocodile was reputed to have rescued from death by thirst a village hunter who had lost his way. The crocodile accompanied him to one of the four lakes, where several crocodile maidens came to keep him company. The hunter settled there and the town of Paga grew. They have lived in peaceful co-existence with man ever since. However what was in it for the crocodiles, you may ask? That's where the business comes to life. Each visitor pays the farmer for a small chicken. For that you are taken to the bank of one of the lakes. You begin to feel this is a fraud. Nothing happens. Then the descendant of the benefactor crocodile suddenly appears like a log in the water. You have no idea of its size and can only see its two eyes and part of its snout.'

'Isn't it frightening?' asked Andreas.

'I was anxious but not frightened. The farmer asked me to stay still and not move, even when the crocodile came out of the water. I did what I was told.'

'I'm not sure if I could do that,' exclaimed Gisela.

'The farmer has the small chicken in his hand and the crocodile hears its tweeting. Ever so slowly it begins to drag itself from the water. It continues to thrust itself forward agonisingly slowly, until even the tip of its tail, some twelve feet from its head, is on dry land. Then the farmer invites you to sit on its back! Or, as I eventually did, lift its heavy tail for a moment!'

'And did you, really?' asked Comfort.

'I must have fully trusted the farmer. Certainly, if you had seen how slowly it came out to the dry land, you would have gained your confidence too. The farmer then throws the chicken across its smiling mouth like the unrolling of a carpet and suddenly this ponderous prehistoric reptile flashes its head with terrifying speed to capture the chicken and in one gulp, the chicken is gone.'

'My goodness. It shows just how trust can conquer a fear of wild animals,' said Comfort.

'So that takes you to the border of the northern territory of the colony. Then you would be in French West Africa.'

'Exactly. So I proceeded along a good straight road to Ouagadougou, where I spent three nights. My schoolboy French got me through quite well. Then I took a day to travel to Ouahigouya where I spent the night at the Hotel de Ville. Not exactly a high quality hotel! Not even an average one, I might add! The ceiling fan did not work, the mosquito net was torn and there was no fresh water to bath, shave or drink. Just bottles of tonic water, all day long, and I needed them. I was so thirsty. It got to 139 degrees at noon. Nothing moved till 4pm. I then boarded a small lorry but it had no sooner set off when there was a call to prayer and the bottles of water were produced to clean the hands, faces and feet of the devout Moslems as they faced Mecca and began their prayer session. It was midnight before we arrived at Mopti. I managed to book into a room, despite the late hour. I wanted to sleep soundly for two days. Surprisingly I felt well after a wash the following morning and I set off to make a list of agricultural supplies I might find. I was prepared to barter them down to a good price.'

'So you spent all the time in Mopti?' Fleur innocently asked.

'No. Due to the recent rains, the Niger was flowing full and so I thought this was a chance to sail and visit Timbuktu. I got on the flat-bottomed boat at Mopti and made for the top deck. It was less crowded there and free from the goats and sheep which were on the main deck amid cooking stoves in action and the multifarious purchases heading home along the river. We stopped at Sarefere briefly, to unload some goods and people. One of the sheep jumped overboard there as the boat was leaving and, amid much shouting and jostling, it was eventually rescued. I think the problem was, not just the value of the sheep and the fear it would be lost, but the simple fact that I don't think anyone, even the crew of the ship, knew how to swim. Even if they did swim, I could not see how they could rescue the sheep wearing such long heavy robes.'

'I would love to sail on the Niger on such a boat. It reminds me of stories I was told when I was young.' Comfort was thinking the trip to be romantic.

'No you wouldn't,' her husband replied solemnly. 'You would be frightened and remember you can not swim either! The mosquitoes would be many by the river too. Have you not read the incident packed adventures of Mungo Park?' Comfort ignored his question.

'It was a pleasant sail, I agree. The mosquitoes were not as bad as I had feared either. The reeds on each side of the Niger were the home of weaver birds and stationary eagrets. They satisfyingly confirmed the progress of the boat as it made its way down river. I eventually disembarked at the port of Kabara. That is the nearest point to Timbuktu.'

'What are the people like there, Hans?' asked Gisela.

'There are different people around this great bend in the river Niger. This area was the ancient seat of Islamic learning and scholarship, that also had a flourishing close business relationship with the caravans in the north and the river-boats in the south. Around that time there was an invasion by the Peul. Now they are a nomadic people, who were called the Bororo when they settled in the east of the region! It is easier to see the difference in the tribes by their clothing, jewellery and culture. So you find the Songhai, the Bozo, the Dogon and the Tuareg all together trading and respecting each other's culture and traditions. However, it is not always as simple as that. The Dogon, for example, find the Peul women more attractive than their own people and many inter-marriages work without any problems. The Peul, on the other hand greatly appreciate the skill of the Dogon in finding and sinking new water wells. So now it is common to find Peul settlements near Dogon villages.'

'Rather like the Gas welcoming the Akan tribes to Accra!' laughed Osofo Akine.

Urged on by the response, he added 'And the Swiss and the Scots getting on, but not the Germans!'

Hans disregarded that remark.

'How long were you at Timbuktu?' asked Fleur.

'Long enough to see the ruins of the city, visit the mosque and see what type of seasonal farming they were engaged in. I was there about four days before heading back to Mopti.'

'Any other travels after that?'

'No Fleur, just the delays and the frustrating promises of

supplies at Mopti. I thought of going on to Bamako, but I had purchased enough agricultural supplies in Mopti. So then I began to set off back home. The goods I bought will follow in due course, I hope.'

Andreas walked round the table with a pitcher of coffee filling several mugs. 'Well, that was quite a travel adventure. I'm glad you came to no harm.'

As he spoke, Andreas noticed a car's lights enter the compound. He could not make out who it was. He was not expecting anyone after dark even though the hour was not too late. Nevertheless, he shared his observation. 'A car has just arrived. I'm not sure who's in it, but it looks like a full car.'

Osofo Okine stood up and made for the door. 'I am not expecting guests this evening. I hope they have already eaten!'

The group left the table and took their coffees to the sitting area. Hans sat down on the armchair opposite Fleur. 'Well, it's good to be back home,' he said.

'Yes,' said Fleur, 'its always useful having extra hands around.' Hans did not detect the attempted pun, which caused Fleur to smile.

'Tell me, how are your Twi lessons coming along?'

'Far be it from me to sing my own praises, but I am not having to go to Nkwatia as often now. I complete some written work and take it along twice a week. My speaking is quite fluent. It's the writing I need to improve on. You can test me tomorrow if you like.'

Hans did not reply. He began to focus on the strangers approaching and listened to their indistinct discussions. They sounded serious. The door opened and Osofo Okine entered with a Police Inspector, a Sergeant and a Constable. The Inspector stepped forward. Silence pervaded the room.

'Good evening. I am Inspector Otu from the Police station at Nkawkaw.' He looked around briefly then settled his eyes between Reverend Andreas Schmidt and Herr Hans Winkler. 'Which of you is Hans Winkler?'

'I am.' said Hans slowly rising to his feet.

'Hans Winkler, I am charging you with murder. On 12th June 1940 in the cultivated farm a quarter of a mile from Abetifi on the Obo road, you did murder Kwasi Amissah, by shooting him with a pistol. You are not required to say anything, but if you do, it will be noted and may be used in evidence against you on a later date. Do you have anything to say?'

Hans could only open his mouth. No words emerged. His eyes looked for support, but none was forthcoming. He dropped to his knees, covered his face with two shaking hands and awaited his immediate fate.

'Sergeant, please arrest this man.'

Hans was led from the dining room in handcuffs, across the compound, into the waiting police car. Hans would spend this night at the bottom of the ridge in Nkawkaw Police Station.

Fleur went to her room and immediately wrote to Sir Ronald about the scene that she had just observed. She also advised him that Hans' account of his travels had taken him to Timbuktu and Mopti, but he had stated categorically that he had not travelled further west. He had clearly denied any visit to Bamako or Dakar. Operation Oboe's file was expanding.

CHAPTER EIGHTEEN

Patches of light danced on the ground beneath Fleur's feet. The spreading flamboyant tree above her struggled to obscure the strong sunlight. The fern-like leaves offered only partial protection but the oscillation between shade and sun perceptibly lowered the temperature. Such peace, such calm. Fleur walked across the compound to a bench. It was set against the upright end wall of the kitchen quarters and provided enough shelter for three groups of banana trees that were well established, though as yet unproductive. She sat down and took off her broad-rimmed hat to let the warmth of the sun bring comfort to her mind.

Fleur examined her rational faith. She knew she was not evangelical, but she had a need to trust a God to see her through this war and to make greater sense of her life. Here in Abetifi, she was so remote from the great conflict. She wondered how the demands made on God in so many other needy situations, could possibly compete with her own. Surely Otto's God had to be more available to him than her? What was the essence of God? What power could he bring? Was it all in the mind?

Fleur pondered her life and what had led her to the Gold Coast. The comfort of discovering a brother justified her decision, no matter what the outcome might be and it made her feel proud. His land was surely hers too. Perhaps after the war, she could settle in Kumasi. What could she do? Teaching was the obvious possibility but the government might have further use for her if she let her intentions be known. For the time being, however, she was pleased to be in the Gold Coast and, to those who asked, she replied she intended to stay.

For some twenty minutes she had been alone with her thoughts, considering the untidy threads of experience in her mind which needed sorting, compartmentalisation and resolution. She noticed Reverend Jurg Fendler approach. Here was a contented man. Perhaps he would have retired to his beloved Swiss Alps, but for the onset of war. Perhaps he had already decided to devote his whole life to the people in Kwahu. Perhaps he would never leave. His tombstone may yet be laid alongside Ramseyer's. There it would rest for future generations to come and contemplate on his life and work. If only such men were the politicians, she thought.

She lifted her hat and placed it on her lap, inviting Jurg to the vacant space created on the bench.

'I am not disturbing you?' he inquired.

'Not at all. In fact I had just tied up all my loose thoughts and packed them away.'

'Private thoughts, or ones to share?'

'Both really. I envy your faith. Yet at the same time if I had the same level of faith as you have, I wonder if I could always accept it. I don't know if that makes sense.'

'It does to me, Fleur. Here we are in West Africa, far from the misery, famine and death in Europe. Yet for us in this moment of time, it is rational. I am a man of faith because I know the world to be inexplicably mysterious and full of suffering. Yet the reality is nevertheless on the side of harmony rather than conflict, of meaning rather than meaninglessness. There is an apparent parallel between my reliance on inner experience as opposed to outer knowledge. It's Sartre's dictum that "l'existence précede l'essence" or Albert Camus' emphasis on the principle of justice that one feels within oneself as opposed to the injustice that one sees operating in the world.'

'How does that relate to your daily work, Jurg?'

'Well, this afternoon, I will visit Hans in Nkawkaw prison. I do not know if he is guilty or not of course. That is not my concern. But his spirits will be low and at such times it is my Christian duty to give him comfort. So you see, his reality is so different from yours. Each has his or her own reality and feelings. Where these are good strong feelings, they support the community. See them on the smiles of faces, the offering of assistance, the comforting word. Concentrate on the principle of justice that you feel around you. That's what I call the Holy Spirit working through you, but you need not dwell on that concept. Sometimes, too much thought gets in the way of being a good Christian. And isn't it better that we each have our own understanding of God?'

'God does indeed move in mysterious ways. That I have often heard. I hope he can put up with my confused thoughts.'

'I am sure yours are no more confused than others, Fleur. After all, you are a mother, a widow, a student and an anthropologist. You have a lot to share with God. You have questions to ask him and trust to place in him. He ensures you are not alone.'

Almost two months later, Fleur was in her room one afternoon brushing her hair when Gisela arrived.

'*Agoo.*'

'*Amee.* Ah Gisela. Good morning.'

'Good morning, Fleur. Guess who I met this morning?'

'Guess? I have no idea. No idea at all.'

'You can not have forgotten. Babatu!'

'Oh really? Any news?'

'Yes, of course. That's why I'm here. I've brought your letter! Anyway, carry on brushing your hair, get your room as tidy as you wish and when that's done I'll give you your letter and leave you to read it. I hope it will have good news for you.'

Fleur felt a rush of adrenaline surge through her body. Yes at last, a letter. From Renate or from Otto, it would not matter. Perhaps it will be the first of a few. Gisela was right, she should make herself comfortable. Savour the moment. Fleur looked in the mirror, replaced her brush and comb on the dressing table and approached Gisela.

'What do I owe you?'

'I have paid Babatu. Let's square up later. It's not too much. Now, is this not what you have been waiting for?'

Gisela opened her bag and produced a long envelope. 'Frau Richter, your mail. See you soon. Bye.' Gisela left Fleur's room closing the wooden door behind her and as the sound of her footsteps diminished, Fleur opened the door once more, took a cane chair from her room to the veranda and, bathed in warm afternoon sunlight, she sat down with her family correspondence.

Fleur ran her finger over the German stamp. Otto's thumb or Karl's had surely fixed the stamp. She turned the letter over, but there was no inscription on the rear. She turned it over again and read her address Frau F. Richter, c/o Babatu, BP169 Mopti, Afrique de l'Ouest.

She arose, placed the letter on the chair and went to her room to get a knife to effect a clean opening. She returned promptly and took the letter with her, after an irrational thought surfaced. Her fear was in the split second she had gone to get the knife, the wind would have blown the letter off the veranda into oblivion, or worse still, to the hands of someone who might report her, Fleur Richter, as a recipient of enemy agent material! She gathered her senses, thought how silly her excitement was making her and resumed her seat, with her knife poised.

The knifepoint easily entered the envelope and with a firm tug along the fold, it was slit open. She gathered the written material and unfolded four pages. That would be a good read she thought. She turned to the last page. It was signed affectionately Karl and Renate. She returned to the first page in excitement.

Dear Fleur Hamburg 18 August 1940

It is our earnest hope that this letter reaches you, following the letter that we were thrilled to receive from you. That was a wonderful surprise. We were delighted that you have found yourself in a safe haven and trust that your health will not suffer in West Africa. We envy your access to fresh fruit! We are keeping well. Do not worry about us.

It is not easy for me to convey what I must tell you about Otto, so permit me to give you an account of his war, which we have as his next of kin here in Hamburg.

Otto was, as you knew, attached to the SS-Standarte Germania, a Hamburg based motorised infantry regiment, commanded by SS-Standartenführer Carl-Maria Demelhüber. SS-Germania was initially part of the reserves of General Wilhelm List's 14th Army in East Prussia. They initially took part in the push through the industrial areas of Upper Silesia. North of Lödz on the banks of the Bzura river Otto's unit came under heavy Polish fire. They engaged in attack and counter attack over two days, with many casualties on both sides. Then on the third day, Otto's unit broke through towards Sochaczev and the river Vistula but they were devoid of air support. Consequently the Polish cavalry rushed through and separated the unit. When air support eventually came, the Poles were outnumbered and Otto was ordered to intercept Polish units retreating towards Warsaw for a final stand.

During one of these engagements, Otto circled round onto higher land under cover of fire. His movement was noticed. A Polish sniper took aim. As Otto turned to check his position from the rear, the crack of the sniper's bullet sped with lethal accuracy into Otto's neck. He momentarily coughed blood then his body lost all its support. He was killed instantly. His death was seen through the binoculars of his friend Gunter Schnellbach, who visited us last week and recounted this sad event.

Fleur, it grieves me painfully to have to inform you that Otto is dead but Renate and I felt that we should spare you no details. He died a hero and has been given the Iron Cross 2nd class posthumously. You can be proud of him. He was popular with his troop. Two of them visited us prior to his action in Poland. They were young healthy lads with a reason to live and a reason to die.

Be proud of him Fleur. Grieve as you must for Otto, but remember also to take comfort in knowing he is at peace. The war is behind him now. He has served his country. It could have been no other way for him as you know.

I have a letter from his commanding officer that I will keep for the day you return to be with us. It speaks of how popular and trustworthy Otto was. It lists the achievements he gained in his training at Bad Tölz and it is enclosed with his certificates, all proudly bearing his name Otto Bruce Richter. .....

Fleur took her tear filled eyes from the page, as she could read no more. She clutched the letter in her left hand and stood holding the wooden post on the veranda with her right hand, resting her forehead against it. Her face was flushed. Tears freely flowed from her hazel eyes. An occasional sob was emitted. She took a handkerchief to wipe her eyes, then clung to it securely as she remembered the moment when she gave birth to Otto, nineteen years before. She remembered how Willy had been present and was given his son momentarily, before Otto was placed at her breast. His little mouth instinctively sought the milk that she provided from her ample breasts. That first moment they became three, lingered in her memory. Otto had been a healthy child, who loved his parents and was proud to hear of the family across the North Sea and the middle name he had been given. He and his father had shared a very happy time in Hamburg. Otto would have made a good sea captain, with his knowledge and interest of the ships of the Elbe and the North Sea. If only he had followed that interest and gone into the German Navy, Fleur thought to herself. Would that have led to a different, a more successful outcome, or would he have had to serve beneath the water where the horrors of submarine warfare would have been worse? There was no answer. There was no comfort in her thoughts. What had Osofo Okine told her and Reverend Fendler? Was this their moment, to impact on her faith? What could she take from their discussions with her?

The will-to-love must be greater than the will-to-live. Yes of course it must and what did Jurg tell her just a few weeks ago? She struggled to recall the exact words, but a rational faith must move on. Otto's suffering like Willy's was over. She felt she had suffered enough. Others would continue to suffer too as this was a world of suffering but love and the constant will-to-love is what Fleur felt was now filling her. It gave her confidence. It gave her strength. In this frame of mind she went to see Gisela.

Gisela saw Fleur approach and walked towards her so that when they met they would not be within the hearing of anyone.

'Good news I hope, Fleur?'

Fleur took a deep sigh. 'Sooner or later, it had to happen,' she began. 'Otto is dead.'

Gisela gasped, clutched Fleur's wrist and placed her other arm on her shoulder. 'Oh no, no. Dear Fleur, My poor Fleur. Come, let's walk but only speak if you wish to.'

They made their way slowly through the compound onto the old Obo road which was no more than a well trodden path, amid the sentinel cassava stalks on one side and the tattered and disintegrating plantain leaves amid stalks of new growth on the other.

'You must feel so lonely but I hope you can trust all at the Ramseyer Centre to share your grief and bring you through these next few days.'

'I know I have everyone's support, even if only you know of Otto's death at this moment.'

'Then let me tell Osofo Okine, to tell the staff. Perhaps he can arrange a service for you that we all can attend.'

'Yes. I think that would help, yet I seem to have taken the news quite well. It was always on my mind when I last saw Otto that we would never meet again. Our parting, the final parting as it was to be of a mother and her son, was a very poignant moment. Willy had died and his death was a great shock to me. After that, Otto was a close son at times, but one sold to the Nazi Party. I could never reclaim him after the Hitler Youth movement grew and absorbed him. In many ways I can face the future now, whatever that might be, knowing that I am no longer a wife or mother with responsibilities. It's just that it will take time getting to realise my new status.'

'Does this cut off your German connections now?'

'No. As long as Karl and Renate and their children are alive, I will have family in Germany and in Scotland.'

They continued along the road leading to the hillside town of Obo. Children greeted them, offering fresh coconuts. Fleur took some coins from her purse in exchange for two coconuts. Once the deal had been made, a young boy took his cutlass in his right hand and with a deft turning of each coconut, reminding Fleur of how a lawn bowler prepared to strike the jack, he cut away at its outer casing until the almost spherical small nut appeared. Then with a blow of the cutlass, of which an executioner would have been proud, he cut off a lid, letting a few drops of the coconut milk spill. He offered the first opened nut to Gisela who gave it to Fleur. She lifted the nut to her lips and let the cool, refreshing, murky milk fill her mouth. The flavour of fresh coconut milk slid over her throat and quenched her thirst. Gisela did the same with hers.

The boy then handed the lids of the coconuts to the women and encouraged them to gouge out the soft white flesh. This tool cut the flesh into dainty strips, which they ate remarking that Europeans could not imagine how soft and sweet was the white flesh of the nut. Nor could they believe it grew in such a large green shell. Coconuts did not remain soft inside after a sea voyage.

They thanked the children and continued on their stroll. Gisela asked if she could tell her a story about death. 'Oh why not? I have no fear of death or dying myself. It seems an appropriate time to tell me,' she smiled.

'Well it's a local story that explains why a snake sheds its skin. Have you heard it?'

'No, I don't think so.'

'And you, an anthropologist! Anyway the story goes that in the very beginning there was no Death. Death lived with God and at first God was unwilling to let Death go into the world. But Death pleaded hard with God, to be allowed to go and of course in time God agreed. Happy so far?'

'Yes, I am with you, I like stories like this.'

'At the same time God made a promise to Man that, although Death had been allowed to come into the world, Man himself should not die. God also promised to send Man new skins, which he and his family could put on when their bodies grew old. Now that would keep us permanently young!'

‘Sounds like a good idea to me,’ Fleur chuckled.

‘God put the new skins into a wicker basket and asked the Dog to take them to Man and his family. On the way, the Dog became very hungry. Fortunately the Dog met many other animals engaged in a feast. So he was very glad to join them in their meal and satisfy his hunger. When he had eaten enough and drunk from the nearby stream, he went into the shade and lay down to rest a while. As he rested, a snake cunningly approached him and asked what he had in his basket. So the Dog told him what was in it and why he was carrying it to Man. A short while later the Dog resumed his rest, this time falling asleep. Then the Snake, who had been waiting nearby, picked up the basket of new skins and slid silently into the bush.’

They approached a fallen tree trunk that had conveniently fallen parallel to the ground giving them easy and safe access to a seat. ‘Let’s rest here a while to hear this story. I don’t think any snakes are around!’

Gisela made herself comfortable beside Fleur and continued her story. ‘Soon afterwards the Dog awoke and discovered that the Snake had stolen the basket of skins, so he ran to the Man to tell him what had happened. The Man then went to God and told him about it and demanded that the Snake be commanded to return the basket of skins. But God said that he would not take back the skins from the Snake and that Man would have to die when he became old. From that day onward, Man has always had a grudge against the Snake and has always tried to kill him, whenever he sees him. The Snake, for his part, has always avoided Man and has always lived alone. And because he still has the basket of skins that God provided, he can always shed an old skin for a new one!’

‘That’s true. So it does. It’s a good story. Such stories help people to understand their environments. I can tell you one if you want. Anthropologists have many to tell. Shall I tell you it? It’s about why the Sun and the Moon live in the sky. Does it sound interesting?’

‘Yes please, Fleur. I’d love to hear it.’

‘Well, many years ago, many, many years ago, the Sun and the Water were great friends and both lived here in the Gold Coast. The Sun often visited the place where the Water lived, but the Water never returned his visits. One day, the Sun asked the Water “Why do you and your relations never visit me? We would be very pleased to see you in our compound."

The Water replied. "I'm sorry, but your compound is not big enough and if I visited you with all of my people, I would be afraid of chasing you all away. If you really wish me to visit you", the Water continued, "you must build a very large compound and I warn you that it will have to be a tremendous place as my people and I take up much room. If it is not big enough we might accidentally damage your property."

The Sun promised to build a very big compound and soon afterwards he returned home to his wife, the Moon. The Sun told his wife what he had promised the Water and the very next day he began to build a truly enormous compound, in which to entertain his friend. When it was complete the Sun asked the Water to visit him the very next day.

The Water arrived and before coming in he called out to the Sun, asking if he was really sure that the compound was large enough and the Sun answered, "Yes, come in my friend."

The Water then began to flow in, accompanied by the fish and all the water animals. Very soon the Water was knee-deep so he asked the Sun if it was still safe and the Sun said, "Yes," so even more water came in.

When the Water was level with the top of a man's head, he again asked the Sun, "Are you really sure you want me and my people to come?" The Sun and the Moon both answered "Yes", not knowing any better, so the Water continued to flow in, till at last the Sun and Moon had to climb on the roof to keep dry.

Again the Water asked, "Do you still want my people and me to come into your compound?" and the Sun, not liking to go back on his word, insisted, "Yes, let them all come in."

Soon the Water flowed over the very top of the roof and the Sun and the Moon were forced to go up into the sky, where they have lived ever since.'

'I suppose that is a simple explanation that has stood the test of time in these parts. But what will you be doing when you start work as an anthropologist, Fleur?'

Fleur was for the first time being challenged on her cover story. She took the question in her stride but wondered if behind its innocent appearance was a challenge to her mission.

'When anthropologists arrive in an unfamiliar society they are rarely in a position to know beforehand, with any accuracy, the problems with which they eventually deal. These problems come from a combination of the theoretical interests of the field worker, which I acquired in training and the particular situation in which I will find myself. You see a situation that may turn out very differently from what the sketchy reports of missionaries, traders and administrators have led me to expect. There is of course a certain uniform culture over the whole area, but it is only relative; for customs change gradually from settlement to settlement like the dialects of a language. The people are more aware of the differences than the similarities, just as you know when I speak German, you concentrate on traces of my Scottish accent and when we speak English, I listen for your German accent. Am I making any sense to you?'

'Yes it's fascinating. I am sure you will do well. Where are you going again?'

Fleur recalled her introductory speech with accuracy. 'It's the Adansi area in the town of Obuasi.'

'I'll miss you, Fleur, when you go there."

'I'll miss you too, Gisela, but that may not be for a few weeks yet. I think I should attend Hans Winkler's trial first. Don't you? I may even be a character witness!'

'Oh, I had almost forgotten about that. Do you know when it is?'

'Not yet. I think it is likely to be in the Kumasi Court or perhaps in Accra.'

The two women eased themselves from the tree and dusted down their dresses before returning to the compound.

'Take it easy, Fleur, I'll pass the word around about the death of Otto. Let me know if you need any assistance and remember people will genuinely wish to share in your grief.'

The two women smiled. Gisela set off to inform Comfort and Osofo Okine. Fleur returned to her room and opened her window to let fresh air circulate. She opened her diary in which she had collected quotes over the years. She turned to the quote of the day that happened to be the last words of the Captain of the Lusitania, before it went down in 1915. She pondered its significance.

Her finger ran over each word gently: *Why fear death? It is the most beautiful adventure in life.*

CHAPTER NINTEEN

On 12th January 1941 the harmattan came down overnight. Despite its annual appearance the harmattan was particularly severe this year. An ochre dust covered the country and in each home a daily dusting became compulsory, to keep on top of the oppressive conditions. There was only one benefit to the harmattan and it was minimal. The sun's strength was weakened and that meant a marginally cooler day but it was always a relief in March to have a severe storm to dispel this seasonal Saharan misery from the land.

The following day Fleur received her citation to attend the trial of Hans Winkler as a witness. She had to report to the Kumasi Crown Court, which would sit on 25th January at 10am.

In mid December she had given a statement to the prosecuting agency of the colony. It was no more than the sum of her knowledge of Hans Winkler at the Ramseyer Centre, her recollection of his account of the death of Kwasi Amissah and his apparent sudden disappearance. When she told the prosecutor of what her employer had told her about his further travels to Dakar, she was reminded that this would not be part of her evidence. It was hearsay and would not be acceptable in court. She wrote to her brother Kwame Bruce to inform him of the case and that she would be in Kumasi from the night of 24th January for the duration of the trial. His reply took five days. It came in the form of an invitation from himself and his wife, Abena, to stay with them during the trial. Kwame felt sure this arrangement would have no bearing on the impartiality of the case as he was not directly involved himself. He told her his only duty was to ensure peace if there was any discord outside the court and his duty court team would service the actual court on the days it would sit. He felt that the case might attract some interest in Kumasi, but not enough to cause disquiet. The presiding judge would be the distinguished Gold Coast lawyer, His Honour Judge Robert A Danquah. Fleur was pleased that an African would preside because, if a colonial judge had been appointed, it may not have been seen to be a fair trial. The King v Hans Winkler, a German speaking Swiss man, during the war would be likely to attract an appeal she thought. Judge Dankwa was what the case required.

Making discreet enquiries at the compound, she learned that

Osofo Emmanuel Okine, Reverend Jurg Fendler and his wife Martha and herself were the only Ramseyer Centre witnesses. Reverend Andreas and Gisela Schmidt had not been cited as witnesses, even though they had also provided a statement previously.

As Fleur prepared for the trial, news reached the colony of Wavell's desert troops, capturing Bardia on 5th January and on 22nd Tobruk. The threatening days of Britain's collapse were behind, the heroism of the Air Force during the Battle of Britain and Hitler's eye on Operation Barbarossa in the east, gave an air of long awaited optimism and the colony remained one hundred percent behind the Allied cause.

On 24th January Fleur set off north to Kumasi to take up residence with Kwame and Abena Bruce, while her fellow witnesses booked into the Presbyterian Church compound rest-house in town.

The following day at 10am promptly, the court usher asked all to rise as His Honour Judge Robert A Danquah entered the court. The prosecution laid out the facts of the case in which the body of Kwasi Amissah had been found with a bullet in his head. The cause of death was not in debate. What the Court had to decide was how Kwasi died and if he died as the result of a freak accident or by the deliberate actions of one man, the accused, Hans Winkler.

The defence was quick to respond that evidence would show that it was the day of a fearful storm and that Hans Winkler had arms, as usual that day, for his own protection and for the protection of those who worked for him at the mission farm. He would also show how distressed Hans had been on finding Kwasi injured, how he promptly went to Kwasi's side to see if he was seriously injured and promptly made the events of that day known to the fraternity of the Ramseyer staff and the police. He had offered his condolences to the grieving family and paid for Kwasi's funeral. These, he contended, were not the actions of a murderer, but the actions of a caring man, working in a caring environment.

The jury had been sworn in. All were Africans. All spoke English fluently, although the judge made arrangements for a

German interpreter and an Akan Twi interpreter to be present during the court proceedings, as was usual practice in such cases.

Fleur was first to give her evidence. She was under oath, but kept to her story that she had come to Kwahu to learn Twi. She had arranged to stay at the Ramseyer Centre in Abetifi, while studying at Nkwatia. She therefore did not reveal her under-cover work. As if to verify her evidence, the judge asked Fleur in the Twi language if she found learning the language difficult. *'Ah slowly, slowly the hen drinks water,'* she replied proverbially in Twi and the judge smiled. Her testimony was holding water too. She went on to confirm that Hans did have a rifle and a pistol which he kept in his room, but he never used them in the compound to her knowledge. Under cross examination she agreed, that it was indeed likely that a man whose occupation was developing farm lands was quite likely to have need for a rifle or similar weapon for reasons of safety, for himself and his employees.

She was asked where Hans had gone after the incident and she told the court that he had told her and the staff of the Ramseyer Centre that he had gone to Mopti to seek French agricultural implements for sale and take some earned leave. When asked where else he might have gone, she told of his visit along the river Niger to the port of Kabara and on by land to the ancient city of Timbuktu.

'Did he travel to any port or large town?'

'He gave an account of his travels on his return before his arrest. He certainly did go to Timbuktu and then back to Mopti. I was told by my employer that he then travelled to…'

'Mrs Richter!' intervened the Judge, 'I must stop you there. Unless you have solid knowledge of what you are about to say, then you will be only providing hearsay or indirect evidence. The court can not accept hearsay evidence. Do you understand?'

Fleur was stopped in her tracks. No less a person than the Governor General had told her about Hans' journey to Dakar yet she could not think of any way to provide this evidence without compromising her position in the Governor's employment, or invite the challenge of hearsay evidence. The prosecutor indicated he would withdraw the question and then quite unexpectedly informed Fleur that he had no more questions.

The judge thanked Fleur for her evidence and invited her to

take a seat in the court gallery. She stepped down from the witness box, passed Hans Winkler who found a slight smile to acknowledge her evidence as neutral and sat down towards the middle of the second row. She felt the case was not going well. If only she had been able to tell the court of her conversation with Sir Ronald, but it was too late now.

Before the lunchtime recess, Osofo Okine and Reverend Fendler gave their evidence. Nothing Fleur had heard so far gave any indication of evidence against Hans Winkler and he clearly thought the same. He was dressed in a light blue open necked short-sleeved political suit. He looked very smart and relaxed.

At lunchtime Fleur strolled round Kumasi town centre taking a bowl of pepper soup and a plate of kenkey and fish stew, at Matilda's Pantry on Bompata Road. A helping of fried plantain with ginger sold as *kelewele* rounded off her lunch. A necessary jug of cool water accompanied her meal.

In the afternoon Martha Fendler gave her evidence. She told the court she had been with the Basel Mission since 1920. In all that time she had enjoyed the company of all the mission staff, the African staff and the Scottish Mission staff she had encountered in the twenties. She had not found Hans as approachable however. She was asked to explain this comment further.

'I have good feelings about people, people I trust give me these good feelings. Hans was not one of those. In my discussions with him I feel he resented living on the Swiss-German border. He has told me of how different life would have been if he had been born only 400 metres down the road.'

'What does that mean?' asked the prosecutor.

'I just feel he would be happier being a German. He seemed deprived of serving in the German army, by being a Swiss.'

Fleur was surprised to hear Martha's evidence. It was the first inkling that Hans had doubts about his Swiss neutrality but then again this did not relate to Kwasi's death. It did remind Fleur however of the feelings of sympathy with the German war effort some Basel missionaries in the Gold Coast had, during the First World War. Yet this had not been an apparent feature of the current war.

The first day's proceedings at court closed and Fleur made her way home to her brother's house. Kwame was waiting to greet her on the veranda. Abena arrived with glasses of freshly squeezed orange juice as the sun, hidden in the harmattan sky, grew dimmer. Abena asked Fleur to recall the events of the first day of the trial. Kwame was glad her evidence was over so she could sit to hear how the case would develop. Fleur agreed that the worst was over for her but she remained disappointed with the evidence so far.

The evening meal was announced. They sat as a family around the dining table with Kwame at the top, Abena at the other end. Alice sat alongside Fleur, opposite the twins Yaw and Sam. Kwame stood up. 'This is a special day for all Scots, like us! The 25th January. It's Burn's night. Let me say grace. But first Abena, the plate please.'

Abena brought in a flat plate bordered with slabs of yam and a mound of mashed turnips at the other end. In the middle was a haggis!

The plate was brought to Kwame who placed it before him. As the steam rose to heighten his taste senses and reveal a hint of the rich flavoured meal beneath the skin, he realised why Robert Burns had worshiped this dish. Addressing the haggis that night in Kumasi, as were Scots throughout the world, Kwame filled his lungs and rendered the traditional address to the haggis. In doing so, he was honouring the Immortal Memory of Scotland's National Bard. The Bruce family watched and listened spellbound to a foreign tongue coming from their father.

Fair fa' your honest, sonsie face
Great Chieftain o' the pudding-race!
Aboon them a' ye tak your place,
Painch, tripe, or thairm:
Weel are ye wordy of a grace
As lang's my arm.

Kwame's performance was quite outstanding as he took pride in his Scottish roots. As he approached the last verse, he spoke more slowly and came to a rousing finish. Alice and Sam joined in at the last line and bellowed it out.

Ye Powers, wha mak mankind your care
And dish them oot their bill o fare.
Auld Scotland wants nae skinking ware

That jaups in luggies
But, if ye wish her grateful prayer.....GIE HER A HAGGIS!

Fleur applauded. 'Well done indeed. I can hardly believe what I see before me. How could you possibly have prepared a Scottish Burns night here in Kumasi?'

'Well I did get some help, Fleur,' said Abena.

'My biggest fear was that the haggis would burst when I boiled it but fortunately it hasn't. Sorry about the tatties! Yam is the next best thing. In fact I got some help from your friend Mrs Hall. It was she who told us about 25th January. She insisted I prepare this food for you this evening. I said I did not know how to cook it or if the family would eat it and guess what? Well, last weekend we went to the Halls and I learned how to cook it and at night we sat down to eat haggis for the first time. Mr Hall was able to get three from Accra somehow. I think it was through the assistance of the Governor General himself. So this is the second haggis. We liked it. We didn't think British food was spicy like ours but this haggis is very spicy with peppers and seasoning. Then we were given a turnip to mash. It goes well with the meal.'

'The difficult part was reciting this address to the haggis,' remarked Kwame, 'but it flows as a poem. Not that I understood all the words.'

Over the course of the meal, Fleur explained the verses and what each word meant. Kwame laughed, 'I didn't think it was possible to write so many verses about one meal!'

Fleur helped to wash up the plates and thanked Abena for preparing the wonderful surprise. When they gathered in the lounge Fleur said she wanted to play some Scottish tunes to round off the evening. The Bruce family sat enthralled as Fleur's oboe played *Scots Wa Hae*, *My Love is Like a Red, Red Rose* and the *Northern Lights of Auld Aberdeen*. As the night drew to a close, Fleur played *Abide With Me* and the Bruce family sang along, singing the hymn in Ashanti Twi. The children had never seen an oboe before at close range. Alice said it was the most beautiful sounding instrument of an orchestra. She hoped she could one day play an oboe.

The following morning, the court resumed. Giving evidence first, were two of the farm workers. Seth Buadu told the court that Hans was a very strict foreman. He did not suffer fools gladly, but he knew his farm work and he had learned a lot about crop rotation and the care of seedlings. When asked what form of discipline Hans used towards his staff, Seth recalled how he had been terrified when he was first given the William Tell treatment. He was asked to explain what this meant.

'Mr Winkler is a very good rifleman. But at first you do not know this. If he wanted someone to work harder, he said he knew how he could get them to concentrate, and work harder. This was the William Tell treatment. He put an object, sometimes a tin or a small cardboard box on your head. He would stand about twelve paces away, raise his rifle or his pistol and put a bullet through the object. He said this was what one of his countrymen did with an apple on his son's head, with a bow and arrow. Every time he did this, he hit the object on the farm worker's head. Nobody ever got hurt. I suppose we were so frightened that we stood perfectly still. I think all of us closed our eyes in fear when he did this. I mean whether he was doing it to you or you were just watching, it always made us work much harder. We were very afraid.'

He went on to say on the day in question, Mr Winkler was very angry. 'It had been very wet and windy and we all wanted to go home. The visibility was so bad that some of us just left. Just before I left I saw him with Kwasi placing stones over the protective covering that was over the seedlings. I thought they would both go home then. There was no point working any more in the storm. So I went home at that point.'

Next to give evidence was Martin Sackey. He too had been working on the farm on this stormy day. His account matched all that Seth Buadu had said but he had been Kwasi Amissah's best friend. When the other farm hands had used the excuse of the storm to set off home, Martin crouched by a banana tree waiting for Kwasi to finish. When asked what happened as he waited, the court fell silent.

'The rain was very heavy and Mr Winkler and Kwasi were placing stones over the sheeting. The wind got under the sheeting and Kwasi pounced on it to keep it from flying away. As he did so, it somehow tore and his pouncing damaged some of the seedlings underneath the cover. This made Mr Winkler very angry. He shouted loudly in German. I don't know what he was saying, but it looked as though he was blaming Kwasi for the tear in the material and all the damage to the crop. At that point he headed back towards where I was hiding. He only got as far as the shelter where we keep our provisions. That's where he keeps his guns too. I saw him take out his pistol. He was still shouting. He raised it up a little and shot once.'

The prosecutor asked Martin to show the court how Hans fired the pistol. Martin pretended he had a pistol in his hand and he raised it only as far as waist level.

'He shot from this position. He did not take care where he was shooting though he knew Kwasi was in that area. But the storm was so strong, I did not see if he hit Kwasi. He certainly did not take aim. I was frightened because of his rage and thought he might shoot again or turn the weapon on me, so I ran away.'

'Was Kwasi in the William Tell position just before the shot was heard?'

'No, there was no time. He was so angry. He did not ask Kwasi to stand up and he did not try to find a tin or some target on this occasion. He just fired the gun as soon as he got hold of it.'

The evidence was turning against Hans Winkler. Hans looked more solemn now.

The next witness was someone Fleur seemed to recognise. She could not place him at first. He took the stand.

'Please give your name, age and occupation.'

'I am Robert Cook, I am aged 35 and I am a civil servant engaged in the Governor General's service, at Accra.'

That was where she had set eyes on him, but she had never spoken to him. Fleur wondered what evidence he could possibly have in this case. She did not have long to wait to find out.

He produced a booklet of photographs. Each photograph was labelled alphabetically. The first was the harbour at Dakar. The second, third and fourth photographs were of the construction of plywood workshop fronts, military camouflaged false oil drums and stores. Each edifice was supported by wooden props, sturdy and facing inland. They were erected along the northern coast of Dakar, clearly as a decoy from the main large harbour and town. Directing their construction and positioning was a white man. The fifth photograph focussed on the face of the man. It was unmistakably Hans Winkler.

The defence lawyer objected to this line of evidence, claiming that Dakar was so far away from the scene of an alleged murder, that it could not have any relevance in his client's trial. The prosecution begged that there was a crucial point to make regarding the accused's honesty and the judge reserved judgement but did not object to the immediate line of questioning.

The disguised shoreline was photographed from the sea. Once more Hans could be seen clearly directing a native labour force on behalf of Vichy France. Hans put his head in his hands. 'This evidence,' concluded the prosecutor, 'shows Hans Winkler as a liar and a traitor. Can he be trusted to tell any truth within this court?'

His story about his visit to Timbuktu may have been true, but he had also been in Dakar at the time of General de Gaulle's failed attempt to bring French West Africa on to the Allied side. The loss at the battle of Dakar was a major setback for de Gaulle, for Churchill and the Allied cause. Hans Winkler had done much in Dakar to bring about this Allied defeat.

Robert Cook was cross-examined at length but the photographic evidence was compelling and damning. Martin Sackey's evidence was equally damning. The next day the medical evidence was to be heard.

Fleur returned to take her seat in the gallery of the court the following morning. 10am duly arrived but nothing happened. By 10.15am there was a general disquiet around the court, but no explanation was forthcoming. Moments later the judge took his seat on the bench but no defendant appeared.

'Good morning. It is with regret I have to inform you, that one hour ago, Herr Hans Winkler was found dead in his cell. It would appear that he took his own life after breakfast this morning. He left a suicide note I have been informed. This is a matter for the police at present. As a direct consequence of this development this morning, the case is now closed. A Fatal Accident Inquiry will be conducted in due course into the cause of death of Kwasi Amissah. I thank all of you who came to the court to give evidence or to sit on the jury. You are all free to leave now. Thank you.'

'Court rise.'

There was a stunned silence as His Honour Judge Robert A Danquah left the bench. Hans was dead. This had been a most unsatisfactory ending to a court case. The court room emptied slowly. Fleur made her way back to the Bruce household and broke the news.

That evening when Kwame returned from work, the full facts became clear.

After breakfast in the Kumasi prison, Hans sought permission to wear a shirt and tie for court in an hour. After some deliberation, in retrospect an ill-judged decision, he was given a red and white, banded tie. The significance of the Swiss colours was not lost in the deception. Hans thanked the prison officer profusely for choosing such an appropriately coloured tie. He went back to his cell to await transportation to court.

In that short time he made a noose of the tie, secured it around his neck, placed the cell chair beneath the light bulb in the centre of the cell and mounted the seat. He secured his tie to the cable above the bulb and then, with a kick of the chair, he hung suspended. The prison staff heard nothing of this commotion. They were running a little late as it happened for the morning's duties. When they came for him to escort him to court, the officers opened the door and stood in shock for a moment. They could not believe what they saw. This had never happened before at the Kumasi prison. They entered his cell and cut him free, but found him motionless. A doctor was summonsed. He pronounced Hans Winkler dead. On his pallet was a letter. It was addressed to Osofo Emmanuel Okine, The Bursar, Ramseyer Centre, Abetifi.

Arrangements were made for Mr Okine to travel back to Kumasi where he was asked to read the letter in the presence of Chief Superintendent Kwame Bruce.

Kwame addressed the pastor.

'The late Hans Winkler wrote this letter. It is addressed to you. I would ask you to open it and read it here. It may or may not be a significant letter. By that I mean one worthy of any further police action.'

'Thank you Chief Superintendent.' Mr Okine took the letter and opened it with care. He read the two pages written in ink on prison lined paper. He nodded.

'Hans was a troubled man but I think this letter was meant to put his mind at rest. Instead, I think it puts ours at rest. Let me read it to you.'

While Kwame sat at his desk, Osofo Okine went to the window and read aloud.

Kumasi Prison
26th January 1941

Dear Osofo Okine

I have let you down. I have let the Basel Mission down but above all, I have let myself down. I was hot-headed and angry but I should never have shot Kwasi Amissah. I have always been an angry man. I'm a loner who preferred the countryside to the town. I had a painful past in Switzerland, which I am not willing to share and feel it irrelevant to mention in this last letter, but it forced me to leave Switzerland and I was pleased to find my farming knowledge could be put to good use in Africa. I am sorry it was the Basel Mission which made this possible for me. They must take no blame. They were civil and supportive of me at all times.

Of one thing I am certain. The war now taking place, will bring a victory for Germany. A new era will bring our people back to Africa, where National Socialism will prosper. The signs are that we are well on our way. Africa can look positively to a sympathetic German colonial power, for at least one thousand years. This will lead all Africans into National Socialism proudly and they will resist communism and fruitless independence. With that prospect in mind, I can end my life knowing I played my part for the Axis powers in West Africa.

Heil Hitler!
Hans Winkler 1912 – 1941.

'I don't think this sheds any further light on your enquiries. A misguided man,' the pastor concluded.

'I agree. There is just one other point of clarification. Clearly he has no relatives in the Gold Coast. Where do you think he should be buried bearing in mind his actions defeated the due process of justice? He did not die a criminal in the eyes of the law.'

'Yes you are right. There is a Presbyterian cemetery in Kumasi. I think that would be more appropriate than at Abetifi. I will arrange to conduct the service.'

'Osofo Okine, for that I am most grateful.'

Four days later Hans Winkler was buried in Kumasi. Osofo

Okine took the service and most of the staff of the Ramseyer Centre attended. They returned to Abetifi the same day but Fleur spent a further night with her family in Kumasi. Alice insisted that Fleur played her oboe once more and she obliged with Pachelbel's haunting *Canon*. To brighten up the evening's sombre tone, Fleur concluded with the allegro third movement of *Kreisler's Liebesfreud.*. Alice was transfixed with delight at the performance and promised that she would start learning to play an instrument soon and hoped to play a simple tune for Fleur next time she visited.

The following morning Kwame drove Fleur to the Kejetia lorry park. He helped her board the Accra bus that would stop at Nkawkaw around noon allowing her time to catch a bus to her much loved Abetifi and the Ramseyer Centre before nightfall. They parted with a fraternal kiss.

Shortly after 11.15am, approaching Juaso at speed, the Accra bus swerved to avoid a wandering goat taking it on to the path of an oncoming vehicle. The bus driver over compensated in bringing his bus back to the left-hand side of the road. The goat was narrowly avoided. The bus however, rocked from side to side exaggerating its movement with each lurch. Then suddenly over it went, off the road into the bush landing on its side and sliding through the dense vegetation until it came to a sudden halt against a ditch by a fallen tree.

In the immediate aftermath there was a moment of complete silence. Then whimpers of pain, disorientated movements and the growing noise of villagers running from Juaso filled the anguished air. Villagers clambered over the bus calling out in an attempt to locate and rescue passengers. The driver was dazed and found sitting on a bank covered in the scythed vegetation created in the wake of the accident. Walking wounded emerged from the bus, unsteady on their feet. Others laid cloth over the jagged glass and emerged from the broken windows. Some had cuts on their faces, some on their hands and legs. All were in shock. When the bus had been emptied and baggage had been gathered, the full impact of the accident was clear. Thankfully seventeen passengers and the driver had escaped with relatively minor injuries. Four had required hospital treatment for suspected broken bones and were transported to the hospital at Agogo, not far away. Three lay dead. One was an African woman of around sixty-five years of age from

Kumasi. One was a northern Fulani trader who had been travelling from Tamale on his way to Accra. The third and final fatality was a baby not yet one year old whose mother was unconscious and also transferred to Agogo.

Fleur was one of the four who was taken to hospital with her left hand and wrist badly injured, a fractured collarbone and extensive bruising. The following week she was transferred to the Accra hospital where Sir Ronald had made arrangements for her to be brought as soon as she was able to travel. He called to visit her the day she arrived, at 4pm.

Sir Ronald first introduced himself to the Hospital Director, Mr Wisdom Ayivor. He asked about Fleur's injuries.

'Well, Sir Ronald, she is a very lucky woman. Her injuries were traumatic and many a woman of her age would have died through shock alone. She is a fighting woman.'

'Indeed I know that,' smiled the Ambassador.

'However she will not come through this accident without some permanent injury.' Sir Ronald grew increasingly concerned. 'What do you mean?' he asked.

'Her collarbone will soon heal and the bruising will too, of course, but we were lucky to save her left hand. At one point I thought we might have to amputate her hand at the wrist. Fortunately there was a less dramatic solution. There was considerable damage to her fingers and I am afraid we had to amputate her middle and fourth fingers, but we have managed to save her hand. So despite the outcome, I assure you it could have been much worse.'

'I don't know. This means she will not be able to play again.'

'Play again?' asked Mr Ayivor.

'She played the oboe. This will be a blow to her. Does she know the extent of her injuries?'

'When your secretary informed me that you were coming this afternoon, I asked that you should come at 4pm. After lunch I spoke with her and judged her well enough to be told the extent of her injuries.'

'How did she react?'

'I was a little taken aback by her reaction.'

'In what way?'

'Firstly, she spoke to me in Akan Twi. That surprised me, but then a proverb! *"Se ahoma tsew na eto a, nna paw aba mu"* which means there is bound to be a knot when two pieces of string are joined together.'

'Was she making any sense to you?' Sir Ronald enquired.

'I understood but told her I was an Ewe and not so sure of Akan proverbs. So she smiled and explained. She said she had a niece in Kumasi. Now that she had lost two fingers on her left hand, she could no longer play her oboe. But her instrument would now find the perfect home in her niece's hands. All this had been made possible from the accident that she survived. Her misfortune was the knot. The new longer and stronger piece of string was the new life the oboe was about to start. What a profound sentiment.'

'That indeed, is Fleur Richter. May I see her now?'

'Certainly, let me take you to her ward.'

Sir Ronald approached her bedside and handed a bouquet of flowers to a nurse to find a vase. 'How kind of you, Sir Ronald. And thank you for arranging for me to come to Accra.'

'It was a terrible shock to hear of the accident. How are you feeling?' he enquired.

Fleur was able to sit up in bed with a cardboard collar supporting her neck. Her left hand was bound in bandages and her facial bruising had given her a jaundiced look though her dimples were as prominent as ever.

'I know I look pretty grim but I'm really feeling better each day. I hope the swelling will be down soon and then I'll look like your employee once more.'

'In a few days I am told you will be well enough to come back to the embassy residence where we will give you a period to fully recuperate.'

'I will like that very much, but what will happen then, Sir Ronald?'

'Well I think you might wish a change. Operation Oboe is complete. You have done a marvellous job. I have been giving some consideration to your post. It would be too dangerous to let you sail home. The Atlantic is not safe with so many U-boats patrolling and claiming so much tonnage. Anyway, I'm not sure if you would really want to leave the Gold Coast. Am I right?'

'It is a wonderful country and I have found my brother here. The Gold Coast has been so good to me. If I left, I know I would miss it dearly in so many different ways.'

'My options include posting you to Tehran in Persia where,

with your fluent German, you would be engaged in a similar sphere of work. That may still be an option for you to consider. However I spoke to the head teacher, Mr Ohene Fianko, at the Wesley College in Kumasi last Tuesday and he was delighted to think that you might wish to teach German at his school. At present he would not consider engaging a native German as you will understand and he certainly knows your true pedigree, through the Chief Superintendent. The school would provide you with accommodation and I would arrange for an adaptation grant of course. Would that be worthy of consideration?'

'I'd love to live in Kumasi and teach at Wesley College. I would also be able to teach my niece how to play the oboe too. She is keen to learn music. It would be wonderful. But, Sir Ronald, I am your hostess. Is my work with you complete?'

'I have no further use for a hostess. I could find administrative work for you at the embassy but if you now wish to teach in Kumasi, you are free to do so with my blessing.'

Fleur did not take long to decide. Her injuries to her hand would make administrative tasks awkward if not impossible. Furthermore, she was neither qualified for nor interested in any secretarial post. Teaching on the other hand would suit her well. 'Then I will go to Kumasi as soon as I am able. Can you let the headmaster know that I am accepting his offer?'

'Of course I will. Now get some rest and I'll call again at the weekend. Do not hesitate to contact my residence if you wish anything.'

'There is just one thing I'd like to clarify.'

'Yes?'

'Well, it's about Operation Oboe. You never told me why you selected it, as a code name.'

'No, you are right. It was done a long time ago and in fact not only by me. When I was in London at the Foreign and Commonwealth Office, I met with Sir Anthony Pitt-Stevenson. He told me he had found the right person for the post and went on to describe you.'

'I wonder how!'

'He described you as a delightful, mature woman with prominent dimples in each cheek! We knew you played the oboe from your curriculum vitae and wondered ...well ....it was the old chicken and egg question really. Were you born with dimples or did the playing of the instrument create them? We had different views on the matter! As I recall we begged to differ. Then it came clearly to us both. Operation Oboe it had to be. So Operation Oboe it was! I trust you were not offended.'

'No, Sir Ronald, certainly not. You know the oboe has a privileged place on stage. It tunes the orchestra but…' she took a long wistful sigh before continuing….. 'I recognise my concert is over now. Yet what pleases me most, is that the oboe is about to start a new life.'

'Yes indeed it will, and Fleur, you will too.'

CHAPTER TWENTY

Kortu Gon
Troon, Ayrshire

28th December 1991

The fireplace glowed with fragile burnt out wooden embers. Miller laid two more logs on the fire causing flames to lick around them and hiss as cold vapours fled the heat. The first few flurries of snow were falling from dark laden skies. A new depth of winter was descending on the coastal town.

Vera removed her glasses and polished both lenses. She replaced them and smiled at Fiona and Laura who sat at her feet on the carpet.

'Well girls, I never thought I would be telling you of these events and recollections which happened so long ago.'

'Why not?' Fiona asked.

'A good question dear. Yes, why ever not! It has taken your innocent question to unveil the past. And yes, a past to remember with satisfaction.'

'And what happened to Fleur?' asked Laura. 'Is she still in Africa?'

'Fleur recovered from her accident and went to Kumasi where she taught German at the Wesley College until 1955. She also gave music lessons to woodwind pupils at the school. She never returned to Scotland. Her niece, Alice, who inherited her oboe, played the open 'A' note to tune the orchestra that gathered in Black Star Square in Accra on 6th March 1957 when Dr Kwame Nkrumah became Ghana's first president. It was a momentous day.' Vera smiled and lowered her voice and she continued.

'But Fleur never saw that day. She died on 16th October 1956 and, at her request, was buried in Abetifi beneath the balcony of her room, at the side of the old Basel mission house.'

Fiona folded the trivial pursuit board that had lain open over the past two days, gathered the dice and the coloured pieces. She neatly packed them into the square box and secured its lid. 'Umm'... she mused .....'Not so trivial after all.'

'Look!' shouted Laura. 'The snow's lying. Come on Fiona, let's make a snowman'.

Epilogue

Ghana, the former Gold Coast, became the first black African country south of the Sahara to gain its independence in 1957 and is today a thriving country, full of natural resources and populated by the friendliest of African people. Democracy has taken root once again and Ghana takes a lead in ensuring a civilian African government can flourish. Little surprise therefore that Ghana's capital, Accra, was chosen in August 2003, as the venue to formalise the end of conflict in Liberia and to lay out a future for that sad, war ravaged West African country.

Driving in Ghana is however much more haphazard, with inadequate speeding restrictions being the cause of so much personal and economic misery. The Kumasi to Accra road in particular has a tragic record of road fatalities. It simply need not be this way.

The author and his wife returned to Ghana in January 2002 to celebrate their silver wedding anniversary in the country that brought them together in 1975.

The Basel Mission continues its medical, industrial, educational and rural mission work in several communities in the country. The Church of Scotland partner church, sends fraternal workers to the Presbyterian Church of Ghana from time to time. It was the author's privilege to serve in Tema on the coast during the period 1973-78.

In 1933 no fewer than thirteen countries, including states such as Nicaragua and Turkey, had admitted women to their Diplomatic and Consular Services. Spain was cited as a pioneer in this field. In 1946 the Foreign Office gave women the opportunity to be employed as diplomats for the first time. In 1998 the FCO received the Opportunity Award for Top Level Commitment. Foreign Secretary Robin Cook stated in September 1997 that he wished "a Foreign Office that is representative of the whole of modern Britain, from all walks of life, both genders." Fleur would have relished a diplomatic post but accepted the politically ambiguous role of 'Ambassador's Hostess' as it was in 1940.

Vera and Tim Wild died within four days of each other in 1992 and were cremated together at the Cardonald cemetery in Glasgow.

In the Forres, Elgin & Nairn Gazette of 2nd September 1914,

subject to wartime reporting, can be found the account of how Vera returned from Germany after the outbreak of war in August 1914. In the report Fleur was referred to as 'a friend' to avoid enemy detection.

During every war, for many, the mind becomes focussed on the unanswerable questions of faith and belief. Fleur attempted to find faith to see her through the traumas in her life but it was the faith she had in the people of the Gold Coast that gave her contentment. In a similar manner it was in Ghana on 15th December 1977 I met a most remarkable man. He is the Reverend Horoshi Murikami. He had spent the previous four months as a guest of the Basel Mission in Germany at Stuttgart and chose to visit Ghana on his return home to Japan. It fell to me to show him the industrial mission work being undertaken in the port of Tema. However I wondered how a Japanese man might have become a Christian. He told me he trained as an airman during the war and in 1945 he was selected to fly as a kamikaze pilot. He prepared for his mission with pride.

Before being sent on his final flight however, the atom bombs fell at Hiroshima and Nagasaki and Japan was defeated. Consequently, he never flew on his fateful mission but was imprisoned instead. He waited for what he assumed to be his only appropriate fate – death. An American chaplain passed by the prison camp one day. Through an interpreter, the airman asked when it had been arranged for him to die. The American told him the most remarkable words he had ever heard.

'In my religion,' he said, 'we love our enemy'.

From that moment he wanted to know more about Christianity and he was now returning to Tokyo to be the head of a Christian seminary.

Loving our enemy and finding the Will-to-Love. These are the most persuasive forces for peaceful change in our world today no matter what faith, if any, we have.

Printed in the United Kingdom
by Lightning Source UK Ltd.
9749000002B

9 780755 200900